Just One Season

CHRISSY HOPEWELL

Content Note

Just One Season is a contemporary romance novel meant for mature readers. It includes swearing and explicit sexual encounters between enthusiastically consenting adults. 2 out of 5.

There are mentions of the male main character's young daughter being a cancer survivor and vague references to the trauma it caused her parents. I am the mama of a cancer survivor, so be assured no children get sick or harmed in this book (or any of my books. Not ever). If you're interested in supporting a childhood cancer research foundation, check out CancerFree KIDS.

Author's Note

I had a group of such wonderful hockey beta readers who read an early copy of *Just One Season*. They truly all saved me from myself. A huge thank you to Lou, Melissa, Jillian, Andrea, Shania, Emily, and Paris.

I beg them (and all hockey fans) to forgive me for ignoring a few pieces of their feedback. Please suspend your hockey disbelief just a teensy bit. Yes... the gate to the rink needs to be closed during practices. And I know, only one NHL team has the same practice arena as game arena. Uh-huh, there's only been one Australian NHL player in the history of NHL players. Yup, the coach's office should definitely not be only accessible through the locker room (but if Ted Lasso can do it, can't I? 😆).

But for the sake of making you laugh (or swoon)... I had to do it.

Hope you enjoy Lucy & Kellen (and their friends)!

love, Chrissy

To my writer friends who talk me off the ledge, listen to unhinged rants about just about everything, reassure me constantly, and come with me almost to the point of no return, threaten to quit, and then shrug it off and keep writing.

You all are the best.

CHAPTER 1

Humiliated by Waffles

LUCY

Wednesday, September 11

"Waffles."

My dog—actually, my ex-fiancé's dog—tilts his head from where he's sitting on the floor of my new office in the building that houses the Fort Collins Blizzard NHL team.

Waffles doesn't look impressed with my most recent attempt at renaming him.

"Let's try it out for a few days, okay?"

He barks once in agreement.

I clip his leash on, grab my laptop bag, and head down the hallway past my new boss's office. Lina's the vice president of public relations and sponsorship and is my manager while I'm here for six months to cover a maternity leave. She insisted I watch a practice to get a feel for Blizzard hockey, so I head to the arena, which is attached to the administrative offices for the team. When I reminded her that Atticus, my little brother—little being a funny word to describe the six-foot-four hulking twenty-nine-year-old man—is a forward on the Blizzard, and I regularly watch his games, she waved a hand in the air and turned back to her laptop and her mug embossed with the words: *Sorry. Can't. Hockey. Bye.*

The hallway cement wall is decorated with framed pictures of past Blizzard teams in between the mostly closed doors of the administration. There's a hallway split into a T shape behind me, and in front of me are more offices and doors I'm not familiar with before the players' gym on the right. At the end is the entrance to the Blizzard's arena.

My phone buzzes in my pocket after I push through the doors to the arena, but I ignore it and head to the stands. Waffles might seem docile and calm trotting next to me, but by now I know his tricks. If I let my guard down for one second, he'll take advantage and escape from my hold to run, bark, jump, and pee in random places.

Which is why he's with me right now instead of back at my brother's apartment. Atticus wants no part of a dog destroying his bachelor pad.

I settle into one of the rink side seats closest to the glass. Waffles sits calmly at my feet, the picture of perfect behavior, back straight and head still like a statue of Zeus or some other godly character. *Ohhh, maybe I should name him Zeus?* I pet his head, and he stretches at my feet and closes his eyes with a soft sigh.

Maybe Zeus is too powerful a name for this little dog—I can't imagine him wielding a thunderbolt.

Ron, my impulsive, passionate ex-fiancé, came home with the Boston terrier puppy in March, after we'd moved in together post-engagement. There was no warning, no planning, just a spontaneous decision to buy a puppy.

I should've known there were far less pleasant surprises to come.

When I discovered he'd been cheating on me for our entire relationship, he begged me to give him another chance. I walked away instead.

And after I moved out, he decided he was allergic to dogs and was going to drop his dog—then Max—off at an animal shelter. We fought over that. I called bullshit. How can a thirty-five-year-old man not know he's allergic to dogs? Later that weekend, he showed up at my short-term apartment rental with a box of my remaining belongings.

And Max.

I'm not really a dog person, but I couldn't bear to see the somewhat lovable animal dropped off at the shelter or given to a random person to be fed to a giant snake or something. Colorado sounded like a better place for a dog anyway, so I brought him with me.

It's not a permanent situation with Waffles, just like I'm not permanent here in Colorado. This is just one little stop on the road to my dream job in England. If things go as planned, I'll be booking a one-way plane ticket in six months. Waffles will be with a new family. I fully intend on finding him a great one before I leave.

And I'll be far, far away from my old life. *Farther* away.

Down on the ice, the Blizzard are doing a fast-moving shooting drill, the forwards trying to put the puck in the back of the net and the goaltender attempting to stop each one.

Despite the fact that Atticus has played professional ice hockey for the past eight years, I still kind of zone out when watching. Soccer has been more my sport as I played from kindergarten through high school. Not that I was exceptionally good. I wasn't terrible, but I know I only made the teams because my father is part owner of the Washington D.C. Football Club (DC FC), a Major League Soccer team—but I love the sport. I loved working for an MLS team, volunteering for the soccer charities we helped fund, sometimes coaching little kids, and watching games live and on TV.

Ron worked at DC FC, too, his office just down the hall from mine. Deep down, I hadn't expected my father to fire Ron when everything went down, but it was a bit shocking when he didn't even pretend to take my side. When I told him what happened, Richard—Dad—just took off his glasses and rubbed his face. He's used to swooping in to help me. He got me an interview—and almost definitely the job—at DC FC after I struggled working at shitty organizations for a few years after college. How could I say no to a job at an MLS team when it'd been my dream to work in professional sports?

And Ron. Dad loves Ron. They went to the same business school. Well, not really, but they might as well have. Ron knows exactly how to kiss my father's ass.

Maybe even by dating his daughter.

And Dad wants me to take Ron back. Return to my old job. My old life. But Dad's on his fourth wife, and I think he doesn't understand why women make such a big deal out of cheating partners. So I'm not really into taking relationship advice from him.

I shift on the uncomfortable seat and set Waffles's leash on my lap. My shoulders are tight, and I will the muscles to relax by pushing thoughts of my father away.

I pull my bag onto my lap and slide my phone out to check new texts, which are unsurprisingly all in a group chat with my best friends. It's been over a decade since the three of us left James Madison University in Virginia, but we're still close, even though we're scattered all over.

JANUARY

How's your revenge plan going, babes? Show your dad what's what yet?

RALEIGH

I can't believe you really left DC. I never thought that would happen! How's Max?

ME

Who's Max?

RALEIGH

...Ron's dog? Er, your dog?

RALEIGH

Also, shouldn't we really want revenge on Ron
since he's the one who cheated on you?

ME

We hate him too, sis, but I have thirty-three
years of resentment for my father
overshadowing a two-year relationship
with Ron

ME

Also, he goes by Waffles now. Or Zeus

JANUARY

You're going to give that animal trauma by
changing its name every other day

ME

Here's Waffles/Zeus

I snap a quick photo of Waffles/Zeus and send it to my friends, biting back a grin and glancing up briefly to watch the hockey players gather around the coach on the ice.

ME

How unoriginal was Ron to name his dog Max?
I mean, no wonder he's a miscreant

JANUARY

This is a case of nurture, not nature

The coach claps his hands five times in quick succession and the noise echoes in the quiet arena, startling me.

And apparently my dog.

Waffles/Zeus leaps into the air and sprints along the glass barrier, pulling the leash right off my lap.

"No! Hey!" I stand and lunge, my phone clattering to the ground along with my bag, which spills my laptop, a notebook, various pens, a stack of tissues, and god knows what else onto the ground.

Waffles/Zeus doesn't just run, he also barks like a freaking mad man. Mad dog?

"Waffles! Hey! Shit!" I push my wayward red curls from my eyes as I stumble over my belongings and after him.

As if in slow motion, I watch the players turn around to find the source of the barking and swearing.

Does that damn dog think there's a squirrel in here? A car to chase? Something besides me running after him?

I remind myself to sign Waffles up for behavior lessons so I can actually leave that menace of an animal behind while I go to work, even though my boss insisted it's fine to bring him in. Lots of people bring their dogs to work in Fort Collins. Weird.

I will my feet to move faster, but I have no hope of catching Waffles before he... oh god.

He's zipping toward an entrance to the rink. Thankfully, it's closed, as it should be during hockey practice.

But—oh no.

It's cracked open just wide enough for a Boston terrier to squeeze through.

"Waffles! No! Zeus! MAX!"

But it's too late. He squeezes through the opening and leaps onto the ice, heading straight for the Blizzard players. I take in Atticus, a wide smile on his face as he shakes his head dramatically, and at least two other players bending down to try to intercept the running dog.

Waffles attempts to stop a few feet away from one of the squatting men, but it's literally ice so he slips and spins and hurtles toward the wall. He kind of looks like me trying to ice skate.

I finally make it to the entrance to the rink but stop there. No use in me slipping all over the ice as well, embarrassing myself further, if that's possible.

"Nooooo," I whisper-scream and bury my hands in my hair.

Atticus calls for my dog, and for a second I think it'll work, but then Waffles, now sprawled against the rink wall, manages to get his feet under him and complete an ill-fated lap around the laughing players. Even the coach is grinning at the chaos with his arms crossed.

Okay. This might be okay. Maybe it'll soften them up to me. No problem. Atticus will grab him and—

Oh no.

Waffles makes it back to the side of the rink.

I know exactly what's going to happen next.

"No, no, no!" I half step onto the ice, but it's far too late.

Waffles lifts one of his hind legs and pees, the yellow liquid spilling down the wall and onto the frozen surface.

That's it, then.

I guess I'm done here.

With the Blizzard. This job. Fort Collins. Colorado. The entire universe. I resign from life.

Atticus is laughing too hard to move, and I glare at him, throwing my hands in the air in the universal *can you help* gesture.

Another tall, broad player slowly skates toward Waffles—who's sitting innocently two feet away from his yellow puddle—and manages to swoop him up in one pass as if it's no problem at all.

"Someone clean that up," the coach yells, then points toward one of the younger-looking players. "You. Get a skate and a shovel from the equipment manager. Scrape that pee off the ice and get rid of it. Go!" The player heads out another exit. "And that door should be shut at all times." The coach turns to look at all the players. "At all times! It's a major safety issue."

The man holding Waffles gracefully skates toward me, stopping when he's a foot away and holding my dog in the crook of his arm.

"This guy yours?" The player is sweaty and wearing a helmet. But his lips are plump, his exposed neck smooth, and dark hair falls onto his forehead above blue eyes.

And I know exactly who he is.

A forward and captain of the Blizzard. A star player. One of Atticus's close friends.

Gorgeous.

And I've just absolutely humiliated myself in front of him.

My heart thumps loudly in my chest and a squeak escapes my throat. I remind myself I'm *not* into hockey players. Really. I've been around enough pro athletes to know they're way too messy to date.

Waffles looks at me with his scrunched-up face, tongue hanging out of his mouth, perfectly happy in the player's arms.

"Max—Zeus—Waffles, whatever your name is, bad dog." I shake my head and plant my hands on my hips. He clearly doesn't understand what I'm saying as he practically smiles at me.

"You don't know your dog's name?" the man asks. He's not smiling, but his face has a hint of amusement.

"Yeah. I mean, he's not really my dog. Well, he is *now*, for a bit. I hated his name—so did he, by the way—so I'm testing out a few new ones." I know I'm giving too much information, but I can't stop myself. My cheeks are warm and must be as red as my hair.

I grab Max/Waffles/Zeus and press him against my chest. He turns his head and licks my neck with his disturbingly long tongue.

"Ugh. Gross."

At that, the man laughs.

"I'm Kellen Bassey." Behind him, the players are skating around into their positions for the next drill.

I know.

"Hi. I'm Lucy. Lucy Knox. Nice to meet you. Atticus... has mentioned you."

"And Atticus has mentioned *you*." He blinks slowly at me, like a judgmental cat, his eyes holding onto mine like a vise.

How much has my brother talked about me to his teammates? He's probably told them all the worst parts of me. Isn't that what siblings do?

I swallow and pull at the neckline of my sleeveless blue top, which I paired with casual jeans for my first day of work.

In one swift movement, Kellen pulls off his helmet and runs his hand through sweat-damp hair. Does my jaw drop, with my tongue lolling out like a cartoon character? Probably. How is it fair that he looks so good when he's this sweaty? I'm not one to swoon over athletes, but Kellen Bassey is something else.

And somehow, that makes my humiliation even worse.

"You alright?" Kellen settles his helmet back on his head.

"Yeah, of course." I make an effort to close my mouth, so I don't look like a gaping goldfish. "My dog, just, you know. He's kind of crazy. Anyway. I'm the new PR person, covering Fiona while she's out on mat leave. So if you need anything to do with PR, I'm your girl." I make a weird swooping gesture with my hand.

What. Is. Wrong. With. Me?

Kellen lets out a noncommittal murmur and raises his eyebrows.

"Kellie!" A player calls from the ice. "Come on!"

"Well, welcome to Fort Collins." Kellen taps the glass panel and gently pulls the door in between us shut until it clicks securely, then skates away with confident, smooth strides.

I groan. *If you need anything to do with PR?* I didn't really say that, did I? And... *I'm your girl?* Oh my god. Way to sound professional. But I guess that ship sailed when my dog peed on the ice.

Good first day.

At least I'm here for just one season. If all goes as planned, at the end of my temporary contract, I'll be packing up to head to my dream job.

So it doesn't matter what this man thinks of me.

I'm not trying to find a new fiancé, or a boyfriend, or anybody like that. What I am trying to get is my dream job with a big soccer club in England: Winchester Football Club.

Farther away from my father. And my ex.

Back to working for a professional soccer team, except this time getting the job all on my own.

I've got a phone interview coming up in a few weeks. If I pass the phone interview, I'll do a video interview... And if I pass that stage, I get to fly to England for a final, in-person interview in January.

I need to kick ass at this temporary PR job because I'm determined not to use my father as a reference. And my work might involve Kellen Bassey, so I'll have to hope and pray that he forgets and/or forgives this unfortunate incident.

The best thing about Fort Collins is it's 1500 miles from D.C., my father, my ex, my old job, my former life entirely.

Do I already need to get away from Colorado?

Good thing that England is—I do a quick calculation in my head—4500 miles from here.

And the sooner I get there, the better.

CHAPTER 2
A Good Father

KELLEN

I'm beat after spending an extra hour lifting at the gym, carefully following the plan I developed with my strength coach. In the showers, I'm still cracking up at the visual of Atticus's sister's dog slipping around on the ice. The look on the dog's face, like he was having the time of his life. That is not a sight I often see at practice.

And the woman. Lucy. She was so flustered, swearing and freaking out on the sidelines. She shares the same wild, curly red hair as her brother, but she wears it much better.

I've heard about Lucy from Atticus. When you're on the road as much as we are—on the team plane, buses, in hotel rooms, out for meals and drinks—things come out. Like his sister's split from her cheating fiancé, and the way she quit her job at DC FC because the team owner—their father—wouldn't fire her ex.

I can relate to asshole team owners.

It's hard not to think about Paul Harrison, the one who's currently keeping me up at night. Who controls my future in Fort Collins with the Blizzard. FoCo is where my job is, my daughter, my friends. My home.

It's more fun to think about Lucy. She was surprising, or at least her dog was when he darted across the ice and peed on the wall. Her cheeks were bright pink when I handed him back to her. I grin as I towel myself off. I should definitely not be thinking of my teammate's sister as I dry my body.

I was the last one lifting, so the locker room is empty as I dress with only Coach Jackson still tucked in his office. He's buried in his laptop and scribbling notes, probably watching last season's game footage to discuss in a future practice.

I slip out into the hallway, planning on cutting through the arena and out to the parking lot. Cement walls with framed photos of teams and individual players from the past greet me. I'm in a bunch of those, and plan on being in a bunch more.

"Kellen," a woman calls from behind me in the direction of the team management and administration offices.

Shit. The source of that voice might be why I'll be left out of future photos.

I stop, take a deep breath, then turn to face the FoCo Blizzard team owner's wife.

Savannah is sashaying up the hallway, looking beautiful as always in a form-fitting blue dress, long blonde curled hair splayed on her shoulders, red painted lips, and dark eyelashes. She's in her late twenties—so potentially twenty-five years younger than Paul.

I got to know her a bit last season when she was first around after marrying Paul. She met him in D.C., and they had a whirlwind romance. Savannah told me Paul paid off all her law school debt, but she didn't realize he expected her to give up her ambitions and just be a trophy wife.

I was a sounding board for her, so when I saw her at the season kickoff event earlier this month, she was catching me up.

But I should've learned the lesson not to befriend Savannah after Paul traded our teammate, Markus, at the end of last season. He was also friendly with her and rumor has it Paul felt threatened.

So he got rid of him.

Maybe it was just a rumor.

But that's what I'm dealing with right now. Rumors.

I look over her shoulder before responding, checking to see if Paul is approaching from the direction of his office. But the hallway is empty. I'm not sure if that makes me feel better or worse, because I *am* sure that I do not want to be alone with Savannah.

"Hey, Savannah. Where's Paul?"

"Somewhere around here." She shrugs and half smiles at me. "Are you still worried about that picture? If so, don't be. I talked to him. Everything's okay."

"What do you mean you talked to him?" Dread creeps up my spine.

My teammate Lachlan—Canadian born but grew up in Australia and has the accent and dual citizenship to prove it—had sent me a link to the picture that started my troubles. It appeared on a hockey gossip website called NHL Tea. The defenseman loves to immerse himself in all the hockey gossip, on our team or off. He was practically giddy.

The zoomed-in cell phone picture, taken from across the room, was of me and Savannah sitting close together at one of the side bars of the venue. She had her hand on my forearm and was leaning close to my ear.

Fuck me.

I get how it looked in the picture. Bad.

But I know exactly what she was saying at that moment. She was telling me how she wants to take the bar exam for Colorado, but Paul isn't supportive. The woman is studying behind her husband's back, and I was trying to be encouraging and kind. It's nuts that she has to study law in secret, like it's something to be ashamed of.

Unfortunately, Paul holds the puppet strings on my life here.

It drives me crazy that anyone even cares about pictures of hockey players. And there was no context to the image—the entire team and administration were wandering around that place. We weren't on some romantic date. We weren't in private or even close to alone.

"I mean, he saw the picture somehow. But I told him we are just friends, and…" she pauses at the look on my face. This woman truly doesn't understand the problem.

I groan. "Maybe it'd be best to not talk to him about it. And I'm really sorry, but we should keep our distance for a while."

The picture's been posted for about a week and seems to have stopped at that trashy website. I'm praying it doesn't get picked up anywhere else.

But now I'm on Paul's shit list, and that is not a place anyone wants to be. Anyone who wants to keep playing for the FoCo Blizzard, at least.

Savannah's face crumples. I feel terrible doing this to her.

"But you're basically the only one on the team who will talk to me anymore." She reaches out and touches my forearm, her face soft and vulnerable.

"Sorry, Savannah." How do I explain this to her? That a friendship with her isn't worth it to any of us if it puts our spot on the team in danger? I gently pull my arm away. I'd be happy to be her friend under almost any other circumstances.

But not this one.

It doesn't matter that I'm the team captain or how many goals I score. I know my spot on the team is now at risk.

I'm only in my early thirties, but they could replace me with a cheaper version. A younger one.

Savannah sighs and looks absolutely crestfallen.

"I have to get home to my daughter." I back up a step.

It's true. Ava is sleeping at her mother's tonight, and Bri lives next door in one of the houses I own on my block. I'll stop by and say goodnight when I get home. It's less than two weeks until pre-season games start, and once the season is in full swing, I'll be on the road all the time.

I hate being away from Ava. It's a group effort raising any kid, but it's even harder with a job like mine. What helps is having Bri live next door, plus we have a full-time *and* part-time nanny. And we're still overwhelmed at times. That phrase about how it takes a village? It's so true.

And with Ava's history, what she's been through... and therefore what Bri and I have been through? We're all still dealing with that trauma.

"Savannah." Paul's tight voice pulls me out of my head. He's now standing right behind Savannah.

Fuck.

"I'm done. Let's go." He sounds annoyed.

At her.

At me.

The man has never been overly friendly, but he didn't used to glare at me. Nope. That's new.

I raise a hand to Paul. He nods and walks past Savannah, assuming she'll follow.

"See you around, Kellie," Savannah whispers, which makes it worse. As does her shortening my name like the boys do, like we're teammates or close friends.

Paul holds the door to the rink open for her and locks his eyes back onto me. It's not a nice look. It's cold. Calculating.

Somehow, I've gotten myself into trouble before the season's even started.

But I can't get traded.

Not with Ava's doctors all in Denver. We've built a life here as a co-parenting family unit over the past five years.

I need to fix this. Convince Paul that I'm not interested in his wife.

But how?

CHAPTER 3

Taco Tuesday (on a Thursday)

LUCY

Thursday, September 12

"So you're fully a dog person now, huh?" My brother leans against the frame to his apartment door, his too-long red curls twisting on his forehead as he casually watches me struggle to control this wiggly dog.

"No. Zeus!" I'm reconsidering the name—maybe he *can* wield a thunderbolt of destruction—and clip the leash onto his collar. "Ha! Got you."

Zeus twists around and licks my hand aggressively.

"Who are you and what have you done with my sister?" Atticus shakes his head and half-chuckles. "I thought it was a joke when you told me you were showing up with that dog. I thought you hated him."

"Gross." I stand and wipe the back of my hand on my jeans. "I hate what this dog stands for. Not the dog."

Ron's impulsivity and untrustworthiness. But that impulsivity made my ex so much fun. He'd do things like drag me around D.C. on a hunt for the best Chinese food, or the best bagel, or the quirkiest coffee shop. He was passionate about everything—soccer

16

and his home state of New York and his parents, who were lovely. Are still lovely, I suppose.

But no matter how much he claimed to have loved me, it wasn't enough.

And he got promoted after we'd been dating for six months. Coincidence?

Had he ever loved me, or was he just using me to get ahead?

After it was over, I still had to face him every day at work. I didn't last long.

"What happened to, what was his name before, Elmo? Edgar?" Atticus nods his chin at Zeus.

"Oscar, Atticus, it was Oscar. And neither of us liked that name." As soon as I brought Zeus home from Ron's apartment, I renamed him. Oscar wasn't a great name, but it was better than Max.

Atticus smirks and holds the front door to his luxury townhouse open for me, locking it after I emerge into the sunny day.

The sky is seamlessly blue, the temperature a perfect seventy degrees, and the leaves are starting to change along the tree-lined sidewalk of my brother's street a few blocks from downtown Fort Collins.

"Is it always like this here?" I breathe deeply. It's hard not to like this place when it insists on being so gorgeous every single day.

"Sunny and beautiful? Yes. I've been telling you to come visit since I got transferred. Fort Collins is perfect."

One of the upsides of coming here was the chance to hang out with my brother. It's been a decade since we spent more than a holiday at Mom's together or talked on a few scattered phone calls a year.

"Mmmm." We'll see if it's perfect. Sunny, beautiful, majestic mountains in the distance. Crisp, cool fall air in the morning, warming to delightful late summer weather by the afternoon. Never humid.

Okay, it's definitely better than D.C.

For so many reasons, I'm happy to be here.

For now.

"And it's the ideal town for a dog lover like you."

"I am not," I scoff as we turn onto the busy main street.

Atticus gestures to the large bowl of water in front of an antique shop just ahead. "Everyone brings their dogs everywhere."

Zeus strains against the leash and dunks his entire head into the water bowl, then shakes aggressively, splattering water on my jeans. A few droplets make it all the way up to my face.

"Hey! Come on!" Zeus runs ahead, causing me to almost trip on the leash and fall on my face.

"There are even dog parades." Atticus calls ahead as I struggle with Zeus.

"Dog parades?" Once I get my balance, I wipe my cheek with a sleeve.

"Over the summer, I witnessed an enormous parade of corgis."

"That sounds ridiculous." Zeus weaves in and out of my legs, threatening to trip me again. "I will never be part of a dog parade."

"There were flags and everything. It was wild."

"Jesus. Heel, Zeus!" Zeus barks, stops, and rolls onto his back. I sigh and tug on his leash until he gets up. "Anyway, it's temporary."

"What's temporary? The dog?"

"Yes. All of this. The dog, me living with you, this job."

"If you say so."

I can feel Atticus staring at my profile, but I ignore him and face straight ahead.

We walk past a few closed businesses. Thai food, Italian, a swanky-looking bar called Black Diamond.

"Right here." Atticus gestures toward a storefront—Deep Roots Cafe. I duck inside ahead of him.

"Ohhh, this place is so perfect!" It's an adorable little coffee shop with a chalkboard list of drinks, a case containing baked goods, and sturdy wooden tables throughout. It smells amazing, like warm muffins and crumb cake. There's a doorway to a cozy-looking bookstore with a sign announcing A Good Book above the wide open internal double doors. A cute guy with a beard and wavy dark hair smiles at me from behind the bookstore counter. I look away.

I have no desire to date any guy, or even flirt. Because I'm not sure I'll ever be enough for someone, even if it seems like I am. I can't trust that feeling.

"And what, exactly, do you intend on doing with this dog when you move to England?" Atticus waves me to follow him.

"I don't have the job yet. I'll figure out what to do with Zeus after I pass the phone interview, the video interview, and the in-person interview." I stop behind my brother in the line for coffee.

"That's a whole lot of interviews."

"You have no idea how normal people jobs work." I huff. "You're a professional hockey player. And this is my dream job." We step closer to the register.

"Is it a dream because the work is so good?" Atticus ignores my comments. "Because you love soccer so much? Or because it's in England, which is almost as far from your life in D.C. as you can get?"

"Oh, shut up." I push his arm and hope he doesn't notice I'm not answering his question. "New Zealand would be much further."

But the answer is all of the above.

The job with Winchester FC would be a promotion from director of marketing at DC FC—a level I've been stuck at for years—to senior director of PR and marketing. And there's potential for growth.

And yeah, it's far, far away in England.

"You're not going to answer the question?"

"How about our father is deeply insecure about DC FC being perceived as less prestigious than European soccer teams, so it would be a great way to piss him off?"

"I can always get behind that." We order our coffees and step aside while the baristas prepare our drinks.

Ever since he was old enough to understand what happened between our parents, Atticus and our father have not gotten along.

Mom left Richard after she found him cheating with a twenty-five-year-old woman. Atticus was one and I was five. It was incredibly painful for her at the time, but I believe our mom has led a much happier life than she would have with our father.

We stayed outside of Washington D.C. after the divorce, spending some weekends with my father. But when I left for college, Atticus refused to even do that.

And as soon as Atticus was out of the house, Mom bought a small vineyard a few hours south into Virginia. She's got her wine and her friends and a boyfriend on occasion, plus a whole lot of money from the divorce.

She's never wanted to remarry.

Our father was divorced from wife number two within a year of remarrying.

"So. Interested in adopting a dog?"

"No way, Luce! I really hope that's not your plan." Atticus crinkles his nose. "I stepped in dog pee on the carpet the other day. Warm dog pee. Do you know how disgusting that is?"

"Yes, I do." I've done that several times since arriving in Fort Collins a week ago. "But you know all about dog parades, and you could probably bring him to the arena—"

"That worked out great yesterday."

"—and you can definitely afford to have someone dog sit while you're traveling. And look at that cute face."

We both glance down at Zeus, who's sitting angelically by my feet, tongue sticking out of his mouth, staring up at me with hearts in his eyes.

"Nope. I will no longer entertain this conversation."

I shrug. I didn't really expect Atticus to take Zeus. It was just one possibility to now cross off the list.

We accept our coffees and step through to A Good Book. I linger right inside the doorway at a local authors shelf, touching a romance book called *Love on the Slopes*. My brother scoffs as he picks up a different romance novel with a girl in the arms of a bull standing on two feet on the cover.

"What in the hell is this?" He looks up.

"Hey, don't yuck on other people's yum, dude."

"I should buy it for Lachlan. He reads all this romance shit." Atticus shakes his head. "But really, who finds this—" then he stops speaking. I follow his gaze, which is directed back into the cafe.

"What? Who's there?"

Atticus tugs me by the arm over to the thriller bookshelf tucked against the wall.

"That's Paul and Savannah Harrison."

"Ohhh, no way." I peek around the bookshelf and take in the couple at the front of the line. The man is tall with a full head of gray hair, sharp lines to his face giving subtle villain vibes, but definitely handsome. The woman next to him is at least a foot shorter and pretty in a high maintenance way, wearing expensive black leggings and a lacy tank top with a fitted jacket over top.

"They come in here every morning at about this time," Atticus murmurs. "I'm assuming it's every morning, because I'm in here at least twice a week before heading to the arena, and they always seem to show up."

I observe the couple for a few more seconds. "He looks exactly like someone our father would be friends with."

"Right? I'm positive there's an actual Rich White Guy Team Owner club somewhere."

I snicker, because it's funny, even though it's not really.

The only downside to coming to Fort Collins to work for the Blizzard is that our father is friends with Paul Harrison, the team owner. That connection is seriously unfortunate. That and the fact that my brother plays for the Blizzard indicates I'm not really forging a brand-new path here.

"She's way younger than he is, huh?"

The barista hands them their drinks and Savannah takes a sip, fiddles with her lid, then hands it back to the woman who reaches for a bottle of flavored sweetener.

"Yup." Atticus gulps from his coffee cup and raises his left eyebrow at me meaningfully. "They live just around the corner from me in a penthouse apartment."

"Should we run away? Or go say hello?"

But at that moment, Paul turns toward us and meets Atticus's eyes.

"Fuck," Atticus says under his breath without moving his lips. The couple walks toward us. We were obviously doing a shit job hiding.

"Good morning, Atticus. Off to the arena soon?" Paul says.

"Yes, of course, Mr. Harrison." Atticus stands up straighter. "On my way now. Have you met my sister, Lucy? She's covering a PR maternity leave at the Blizzard."

Paul turns his gaze to me, and Savannah tentatively smiles and says hello before staring down at her phone.

"Nice to meet you, Lucy. Richard told me to watch out for his daughter."

Oh my god. I can't get away from him. The idea of my father asking the Blizzard team owner to keep an eye on me makes my toes curl.

"Nice to meet you. I assure you, I don't need to be watched." I throw in a smile. I'm thirty-three years old. I don't need a chaperone.

"I keep telling him to come out here to see a game in person," Paul says, not acknowledging the fact that Atticus playing here should be enough reason for Richard to come to Fort Collins. "But I suppose he's more interested in soccer."

Atticus's shoulders tense. Our father has never come out here to see him play. Even though I think I have it bad with Dad trying to control my life, providing me a constant narrative that I can't survive without his help, Atticus has it worse. Our father barely acknowledges his existence.

"Yes, I think you're right. Maybe you can finally convince him." I cock my head and give Paul a big smile.

Atticus lets out a quiet scoff just for me to hear.

"I'll have to let him know I met you. Welcome to the Blizzard, Lucy." With a nod at Atticus, Paul leads his wife out the front door of Deep Roots Cafe.

"Dad asked him to watch out for me?" I stare at their departing backs.

"I'm lucky Richard doesn't give a shit about me, because Paul might have been reporting back for years." Atticus gently elbows me.

"This is why I have to go to England. I can't escape."

Something clicks in my brain. I thought I was getting away from my father by being in Colorado, but really, there's always going to be someone watching and reporting back.

I can't fail here.

I can't prove my father right, that I can't do things on my own. That I'm not good enough.

Once we're sure Paul and his wife are gone, I follow Atticus out the bookstore exit to the street and back toward his apartment.

"Hey, you should hang out with the guys at some point." We're back at the door to Atticus's place.

"Socialize with a bunch of hockey players? Pass."

"These are good guys, Luce, I promise. And we're normally pretty boring. We mostly sit around and watch a movie and then go to bed early and sober so we can get up and work out again."

"I have no interest in hockey players."

"I'm not suggesting you date them." Atticus rolls his eyes. "Just make some friends or something. I worry that Raleigh and

January live so far away. I can't let you get sad and lonely in Fort Collins."

"I'll think about hanging out." I sigh deeply. "But don't worry about me. I'm doing fine."

But am I? Because I thought I'd feel all independent and strong as soon as I put some space between me and D.C., but I kind of don't feel like it worked. Not yet anyway.

"Basically you won't be able to avoid them since you live with me."

Atticus offers his fist and I bump it with mine. I head off to do another lap around the block with Zeus, and Atticus gets in his parked car.

The next street over has a restaurant called Taco Tuesday. Zeus barks at the sign.

"Tacos?"

He looks up at me.

"Taco Tuesday? On a Thursday?" I crack up at my own joke.

Zeus just looks at me.

"Sure, okay. Taco. We'll give it a shot."

Taco wags his tail and barks happily. He smiles for the picture that I snap and send to my friends.

ME

Meet Taco.

CHAPTER 4

A Family that Works

KELLEN

I open Bri's front door without knocking, a habit I should probably break at some point.

"Morning," I call into the foyer of the four-bedroom house next door to mine. The house that technically belongs to me, but it's helped Ava's mother to have someplace nice to live, and I get to see my daughter more often. It's a win-win.

"Daddy!" Ava calls from the kitchen. A second later, she's sprinting around the corner and throwing herself at me, wrapping her limbs tightly around my leg.

"Hi, sweetie." I peel her off and lift her into my arms so I can kiss her cheek. "I love your outfit."

"Thanks! I picked it out myself!" Ava's wearing a bright pink tutu, a purple t-shirt depicting three dogs wearing Christmas sweaters, and rainbow socks enveloped with bright yellow crocs. Top her ensemble off with two crooked ponytails that I'm betting she insisted on doing herself and you have my daughter's typical look.

"Kellen." Bri follows Ava from the kitchen and stands with her fists on her hips, legs wide in a fighting stance.

"Hello, Bri." I know the argument she's about to have with me. It's the same one we have every few months.

"Why did you transfer half my rent back to my account?"

I sigh. "Because. You don't need to be paying rent here at all, and definitely not that much. I make many, many multiples of what you do, remember?" Ava tugs at the neckline of my t-shirt with one hand and pulls my face toward hers with the other.

All I want in life is to take care of Ava and our family, which includes Bri. NHL players get paid shit-tons of money. What's the point if not to help the people you love?

"You don't let me forget it." Bri crosses her arms.

"Daddy," Ava whispers close to my face. "We're eating pancakes."

"Can I have some?" I turn to her.

"Nope." She shakes her head. "All for me."

"The amount I sent you is the going rate for a house like this in Fort Collins." Bri sighs and drops her arms. "I don't need your charity."

I know better than to argue further with Bri, so I bite my tongue and instead tickle Ava in the side until she squirms out of my arms and sprints back to the kitchen.

When Bri showed up at my door six years ago with a pregnant belly claiming I was the father, I was horrified and disbelieving.

Bri had been the pretty but nerdy girl in high school who played the flute in band, with messy hair and glasses. I was all hockey, all the time, so I never even tried to date her back then, but I had a crush on her from afar. I lost track of Bri after high school, but apparently, she'd gotten her associates degree from a small community college and was sucked into our hometown of Pueblo by her loser boyfriend.

Six months before she showed up at my door, I'd run into Bri at a bar in Fort Collins. She told me she was in town for a bachelorette party weekend, three hours from Pueblo. She'd broken up with her boyfriend a month earlier. We had one night together, then she went back home without even leaving her number.

And when she found out she was pregnant, and the doctors told her the estimated due date... she knew it was mine, not her ex's.

Bri didn't have one baby item with her when she arrived. Her parents weren't willing to help. That town is full of useless, dead-beat, lying parents, which I know all too well.

How could I turn her away?

"Daddy! Come sit!"

I shrug and slide past Bri into her kitchen. We never tried to be together after that, and neither of us wanted to. These days, Bri is family. And when Ava had serious health issues a few years after she was born, we got through it together while she was treated at the fantastic children's hospital in Denver.

"What's up today, pumpkin?"

"I have kindergarten. Again! Then soccer practice. Are you picking me up?" Ava pours about a gallon of syrup on her pancakes before murdering one with a fork and taking a too-big bite. I subtly slide a banana closer to her.

"Sorry baby, I'll be at hockey practice till late. Grace will grab you from school and take you to practice, okay?"

"Daddy, we still don't have a soccer coach since Bella's dad stopped helping. Are you sure you can't do it?"

"I wish I could, but I can't be there for most of the practices and some of the games. I'm sorry." If there was a way I could do this for my daughter, I would. Not because the kids need me in particular to be their coach, but because it'd be another way to show her she's my top priority. But I just can't. Not with my schedule.

"Aw." Ava sticks out her bottom lip.

"Hey, I have a funny story for you."

"What, Daddy?" Ava pours more syrup on the last two bites of her pancake. My blood sugar spikes just watching her. "Want some pancake?"

"Definitely not. I'll eat at the arena. And pancakes soaked in maple syrup will not be an option." Sometimes I wish I could eat like my daughter, but my hockey career depends on me taking care of my body. "Ava. There was a dog on the ice yesterday."

"A dog??" Ava gasps with delight, fork halfway to her mouth. "What kind of dog?"

"I don't know. It had a scrunched-up face."

"Was it a pug? I love pugs!" She shoves the dripping bite of pancake in her mouth.

"I don't think so."

"A bulldog? A Boston terrier?" I should probably stop her from talking with her mouth full, but she's too cute. I'm sure I'll regret that rationale at some point.

"Maybe? How do you even know all these dog breeds?" I chuckle.

"I got a book from the library! Was it a big dog? A small dog?"

"Um, I'd say small."

"She's obsessed with this dog breed book," Bri says. "I'll have her bring it to your house."

"What was the dog doing there?" Ava's eyes are open comically wide as she absorbs every word I say.

"Well, it was running away from its owner and got into the rink, slipping and sliding everywhere. And then—ready for this?— it peed on the ice."

Ava cackles wildly.

"Gross. Whose dog was it?" Bri asks from the kitchen sink.

"Atticus's sister."

Lucy's face pops into my mind, a vivid image of curly red hair, light freckles, and pink cheeks.

Ava groans. "Daddy, why can't I get a dog?"

"Because I travel too much."

"Mommy doesn't travel." Ava sits back in her chair and crosses her arms.

"Not this again, Ava." Bri shakes her head. "What was Atticus's sister doing with a dog on the ice?"

I stand and head over to the coffee machine, grabbing a clean mug and helping myself to the fresh pot.

"She's working for the team for the season. PR stuff." What'd she say? Something about how if I need anything to do with PR, she's my girl? I hold back a chuckle at the memory of the conversation.

"Daddy, what was the dog's name?"

"That's another funny story."

"Why?"

"Because she—Lucy—didn't even know its name."

"What? That's weird. She sounds weird." But Ava's grinning from ear-to-ear.

Bri hands me a container of pumpkin spice creamer. I make a face but pour it into the coffee anyway. I won't tell the nutritionist.

"It was either Zeus, or Waffles, or Max."

"I like Waffles!"

I lean against the counter, sipping from the steaming mug.

"Why are you smiling like that?" Bri narrows her eyes at me.

"I'm smiling?"

"Yeah. It's weird."

"So now I can't smile?" I press my lips together.

"I want to meet Waffles!" Ava stands and jumps up and down.

"Well, maybe I can arrange that."

And then maybe I can see Lucy again. Not that I have any real interest in that woman. Or any woman, these days.

But Lucy was... well, interesting. She was kind of babbling and flushed and not at all what I expected from Atticus's sister.

And she was hot. Hot mess hot.

"Yay! I love Atticus!!"

"Ava, honey, go grab your backpack so you can pack your

lunch and water bottle, okay?" Bri waves our daughter out of the room, and I gather up Ava's breakfast dishes and walk them over to the sink.

"Did you decide to apply for that role?" I run the lake of maple syrup off Ava's plate.

"Yeah." Bri leans against the counter. "I filled out the internal application yesterday. And if I get it, it'll be a significant pay increase, so no more sending back rent."

Bri works at the University of Colorado in an administrative job and is ambitious to do more.

"Fingers crossed."

"It is what it is." Bri waves me off, but I know how serious she is about this. "Don't you have to get to the gym or something?"

"Actually, yeah." I check my phone. "Have a to-go cup?"

Bri's already pulling a Yeti out of her cabinet.

"This is yours anyway. I grabbed it last time I was over your house."

I kiss Ava and wave at Bri.

Maybe our situation is a bit weird, but everything is good here in Fort Collins. I have a job I love, Bri's happy at work, Ava's settled, and we're close to her trusted doctors.

I don't want anything to change. I like being single, stable, and a provider for my family. I'm not interested in dating or a relationship, and I don't have time for one-night stands. I've got too much going on. Ava's depending on me.

And when I did try dating someone last year, it was a disaster. Lesson learned.

I slide into my car and close my eyes for a second.

I need to keep my spot on the team. That means convincing Paul that nothing happened between me and his wife, and that nothing will.

These rumors could be disastrous for my career. I don't want to get traded. I don't want to leave Fort Collins or Colorado.

The problem is, I have no clue how to fix the mess I've gotten myself into.

CHAPTER 5

Waiting Behind the Door

LUCY

Monday, September 16

Ilook down at my phone again, checking the video feed at the Delightful Doggy Palace, the new doggy daycare I dropped Taco off at this morning. He's currently running some kind of obstacle course. Through a tunnel, up some steps, down some steps, then jumps over a big log. Looks ridiculous, but he seems to be having a blast. I mean, *I* kind of want to go and do it. I let out a deep breath and lay my phone on the desk. Phew. I'm relieved he's having a good first day.

I don't care about this dog nearly as much as it appears.

It's just that I'm a responsible human being. I couldn't let Ron drop him at the animal shelter just because he didn't realize Boston terriers aren't completely hypoallergenic. It's not Taco's fault.

And even though I can bring him to work with me, he needs at least some time socializing with other dogs. And exercise, and nice pets from humans, and overall stimulation. The Delightful Doggy Palace was amazing when I went to check it out last week. Taco deserves some kind of fun, doesn't he?

Anyone would do the same thing.

32

My onboarding meeting with Coach Jackson, the Blizzard head coach, isn't for another fifteen minutes, but maybe I'll walk down early to make sure I can find his office. My scribbled note says he's in the second to last door on the right. I think that's what it says, but I might have been paying attention to the continuous reel playing in my head of Taco peeing on the ice instead of details about the office floor plan from Lina. But it can't be hard to find.

I stand and grab a notebook and pencil, then smooth down my curls—which I've hopelessly tried to tie half-back—and straighten my thin green sweater before walking out the door. The dress code is casual in the team administrative office so I'm wearing gray jeans and short heeled boots.

I'm excited to meet Coach Jackson. Atticus said he's a great guy, treats the players well, and is kind and friendly. Hopefully the coach can help give me some tips on working with the team.

One part of my role while here is to follow up with key publications on getting features written about some of our top players. Then I need to make sure they are media trained—most already are —but department policy dictates we do a refresher before interviews. I'll also need to ensure we have the right catalogue of photos. Including ones in suits. Apparently, everyone loves it when the hot hockey players walk into the games in full suits.

Not me. Hockey players aren't my jam.

Obviously, I can see the appeal—I'm not *completely* dead inside —but it'd be best to not get involved with anyone who's connected to the team I work for.

I wish I'd learned this lesson earlier and not dated Ron at all.

Kellen's face from last week appears in my mind. Those dark strands of hair on his sweaty forehead when he pulled his helmet off, the light blue eyes. He might have made an impression on me, and I definitely made one on him. Not in a good way. Could it have been any worse? My escaped dog peed on the ice. Peed! In the rink! And that poor player scraping the stained ice off with a skate. Lordy.

None of that matters though. I just need to do well in this role so I can impress Lina and get her to agree to be a reference.

I can't have things like Taco or fantasies about one of my brother's teammates distract me from that.

I shake my head and pause in the hallway, counting doors. The farthest door on the right—before the exit to the arena—is the player gym. It's got a fierce abominable snowman painted on the entrance in Blizzard colors of purple and yellow. The second door from the end of the hallway is less fancy but also decorated with the Blizzard logo. Makes sense for the coach.

It's a keycard access door but it's propped slightly open with a rubber door stop.

"Hello?" I pull the door and step inside a small area leading to another door. Weird. My phone buzzes with a ten-minute reminder for the meeting.

Exude confidence. Project how much value you're going to add to the team, not just be a pain-in-the-ass PR person. Don't think about the Taco incident.

I knock, but there's no answer.

So, I push through the door.

A split second before it opens, I wonder why his office has double doors. And why it doesn't have a normal doorknob. This one is just one of those swing doors that pushes out into...

A locker room.

A locker room full of men.

A locker room full of men in various states of undress.

My body turns into a statue. Holy mother of god. I'm a tree. A giant, trembling, out of place tree in a landscape of not-trees. Do I blend in? No, I definitely do not.

I'm a purple tree. The carpet in the locker room is a deep purple and there's a yellow Blizzard logo in the center. Maybe no one's noticed me. Maybe I blend in. My eyes dart around the room in terror.

There's a bare ass. A man ass. I can't help the gasp that escapes my throat. A bare, round, man ass that leads to long legs and feet that are stepping into a pair of boxer shorts. That man—I squint my eyes—is mostly naked.

One of the guys sitting on a cushioned bench in front of a wall of wide, neat cubbies looks up at me and raises his eyebrows.

"Are you lost?" His hair is wet, and he's blessedly wearing a shirt and a pair of athletic shorts. He tosses a towel into a wheeled laundry bin. I try to keep my eyes on him, but there's just so much skin on display in this room, and somewhere deep down inside me a voice screams to turn and run, don't just stand there, remove yourself from this situation immediately.

But I cannot.

Because trees have roots and are not mobile. And maybe some blink like a malfunctioning neon sign so everyone will notice them.

Just like me at the moment.

"Hey," that same man says. "You're the woman with the dog that peed on the ice."

"No," I whisper in despair. I shake my head and another pair of shirtless dudes with abs for days turn in my direction, pausing their conversation.

"Oh my god." Am I whimpering? Impossible to tell through my veil of horror and fear. I whip my head away from the shirtless men.

My body comes to life starting from the tips of my toes, and as I'm about to try to leave this place, around the corner walks a man who's obviously fresh out of the shower with hair dark and wet and a towel wrapped so very low around his waist. My eyes rake up his body and land on his face. His eyes meet mine, and he stops in the doorway to the showers.

Oh no. Blue eyes I can see from across the room, the same dark hair that was peeking out from his helmet last week when he handed Taco—then Waffles/Zeus—to me at the edge of the ice rink.

Kellen Bassey.

"Lucy. Good to see you again." Kellen leans an arm against the doorframe, posing like he's in a damn cologne commercial on a yacht off the coast of Italy. His six pack—sparkling with droplets of water that must've evaded his towel—twitches.

I'm not sure I've ever seen a more gorgeous specimen of man. The side of his mouth quirks up. That smile. I'm melting. Dying.

And... is his towel *slipping*?

He doesn't seem concerned.

A few of the other guys chuckle, and I open my mouth to say something, anything, but words have left the building.

With much effort, I swallow, my burning face about to catch flames. Which might be a blessing. Then I could burn to ashes and cease to exist in this world and therefore not have to face this man or any of the Blizzard players.

"Are you looking for someone? I think Atticus is still in the showers." Kellen gestures behind him.

"Oh sweet baby Jesus." I didn't even think of that. What if my little brother walks through that doorway butt-ass naked? I see him in a towel on the regular since moving into his apartment, but I can't handle his bare ass.

Or worse.

"Pretty lady, are you okay?" one of the fully clothed players asks me, but I cannot rip my eyes from Kellen's face.

"I have a... uh... a meeting. With the coach. Coach, uh, Coach Jackson..." I back up slowly, like I'm escaping from a bear without turning my back to it. That's what you're supposed to do with bears, right? Back away slowly, not run. But I'm not a hiker, so how would I know that? Maybe you're supposed to sprint as fast as you can.

It's then that I notice the coach's office through a clear glass wall.

Ah. I understand now. His office is through the men's locker room, and if I hadn't come early, I probably wouldn't have experienced any naked men. Or as many.

"Door to his office is this way." Kellen nods behind him. "I can take you to him." He raises his eyebrows and lowers his hand from the doorframe, crossing his arms instead and emphasizing his biceps and forearms.

I swallow with a loud, dry click that must echo against the lines of player cubbies.

Why wouldn't Lina warn me about this? Why wouldn't she specifically tell me that the head coach's office is through the hockey players' locker room? I feel betrayed.

"I'm just gonna go." My feet finally cooperate, and I spin around and slam against the door, which doesn't budge. "Oh no. No, no, no." I push harder. Nothing happens. Am I somehow locked in here?

"Lucy," Kellen calls. "You gotta pull, not push."

I squeak and manage to pull the door open and fall out, leaving a locker room full of laughing men behind me.

I sprint down the hallway and dart into my office, slamming the door shut and wishing there was a lock. With a shaking hand, I tap my phone until I get to Raleigh's contact.

"Lulu?" she answers immediately.

"I saw naked hockey player ass." I close my eyes and lean my forehead against the door. Remnants of terror seep into my stomach and make me want to throw up.

"Finally!!" She laughs. "But I'm gonna need more details than that. Hold on, let me take my break." Her voice goes muffled for a beat.

"Hurry, I'm dying." Visions of naked ass, abs, and Kellen Bassey leaning against a doorframe in a low-slung towel fly through my head.

It's not a terrible vision.

"Okay, tell me in great detail what happened."

"Raleigh, I walked into the locker room. Full of hockey players. Mostly naked hockey players. It was horrific."

"That sort of sounds like a dream."

"No, it wasn't!"

"Did you see all the goods?"

I gasp. "Thankfully, no."

"Aw. I could really benefit from seeing hockey player ass, or dick, or any body parts." She laughs and it's infectious.

"Well, sis, you should come visit, because I'm sure that could be arranged." I groan and cross the room to my desk chair.

"Was Atticus there?"

"Thankfully, I didn't see him. Why? Do you want to see his ass?"

"Gross, no, he's your little brother. I still think about him puking in the bushes outside of our dorm."

I laugh at the memory. "He made quite an impression on you and January from the first moment."

"Sure did. Remember how he'd follow us around to parties when he was a freshman?"

"God, he was the worst." My heartbeat slows down, and I slump in my chair. "Oh. Raleigh *Durham*." I emphasize the nickname January and I gave her during college. January has one too—Janny—and they gave me Lulu.

"What?" She huffs.

"I see what you did there."

"I don't know what you're talking about."

"Distracted me."

"Did it work?"

"Yes, but I still want to hide under this desk for the rest of my life." But I'm smiling now. Talking to Raleigh and January always makes things better.

"I'm sure it wasn't that bad. But seriously, I'm coming to visit as soon as this divorce is final. As a celebration."

"Yes! That would be amazing."

"What do you think about around New Year's Eve?"

"Really? Perfect." I need my old college roommates. Who knows what other messes I'll make while in Colorado?

"And I think January is planning on being in the US for the holidays, so she said she might be able to come too."

I sink down into my chair and shut my eyes. Seeing them is exactly what I need. Raleigh and January are my best friends, and even though we haven't lived in the same place since college graduation over a decade ago, we've stayed close.

Raleigh gives me the latest details on her (second) divorce, which is almost final. She's been back in her hometown in Connecticut since college and has had two rough marriages.

January is the wild one of our trio. She wanders the world. Paris, Sydney, Bangkok, and London, her current location. I can't even remember when she's been in one location for her freelance consulting job for longer than six months.

I was the one who settled a few hours from JMU in Washington D.C., back home where I grew up. I didn't think I'd ever leave.

I try to be a good listener to my old friend, but my mind is stuck on the way Kellen's biceps rippled when he crossed his arms on his bare chest.

My phone buzzes, and I look down at a text from Atticus.

ATTICUS

What on earth did you do??

I will never live this down.

CHAPTER 6

Just Be Nice

KELLEN

"Atticus's poor sister." Harley stops next to me with his hands shoved in his pockets.

I'm still lingering in the doorframe, a grin on my face, a chuckle in my throat.

Harley's always the one who thinks about other people's feelings. Which is probably why he's been in such a stable long-term relationship, even if his girlfriend is back in his Maine hometown.

I let out the laugh. Poor girl? Yeah, okay, I can see that. But she's the amusement I need in my life right now.

"Did you see her face? That was the funniest thing I've witnessed in a long time." Lachlan says in his Aussie accent. There aren't many Aussie NHL players—just one other in the league.

"It really was." I head to my locker, dropping my towel to step into boxers. "She was especially horrified to see your hairy ass."

"My ass is not hairy, mate. It's smooth as a baby's bottom. That's what waxing is for."

"Christ." I shake my head and pull on jogging pants.

"Want to see? Maybe you should take care of *your* hairy ass."

"My ass isn't—" I stop. "You know what? Fuck off."

Lachlan laughs and reaches for his hoodie. "I can't wait to tell

Atticus." He runs his hand through his long, blond curls, securing them back into the man bun we mercilessly make fun of him for.

Doesn't seem to stop him from getting women.

Being a professional hockey player plus that damn Australian accent gets them every time. The tattoos and beard haven't hurt him either.

"Tell me what?" Atticus emerges from the showers in a towel.

"You missed your sister, Atter."

"Lucy?" He furrows his brow. "In here?"

"Yeah." I answer Atticus because Lachlan is laughing too hard. "She walked right into the locker room."

"Why the actual fuck would she do that?" Atticus groans.

"Apparently she has—had?—a meeting with Coach."

"Oh, shit." Atticus glances back over his shoulder through the glass, where Coach Jackson is typing something painfully slowly with two fingers.

"Yeah."

"Was everyone dressed?" With a slight panic in his voice, Atticus scans the room, where there are no asses or dicks on display.

At least not anymore.

"Absolutely not," another player calls out.

"It could've been worse," I say helpfully. "I think it was only Lachlan's ass that was visible."

"And my dick," Lachlan adds, now that his laughing has died down. "But I don't think she saw."

"For fuck's sake." Atticus rubs his hands on his face. "Alright. Listen up, assholes!" he yells to the room. The side conversations die down.

I turn to him and cross my arms, biting back a smirk. This should be good.

Atticus turns in a circle, looking each of our teammates in the eye. Trying to look intimidating? Which normally I could see happening, given his height and bulk. But it's not quite working right now. Probably because when I look at him with his red curly hair, I think of his sister's expression when she realized she was in the same room as a half-naked hockey team.

"My sister Lucy is working for the team for just one season to cover Fiona's maternity leave." He pauses. "Please be nice."

The room bursts into laughter.

"Seriously. She's had a rough time recently and could use some friendly faces."

"You're not going to tell us she's off-limits?" Lachlan raises his eyebrows.

"I don't think I have to as we're not supposed to date team staff." Atticus glares at Lachlan.

Of course he thinks Lachlan is the most likely to cross that line. He usually is. But this time, I wonder if I'm the one more interested in the pretty new staffer. Not that I'll do a thing about it. I don't need woman drama in my life. More woman drama, anyway.

"She just broke off her engagement and is figuring out her life. Don't mess with her."

The laughter fades away.

"We'll be nice," I say. Lachlan nods in agreement.

I pull on my gray t-shirt, tugging down the hem.

I don't date because it makes my life too complicated. I'm always on the road during hockey season—which is most of the year—and when I'm here, I like to focus on Ava.

And the one recent time I took a chance on someone, it backfired.

Last fall, I'd gotten involved with a woman who worked for one of the craft breweries in town. I'd met her on a night out with the boys. She and her two friends had sung "Like a Prayer" by Madonna, then Lachlan and Atticus sang that 500 miles song by the Proclaimers.

Sam seemed sweet, but she was twenty-five, more than five years younger than I am, which is usually not my jam. She got attached quickly. But after she came with me to the fall festival last October—most of the team volunteers at the event—and couldn't figure out how to interact with Ava or Bri, I broke it off. I wasn't feeling it anyway.

But she sold me out.

Literally sold pictures of me and Ava to the same sleazy hockey tabloid that has the photograph of me and Savannah. NHL Tea. What's worse is she told the tabloid about how I'd recently taken Ava down to Denver Children's Hospital for her annual oncology checkup. Ava's one hundred percent healthy these days, but we still do annual visits to make sure she stays that way. I've always kept that out of the press.

As if I don't have enough PTSD about Ava's treatment and long-term care. Bri does too. I don't need to see it in the press.

The team had my back.

They turned the publicity into a fundraiser for childhood cancer research and raised a shit ton of money.

It was another lesson in how I can't let anyone near my family. I need to protect my daughter in every way I can. And that includes not dating women who could get close to Ava and hurt us somehow.

So just because I have the tiniest little crush on the new PR person doesn't mean anything will happen.

It'll stay just that—a secret crush that never sees the light of day.

"Hey." Atticus is now dressed and steps next to my locker, which I'm staring into blankly. "I know I can count on you to be friendly to Lucy."

Christ. I'm such a non-threat to women that Atticus is asking me to watch out for his sister. My image is too soft.

"Sure, I guess."

"And listen—" Atticus slaps his hand on my shoulder. "I was thinking about Ava's soccer coach situation."

I chuckle. "Yeah? Why? You have time to coach?" Clearly, I

overshare with my teammates. They're my extended family, especially Atticus, Lachlan, and Harley.

"No, but my sister coached little kids when she was living in D.C. She loved doing it. I bet she'd be happy to help you out."

"What? Oh." There's no way I'd let someone I don't know around my daughter. I shake my head. "That's an idea, but—"

"Kellen." Atticus removes his hand from my shoulder and stands up straight. "She's not some stranger. She's my sister. You can trust her. I promise." Atticus walks away.

Past experience and being a professional athlete have taught me to be overly cautious about who I trust with myself and, even more so, my daughter. Ava's face pops into my head, begging me to be her soccer coach. I know she's only in kindergarten, but I want to give her everything in life. I'll have to find another way to help her. Maybe I'll hire a background-checked professional soccer coach to come in to train her team.

Throwing money at problems doesn't always solve them, but maybe in this case, it would.

CHAPTER 7

Abs for Days

LUCY

Monday, September 23

I stare at the email in my inbox, my cheeks high with a smile. I was hoping to hear back quickly from Friday's phone interview with Winchester FC, but first thing Monday morning —so the afternoon in England—was even faster than I imagined.

To: Lucy Knox
From: Marcie Lancaster, Winchester FC HR
Date: Monday, 23 September
Subject: Congratulations & Next Steps

Dear Lucy,

We were all very impressed with your phone interview on Friday. We'd love to move you on to the next stage of the process for senior director of marketing and public relations for Winchester Football Club located in Winchester, England.

The next step is a video interview in November. I will send you a list of dates and times to see if any work for you. If you progress after that interview, we'll ask for references and schedule you for an in-person interview in January. The job will start on or before 05 May 2025.

I squeal and read the rest of the email, the blood pumping through my veins. I *so* want to do this on my own. I do not want to use my father or my old boss at DC FC as a reference, but after eight years there, I don't have much choice.

That's why I'm here.

I want to prove to myself—and Winchester FC—that I'm the best person for this job. That's why I have to kick ass at this job for the Blizzard.

After starting at DC FC, I got promoted to manager within a year and director a few years after that. But with each promotion, I got the side eye from coworkers who assumed I was moving up because of my father. I'd been so frustrated to be stuck in the same job with the same responsibilities for the past five years. Richard kept telling me to be patient, that he'd give me progressive work soon.

I started to think my father was holding me back on purpose. To keep control of me.

But my coworkers had made a fair assumption. My father had helped me with so many things in my life.

In high school, I'd made the top team at a big youth soccer club but sat on the bench for most of the games. I preferred to be on the sidelines cheering anyway, or the admin offices working, or even helping coach the local elementary school kids.

I'm sick of my father assuming he knows what's best for me. I'm thirty-three years old, and I'm done with men trying to control me.

But when I got a text from Ron this morning, it really threw me. We haven't spoken since he dropped off that box of stuff.

And Taco.

Hey. Can I call you sometime today?

I ignored the shit out of that text. What could he possibly want to talk to me about? At first I was hurt that he'd not reached out after we broke up. But then I realized it was a blessing that he was just going to let me get on with my life without him.

Something that wouldn't have been possible if he'd been down the hall at work.

I gather up my laptop and notebook so I can head to Lina for our one-to-one, then pause at the door to my office to take a few deep breaths.

Each morning since last week's locker room incident, I have to pep talk myself into coming into work.

The humiliation of walking into a locker room full of half-dressed hockey players.

The laughter of the entire team.

The bare asses. Lachlan's ass, Atticus informed me.

Kellen Bassey in a towel.

I wave my hand at my face to cool down from just the thought of it. Those broad shoulders, moisture covering ripped abdomen muscles, the V leading down into the towel, hooked criminally low on his hips. Barely staying on. One sneeze could've caused it to fall completely off and then I would've seen everything.

Everything.

I grip the doorframe of my office.

I've been officially broken up with Ron for three months. Three months since I picked up his phone and discovered a text chain with another woman. Then I scrolled down and found another from several months back. And another.

He didn't try to deny it, just broke down and begged my forgiveness. He told me he'd get help. He admitted he had a problem. And if it had been just once, maybe I would have considered.

But he'd been cheating on me the whole time, when we were happy, in love, laughing, sleeping together. When he'd proposed.

I don't know what I missed. How can I trust my gut when it was so wrong about Ron? I don't think he'd been faking with me, but apparently I wasn't enough to satisfy him.

I broke up with him and told him not to contact me again.

But now he has.

Maybe if I ignore him, he'll go away.

I knock on Lina's door, and she waves me in.

"Hey! How's it going? Feeling okay after..." she waves her hand vaguely to her door.

"After what?" I pretend to look confused. "Oh, the locker room thing?" I shrug and make a face that I hope conveys nonchalance. "I haven't even thought of it since it happened." I sink down into one of the hard-backed chairs in front of her desk.

"Excellent." Lina presses her lips together, but her eyes crinkle slightly. "I wouldn't want you feeling awkward around the players."

"Never," I say, but my voice betrays me with a tiny squeak at the end. Lina pretends not to notice.

"Alright, let's go over your projects." Lina taps her mouse a few times. "Where do you want to start?"

I give Lina a status update on the work I'd picked up from Fiona and some new ideas for pieces to pitch to publications.

"I think Kellen would be great for that idea, Lucy."

She looks at me expectantly, so I glance down at the document open on my laptop and type Kellen next to the piece I just pitched to Lina. My brain stutters a bit, and I mentally get sucked back into that locker room.

"Lucy? You okay?"

"What?" I snap my head up. "Yes, of course. Sure, Kellen's a great fit considering he's the captain."

"He's good with interviews but prefers the questions vetted ahead of time. His private life is mostly off-limits."

"Okay."

"There was a whole incident last year with pictures of his daughter that some hockey gossip site picked up."

A daughter? Did I know that?

"Got it. Is he married?" The bottom of my stomach drops out at the idea of there being a Mrs. Kellen Bassey.

"Nope."

Kellen, a single dad who's protective of his little girl. I bite my bottom lip. Why does that make him even more attractive?

"Oh, and Lachlan will be a good fit for your first idea. Journalists love his accent."

"Does he need media training?" I ask.

"A quick review won't hurt, but keep your pants on."

I burst out laughing. "I will. I'm not into hockey players."

Lina gives me a funny look.

"What?"

"Lucy, everyone's into hockey players." She looks at me over the top of her glasses. "But remember that the official team policy is that players and staffers shouldn't date, and if they do, they need to disclose the relationship to HR right away."

I laugh. "That won't be a problem. I promise."

When I leave her office thirty minutes later, there's a string of texts from Raleigh and January. The first one is a picture of some of the Blizzard players taken from a charity calendar. They're all standing in front of a snowy mountain with their shirts off. I jolt to a stop in the middle of the hallway.

Holy hell. My eyes roam over their bare chests until I find Kellen.

JANUARY

Honestly, you need to hit some of that while you're in Colorado. Bang the breakup out of your system

RALEIGH

January, you leave her alone. That's the last thing she needs

JANUARY

The last thing? Look at the one named Harley. Second from right in the back row

RALEIGH

👀

JANUARY

Oh, and the one with the man bun. Smoking. Babes, maybe you need to bang your divorce out as well

RALEIGH

I'm not even officially divorced yet. Let's focus on Lucy

JANUARY

Lulu? You there? Pick one of those guys. Not your brother, obviously. Atticus is looking pretty hot these days though

RALEIGH

Gross

JANUARY

There is no way you really think Lucy's brother is gross in that picture

RALEIGH

He will never not be that annoying freshman kid

JANUARY

Bullshit. LOOK AT HIM

Finally caught up on the messages, I crack up as I slide back behind my own desk.

ME

Get your asses over here and maybe we can all
bang it out with some hockey players

JANUARY

YES LUCY

ME

Janny! I'm kidding. I'm a professional woman,
plus there are HR rules

I flip my phone over and bite back a smile.

We can laugh about it all we want, but I need to keep it professional while I'm here. I can't let hot hockey players distract me.

Even ones with abs for days.

My phone vibrates again, and I flip it over with a grin.

It's Ron. Calling.

A string of thoughts flies through my mind.

I should ignore the call he has no right to call me no reason that I need to answer what if it's important—

Or I could take the call and get it over with. Something tells me he's not going to leave a voicemail or let this go.

And even if he does, there's no way I'll call him back later.

"Hello." My voice is tight, and my shoulders bunch up around my neck.

"Lucy?"

"Yeah." I squeeze my eyes shut. His voice feels half like coming home and half like stepping on a stray thumbtack. "Why are you calling me, Ron?"

There's a brief silence.

"I wanted to check in on you. And... Max. See how things are going in Colorado." He pauses. "I miss you, Lucy."

My stomach twists at the tenderness in his voice. He has no right. I shake my head, even though he can't see me. I won't let him suck me in again.

"Things are great here." If he thinks I'm going to chit-chat with him about my life, he's mistaken.

There's a silence as he presumably waits for more.

"Listen, Lucy. Richard—sorry, your father—talked to Paul Harrison, the Blizzard team owner."

"I know who Paul Harrison is. And I know Richard is my father."

I can't believe I came all the way out here, and I have the Blizzard team owner looking over my shoulder and reporting back to my father, who's reporting back to Ron. I knew about Paul and my father's connection before I got here, I just didn't really think through the implications of that connection.

"Richard is worried about you. I am too. We all know that the farthest you've ever lived from D.C. is two hours away for college."

"Neither of you need to worry about me." My insides twist. "I'm a fully grown adult. And it's none of *your* business what I'm up to." I hate how defensive I sound.

"How's Max?"

"Who?" It takes a second for his question to register.

"I'm sorry about dumping him with you. I kinda hoped you'd invite me in, and we could've talked about things—"

"There's nothing to talk about." That's what he apologizes for? Dumping his dumb dog on me? What about cheating and lying and completely betraying me?

"Your father wants you to come back to DC FC. And I... I'd love for us to have another chance." He stops and sighs. "I miss *us*."

I hate how sincere he sounds. Like the Ron I fell in love with, the one I said yes to.

"The *us* that you were cheating on the entire two years of our relationship?" I summon the fury he deserves and let it smash whatever fond feelings are crawling out from where I'd buried them.

"I know. I'm sorry."

"I don't want to come back. To DC FC or to you."

"Lucy—"

"And it's Taco, not Max."

I can't stop the tears from running down my cheeks. I thought I was over this. Over him. But hearing his voice again makes me remember the way I felt at the end. Discarded. Not good enough. Alone.

I click off before he can respond.

CHAPTER 8

The Best Idea

KELLEN

Friday, September 28

My chest burns as I bench press one and a half times my body weight. Harley is spotting me, and we'll swap as soon as I'm done with my reps. I'm already sore from practice today, where Coach Jackson drilled us relentlessly to prepare for the season, which starts in less than two weeks.

I need to be top of my game in every way so there is no excuse to trade me, at least from a hockey perspective. That's what I can focus on right now. Working out. Practices. Playing my best.

Not pissing off the team owner any more than I already have.

Paul and Savannah have been around the arena every day lately. He's always been present more than most team owners, at least the ones I've experienced in my time in the NHL. Some might take it as a compliment that he's so interested in how the team works... I find it annoying as hell to always feel like we're performing for him.

I'm avoiding Savannah, and she gives me sad puppy dog eyes each time she sees me. She's friendly with the VP of finance—I wish she'd focus more on uncontroversial friendships like that one.

"Listen up!" Coach Jackson strides to the middle of the

weights area, where a dozen of my teammates are in various states of lifting.

I sit on a nearby bench, rotating my wrists, appreciating the creaky stretch.

"We had a great practice today, and a strong showing at the pre-season games last week. But pre-season is literally only the beginning. We need to focus on our individual conditioning and executing our new plays."

"We got it Coach," one of the players calls.

There's a rush of air at my back and we all turn to the entrance to the gym.

Paul Harrison strides confidently to the middle of the room, dressed in an expensive-looking tailored gray suit. The mood of the room tenses.

"Excuse me, Coach Jackson, I just want to say a few words. First, encouragement. Keep working hard. This is a strong team, but you need to really bring it to every single practice, workout, and especially games. I expect a lot of you all."

Heads nod all around the room.

Paul keeps talking about focus, but my mind wanders. Of course we're all working our hardest. We need to earn our salaries and keep working, improving, winning.

"Second, we need to keep the reputation of this team top notch. Our PR team is working on that, so make sure you make cooperation with them a priority."

Cooperate with Lucy Knox? She's already emailed me asking if I want to set up media training. I haven't responded yet, because while I'd like to spend time with her, I've been to endless media training sessions, and I can do it all over email.

I'm staring at the mat with my hands clasped between my knees when the room quiets, and I feel eyes on me. I look up, and Paul's staring directly at me.

"Are we clear?"

There are murmurs of agreement from around the room and I nod my head.

"Mr. Bassey? Will you step outside with me for a moment?"

My muscles tense, and I go into fighting mode. All eyes are on us as I stand and follow Paul as he strides out of the locker room, through the doors and into the hallway.

He stops and spins toward me.

"Will you be cooperative with the PR team?" Paul says it like an accusation. One I don't deserve.

"Of course." My chest tightens. I don't need any added attention from Paul Harrison. But that's exactly what I'm getting. There's no reason for him to target me on this topic. I've been nothing but cooperative with PR.

This is only because of that photo with his wife.

Paul's hard eyes drill into me.

"Cooperate with PR. Have the best season of your life. And no bad press. Or any press, preferably, unless it's about the record number of goals you've scored." He spits the words out.

I breathe in deeply. I want to punch this guy. Shove him into the wall and see him bounce off it and onto the floor like what happens on the ice.

"Because your job depends on it."

I clench my fists at my sides and swallow. Paul's words sink into every cell of my body.

"Yes, of course, Mr. Harrison."

He stares at me for another moment. Maybe we should just talk about this directly. I could explain to him that there is nothing between me and Savannah. That she was just talking about her career plans. How she wishes he was more supportive—

I hear the conversation in my head. Yeah. It wouldn't go over well.

"Good. Then get back to it." Paul walks down the hall toward the executive hallway, and I've lost my chance.

Shit.

I honestly wondered if maybe I was imagining him hating me. At least hating me more than the others. For a NHL team owner, he doesn't seem to enjoy hockey or hockey players or anything about the process. It's all business for him. Which, I suppose, isn't that rare. But I've known more casual, friendly, collaborative owners, and it's a much better environment.

But after that interaction, I know it's not all in my head.

I avoid the questioning looks from my teammates and finish my work out before heading to the showers.

How can I convince Paul to back off? How can I show him I have no interest in his wife? I strip down and step into one of the stalls. The hot water washes over me, and I let it burn my skin, just a little.

I only want to have a great hockey season and hang out with my kid, my family, and my friends. At least Paul and I are on the same page on the topic of having the best season of my life. Back at the lockers, I pull my arms into a long-sleeved raglan t-shirt and sink onto the bench as my mind conjures a picture of Lucy's red curls and the smooth line of her neck. There are worse people to spend time with.

"Kellie, what are you thinking about?" Lachlan says from his seat on the bench, yanking me out of my daydream. Harley is standing in front of his cubby watching me as well.

"Just how much Paul hates me." I toss my wet towel into the laundry bin for the equipment manager, who is wandering around picking up anything from the floor that didn't make it to the right bin.

"He sure does." Atticus looks around. "And he's watching Lucy for our asshole father. Keeping an eye on her. Paul told us that directly when we ran into him at Deep Roots Cafe the other day. *Richard told me to watch out for you.*" Atticus uses a sing-song voice to mimic Paul.

"No way," Harley says.

"Yeah. Richard doesn't care enough to watch me, thank fuck.

But he wants to get Lucy to come back to DC FC and, according to her, take her ex back."

The guys murmur their sympathy.

"After we saw him, Paul must have called Richard, who talked to her ex, who called her earlier this week. He told her to consider coming back to her old job and getting back together with him, even though he's a cheating asshole."

Indignation twists in my stomach. That's an unfortunate string of connections between Paul and Lucy.

"She's pissed." Atticus ties his second gym shoe.

"Understandable," I say.

"I was thinking about Paul hating you, Kellie." Lachlan pulls his Blizzard-branded string bag out of his locker and drops it on the bench next to me with a clunk. The man's always got a book with him.

"Wonderful. I also think about that."

"I had an idea on how to convince him you don't have a thing for his wife."

"Christ. Don't even say those words out loud." I squint my eyes shut for a beat. "But please, tell me how to fix this."

"Date someone." Lachlan throws his arms out like it's some big surprise idea.

I snort a laugh. "No. Have you met me?"

"Hmm." Harley runs his hand over his chin, creating a sound like sandpaper on wood. "It's not the worst idea." Harley's approaching retirement, and I can't imagine what life will be like at the Blizzard without him. He's only thirty-four, but most hockey players are retired by around thirty, an age in both of our rear-view mirrors. He said he'd go for another season or two and then he'll head back to Maine to his girlfriend. Get married and pop out a few kids probably.

"I am zero percent interested in dating someone."

"Yeah, but if you have a girlfriend, mate, it might get Savannah to actually back off you. And since she tells her husband everything

—" Lachlan knows about how Savannah voluntarily showed Paul the picture of us on NHL Tea gossip site. "—it'll certainly be a topic of conversation."

"Where the hell would I find a girlfriend?"

"Anywhere." Lachlan shakes his head in disgust. "Literally anywhere."

"It's not that easy." I sound like a whiny child. While they all know how sensitive I am after the Sam situation from last year, I think they're a bit sick of me swearing off women.

"You don't have to find the love of your life." Harley cocks his head to me. "Just someone to throw them off your trail."

"So I just fake it?"

"I didn't say that." But Harley raises his eyebrows and seems to consider it.

"Fake dating. That's perfect." Lachlan nods his head and grins, flashing perfectly pearly white teeth. At least one of his perfect front teeth is an implant after having it knocked out on the ice two seasons ago.

"I hate to agree with Lachlan, but I kind of do here. Fake dating a woman to save your hockey career would be epic." Atticus surveys his locker before closing it and taking a step toward the exit.

"That's ridiculous. What woman would agree to be a fake girlfriend? And again, where would I find one?"

"Yeah, true." Harley shrugs.

"I think it's a good idea. Let's take a vote." Lachlan shoots his hand up in the air. "All in favor of Kellie finding a fake girlfriend, raise your hand." He looks pointedly at Atticus and Harley.

Harley chuckles and raises his hand.

"Yeah, sure." Atticus raises his as well.

"Three to one. It's settled. Figure out how to make it happen." Lachlan points at me, then nods to Atticus and Harley. "You two walking out?"

My traitorous teammates leave me alone in the locker room to question why I'm friends with them.

I don't have time to find a real girlfriend. Or a fake one. Were they really serious about that? And I don't want to have some random woman who I can't trust all up in my family's business.

If only there was someone convenient, who I could trust, who would have a reason to go along with—

I let out a chuckle as the best-slash-worst idea occurs to me.

Lucy.

I could fake date Lucy Knox.

It's kind of perfect.

I can trust her because she's Atticus's sister. We can say we got to know each other over media training. And it'll be easy to show Paul and Savannah the relationship as we're all often in close proximity.

And the best part? She has a reason to do it as well.

Maybe she wants Paul to report to her father—and therefore her ex—that she's getting cozy with a star Blizzard player.

Are there red flags here? Maybe one or ten.

But I can't deny that the idea of getting to know that woman —even under ridiculous pretenses—is appealing.

She can help me convince Paul I'm harmless when it comes to his wife. Help me keep my spot on the Blizzard.

I can help her piss off her father and her ex.

A grin crosses my face as I pull the first door out of the locker room, then push the second one into the hallway.

I have one more stop before I head home for the day.

CHAPTER 9

What Just Happened?

LUCY

> **DAD/RICHARD/ASSHOLE**
>
> Hello, darling. I heard you met Paul Harrison. If
> you need anything, go talk to him.

I don't respond. There are more little dots as my father continues to type, and my blood pressure continues to rise.

> **DAD/RICHARD/ASSHOLE**
>
> I know you have to do this thing. This little
> adventure working in Colorado.

> **DAD/RICHARD/ASSHOLE**
>
> I want you to know your job is still here. It's
> where you belong. You know you can't do this
> on your own. I can help you. I will always help
> you. You know that.

I look up from the texts, attempting to unclench my jaw. He's still typing, but nothing good is going to pop up on my phone. Just more of the same nonsense.

Two pairs of footsteps echo from outside my open office door.

Of course he thinks I need him to succeed.

He's right. I've never done it without him. He thinks women need a man to define themselves, and if I ever attempt to reason with him, his eyes glaze over and he stops engaging. Some men in his generation are impossible to reason with. They always think they're right.

Paul Harrison zooms past my office, and then the click of heels reveals his wife, Savannah, close behind.

"Paul, wait up." She sounds flustered, and she's practically running in her heels. "Can we talk about the bar later?"

What's she talking about? *A* bar, with alcohol? *The* bar, as in the bar exam? January went to one semester of law school and then bailed. She said it was the most boring shit she'd ever experienced, so she never came close to taking the bar exam.

I hope I never chased Ron down the hall like that. As much as the DC FC staff were nice to my face, I bet they hated me. The daughter of the team owner. Engaged to a VP who was the team owner's pet.

I should call my mother.

When I was in college, I asked her why she and Dad divorced. I knew, but I wanted to hear it from her, adult to adult. She'd caught him cheating. Mom suspected there'd been others, but this one was right in front of her face. Mom was in her early fifties and decided there was no way she was putting up with a cheating husband for the rest of her life. One who thought she was not pretty enough. Not funny enough.

Not good enough.

She didn't say I told you so when I broke it off with Ron.

I'm instinctively suspicious of Paul Harrison. Rich older man, much younger woman. It's an uncomfortable power imbalance. Makes sense he's friends with my father, whose fourth wife is only five years older than I am. I remember what Atticus said—they're part of the Rich White Guy Team Owner club.

I clench my jaw and spin a pen on my desk, attempting to grab it as it shoots past my laptop and off the desk, skidding to a stop outside my office door. I prop my elbows and drop my head into a palm.

It's no wonder Dad didn't understand why I had to leave DC FC. For him, this behavior is normal. Cheating and trading down for younger models.

If he'd have fired Ron, would I have stayed? Maybe. Probably.

I pick up my water bottle and lift it to my lips, filling my mouth, lost in thoughts of the destination wedding I'd started to plan with Ron, and how it all went up in flames with one scroll of his texts.

"Lucy."

I gasp and then spew water all over my laptop, my notebook, and the man who's appeared in front of my desk holding the pen that I spun into the hallway.

Then I proceed to choke on water I inhaled with the gasp.

"Christ, are you okay?" Kellen darts around the desk and pats me on the back with increasing intensity until it feels like I'm being whacked from behind with a baseball bat.

I wave a hand in the air and end with a thumbs up.

"I'm fine," I rasp, clearing my throat.

A thumbs up. I am the least cool person ever in the history of people.

Still catching my breath, I scrunch my face and can't bring myself to make eye contact.

Kellen walks back around to the front of my desk. I'm hoping he walks out the door and saves me even one more humiliating moment.

"Here."

I jolt my gaze up. He's holding out a tissue from the box on my desk, and when I take it, he grabs one for himself.

He's got droplets of water on his face.

For the love of god.

I wipe my face with one tissue, and after dropping it into my trash can with foundation smears, I grab another and dab my keyboard.

I'm a hot mess. Like, the hottest mess. If I was on a planet that was covered entirely in lava and trash, I'd still be the hottest mess there.

"Uh, sorry about that?" I think this is the universe's way of ensuring I'm not tempted by the most attractive man I've ever seen without a shirt on.

Who is in my office.

Alone.

With me.

On a Friday afternoon. Not looking like he's planning to leave. Lordy, why? At least he's not shirtless.

Beads of sweat pop on my forehead. Or maybe I just missed some water droplets. I ignore them, even as one starts to trickle down my face.

Help.

I'll go ahead and add this little event to the list of reasons why I need to get out of the United States of America.

"No problem. I'm sorry I surprised you." He glances down at the chair. "May I?"

"Yeah, yeah, of course."

Why. Why, Kellen? Please go away and let me drown in this lake of humiliation.

"How are you settling in?" Kellen lowers himself down, leaning back and laying his arms on the armrests. He then lifts his forearms suddenly. "Oh, it's just a bit wet."

"How much water did I spit out? I'm like a freaking sprinkler system over here."

Kellen chuckles, and I'm mesmerized by the rough stubble on his jawline and neck, as if he hasn't shaved for a few days.

"I have to say," he says, "you have made me laugh more in the past few weeks than anyone has in a long while."

"As long as you're not laughing *at* me." I cross my arms and try to look indignant, but it just makes him laugh again.

I don't hate the sound. It's deep and kind of throaty, raspy, like maybe he's telling the truth about not laughing much.

"Where's Waffles?"

"It's Taco now, not Waffles." I shove a chunk of curls off my forehead. "Wait, no, now it's Harry." I'd been reading an article about Prince Harry last night online and Taco seemed excited. I think people names are funny for pets, so now I have a dog named Harry.

My friends liked Taco better.

"Harry?"

"As in Prince Harry. Oh, maybe it should be *Prince* Harry then? Hmm. That sounds better."

"Right." One side of Kellen's mouth quirks up into another smile.

"Anyway, he's at daycare."

Kellen's eyebrows shoot up.

"The Delightful Doggy Palace."

"That's a thing?"

"What do you think dogs do when their people are at work? Prince Harry would just pee everywhere. Anyway, he loves daycare. It's going great."

It's not going great.

Prince Harry keeps picking fights with other dogs. He does this by peeing on them.

The other dogs do not like this.

And the daycare people give me crap for changing his name. Something about consistency and training. Whatever. What do they know about dogs, besides most things?

"Well, good for Prince Harry." Kellen runs his hand through dark locks, and I suppress a wistful sigh. "Sorry to stop by so late on a Friday, but I thought I'd finally give in to your messages to meet up for media training."

"I assumed your lack of response to my latest pings meant you didn't really want to do it."

"You sent quite a few messages."

"Did I? I don't remember, how many?"

"One or two, I think."

Five. It was five.

"But I hadn't noticed you didn't respond." *Lies.* "When do you want to meet? Have any time next week?" I click through to my calendar, then glance up when he hasn't responded.

"What do you think about going on a hike tomorrow?" Kellen crosses his arms.

"Tomorrow?"

"Yes."

"Saturday?" I blink.

"Yup."

"Like, the weekend?" I tilt my head. He wants to meet up with me on the weekend?

"Uh-huh." Kellen nods. "Today finishes up, then you go to sleep, and when you wake up, it's tomorrow. Saturday. The weekend."

"You want to hang out with me on a Saturday?"

"I feel like I'm talking to my five-year-old daughter."

I laugh. "Sorry. It's Friday afternoon and it's been a long week." I'm still confused, but I'm definitely not going to ask for clarification again.

He clears his throat and rubs the back of his neck. "While you're thinking about your Saturday schedule, I have another topic."

"Go ahead. But just so you know, my Saturday schedule is very busy."

"I'm sure."

"I have to walk Prince Harry at least three times."

The other corner of Kellen's mouth turns up. I like making him smile.

"Well, you should bring him on the hike."

"I'll do that. What were you going to ask?"

"It's weird as fuck." Color creeps up Kellen's neck, and I'm super curious to hear what's making him so uncomfortable.

"I can be a bit weird, so no worries."

"Okay." He cracks a smile. "I have this issue."

I cock my head and wait for him to continue. The man looks so nervous that maybe he'll forget about me spitting water all over his face.

"Paul Harrison hates me."

"Wow." I huff a laugh. "That's not at all what I expected you to say. Why does he hate you?"

"What did you expect me to say?"

"No idea. Literally. But if I'd had a list, that would've been at the bottom of it. Or... not on it at all."

"Right." Kellen presses his lips together for a beat. "He thinks—but is completely wrong—that I am interested in his wife."

"Oh. That's... really bad." I'd gotten the impression from Atticus that Kellen is a good guy, but is he?

"Yeah."

"Are you?"

"No," he says firmly and shakes his head.

I blink about a million times. Why is he telling me this? Kellen clears his throat. I push my hair off my forehead and sigh.

"Well, Paul and my father are friends, and I'm pretty sure he's spying on me for him."

"I've heard that." Kellen nods.

"Atticus." I make a mental note to chastise Atticus for sharing too much information.

"Yup. I also heard that your father is reporting what he hears to your ex-boyfriend."

"Ex-fiancé. Shit, my brother really needs to keep his giant mouth shut."

Kellen fidgets in his seat, smoothing his jogging pants and then scratching his forearms.

"Ok, I give up. I'm enjoying our heart-to-heart conversation, but how can I help with your problem?"

"I was hoping we could help each other."

"How so?" I furrow my brow. "By murdering Paul? Or my father? Or my ex? Oh, all three??" I fake excitement.

"Nothing illegal." Kellen's eyes twinkle. "But what if there was a way for your father and your ex to hear how fantastically you are doing here in Fort Collins? How your life is happy and perfect?"

"That sounds amazing."

Kellen swallows.

"Dude. Spit it out. You're making me nervous."

"If you and I pretend to date—"

I literally gasp, and then laugh, and then quiet at the solemn look on his face.

"Shit, you're serious. Okay, go on."

"—then maybe Savannah will back off, and Paul will turn his attention away from me. Then I don't have to worry about getting traded because the team owner hates me. And you can show your ex-life how happy you are without them."

My eyes must be as wide as one of the communal dog bowls at the Delightful Doggy Palace. Which is kind of gross, when you think about it. All these dogs sharing drool and mixing it together in big bowls? Yuck.

"Then they'd think—know—how well you're fitting in here. How great your job is going."

I'm incapable of responding for a full minute. Is he serious?

"You want to fake date me?"

"Mmm, yes. That's what I'm suggesting."

I laugh again at the absolute absurdity of it all. Not only the general concept of fake dating, but that anyone would believe that I'd end up dating Kellen Bassey, a gorgeous star hockey player.

"Fake date so you can help me create a certain image of my life to my father and my ex?"

"And I can keep my spot on the team."

"Wow."

"Don't answer now." Kellen holds up a hand. "Why don't you think about it, and we can talk about it on our hike tomorrow? If you want to talk about it. We don't ever have to speak of it again."

"Oh, the answer is definitely yes." Something akin to joy rushes through my veins. This is ridiculous. Hilarious. Perfect.

"Really?" Kellen's cheeks lift with a grin.

"Yeah. Really. I think we have some serious plot holes to work out, but I'd love to help you with your Paul Harrison problem. And I'd also love to get my father off my back."

"Excellent. Thank you, I guess." Kellen stands. "So I'll pick up you and Waffles tomorrow morning. Taco? Prince Harry."

"Prince Harry. What kind of hike is this?"

"An easy one. Good views."

"So when you say easy, you mean someone who never hikes could do it?"

"Yes."

"And I should let a random man take me into the mountains?"

"Fair point. But you'll have Prince Harry to protect you." He blinks slowly and is painfully charming.

"I'm not really a big hiker."

"No problem. Wear layers. And sturdy shoes. I'll pick you up at eight." He steps backwards toward the doorway.

"Eight in the morning? Is that necessary on a Saturday?"

"Yes. You're still staying with Atticus?"

I nod, and Kellen pulls out his cell phone.

"What's your number? Just in case I need to get ahold of you."

I tell him my digits and he smiles at me. Yes, I just gave my number to a hot professional hockey player.

Kellen starts to walk out but pauses in the doorway and turns back to me. "And I'm not a random man. I'm your fake boyfriend."

And with that, he disappears from my office.

"Oh, for fuck's sake." I laugh in the empty room. I feel like an insane person.

What just happened?

I'm just going to go ahead and fake date a hockey player? How can I possibly pull this off?

It's almost five o'clock. Maybe I'll head out early and go buy some hiking boots. I definitely don't own any sturdy shoes. I pack up my stuff and tap my phone as I leave my office, flicking the light off and pulling the door shut behind me.

ME

You'll never believe what my plans are for tomorrow

JANUARY

OoooOOooo do tell

RALEIGH

Story time!

I smile and keep typing as I walk down the hallway, through the arena, and out to the parking lot. Before I can press send, another message pops up.

KELLEN

Hey, love muffin, it's your fake boyfriend

I burst out laughing.

ME

Love muffin?? What the hell?

KELLEN

We should probably come up with cute pet names for each other. Isn't that what boyfriends and girlfriends do? If you don't like that one, I can keep brainstorming

ME

Are we twelve years old? And... how do you not know what people in a relationship do?

KELLEN

You don't have to be mean

I look around the parking lot and see a pair of squirrels frolicking up a tree.

ME

Sorry, squirrel

KELLEN

Squirrel?

ME

I'm not good at this either, okay??

Kellen sends a laughing emoji, and I don't lift my eyes from my phone until I get into my car.

This might actually be fun.

CHAPTER 10

Not a Lion

KELLEN

Saturday, September 29

"How far is this mountain, kitten?" Lucy asks.

I chuckle and glance over at the passenger seat. Lucy looks adorable in an oversized hoodie, jeans, and —I swear to god—brand new hiking boots.

It's clear she's not a hiker, just like she said.

"It's right outside of town, cookie."

"That one's terrible." Lucy groans.

We texted all yesterday evening, mostly discussing pet names for each other. I insisted that food related names are the funniest, but she decided on animal names.

"You're right, it's pretty awful."

Prince Harry sits on her lap, tongue hanging out, gazing at me with a look that might be adoration. Or it's his natural face, I'm not sure.

Ava would love this creature.

"Do you have layers on?" I put my car in reverse.

"Layers?" Lucy furrows her brow.

"It's warmer than it looks out. There's zero shade up at the top by Horsetooth Rock, so you'll get hot."

"Yes, *Mom*, I have a tank top on underneath my hoodie."

I bite back a grin and pull out from in front of Atticus's apartment building.

Atticus might not be pleased when I tell him, Harley, and Lachlan my plan when we hang out tonight. He might have been supportive of me fake dating someone, but his sister? Then again, he did tell me to be nice to her. Which I am.

"What'd you tell Atticus?" I turn at Colorado State University to drive along the straight road that'll quickly lead us to the entrance to the Foothills Trail.

"Nothing. He's still sleeping. Oh, that's really pretty."

I glance over, and Lucy's gazing out the window at Horsetooth Mountain, which is a modest size mountain that towers over a large reservoir right next to the town of Fort Collins.

"We should talk about a few things."

"We definitely should."

"There's a lot of wildlife in these mountains." I give her a quick glance, and she's staring at me intently. "This is a fairly busy trail, so we probably won't run into any lions."

"What."

"Like snakes, bears, mountain lions." I smirk but don't turn my head.

"Lions??"

"*Mountain* lions. They're about the most dangerous creature we'd encounter. But it's very unlikely they'll come near a crowded trail." I turn into the parking lot and grab the first empty spot.

"What do we do if we see a mountain lion? Run?"

"God, no, woman, don't run." I rotate in my seat to face her. "They'll take you down with one swipe."

Lucy's face drains of color. "Seriously?"

I reach over and gently tap underneath her jaw. She breathes in quietly, her eyes widening.

"Very unlikely."

Prince Harry reaches up and licks me with a long, squishy tongue. I laugh and pull back. I open my door and hop out, resting a hand on the roof and leaning my head down into the car.

"If we see a mountain lion, we face it directly. You get right next to me. We raise our hands and try to appear as big as possible, then make a lot of noise to show it we're dominant. Then we slowly back away until we are very, very far from it."

"Got it." She nods solemnly.

"Oh, but make sure to grab Prince Harry. If he runs, the mountain lion would catch him in about two seconds flat."

"Jeez," Lucy mutters under her breath and ducks out of the car, gently placing Prince Harry on the ground with a quick pat to his head. She might be murmuring reassurances to him, probably about how she won't let a mountain lion get him, but I can't quite hear.

"Honestly. Don't worry."

"What kind of noise do we make?" She stands up straight.

"Roar and yell. Or growl like a bear." I lock the car and wave her toward the entrance to the trail.

"Can you give me an example? Of the kind of roar you're talking about?"

"Just a normal roar."

"I really don't know what that means. Like this?" Lucy makes a pathetic roaring sound.

"No," I laugh. "Like this." I make a much more impressive roar, but when I look back at her, she's cracking up.

"You're good at that."

"Oh, shut up." I bite back a grin. "Come on."

Lucy walks by my side onto the trail, Prince Harry on his leash trotting happily beside her.

"There's a nice waterfall and a lake that we'll head toward. Should take about an hour and a half total, so fairly easy."

Lucy stumbles on what appears to be dirt and reaches out for my arm, catching herself. She leaves her hand on my forearm for a few more seconds, and I glance down at her fingers on my sleeve, interested to see how much I like the feeling.

"Sorry." She slides her hand off. "New boots."

"I thought they looked too clean." I sigh. "Wearing brand new boots on a hike isn't a great idea. You should break them in first."

"Too late now, I guess." She shrugs.

"So, should we get started?" Fall leaves crunch under my (broken in) boots.

"With the media training?" Lucy looks at me innocently, and I raise my eyebrows back.

"Haha. With fake dating, peanut butter pie." I can barely get the words out without chuckling.

"Now you're just making me hungry."

"Sorry." I sneak another look at her. "After a night's sleep, you still up for this? I would be okay if you wanted to back out."

"No way." Lucy shakes her head and crosses her arms, like she's protecting her chest. Or her heart. "I don't want to back out. I'm fully invested."

"Great."

"But we might have an HR problem."

"Hmmm."

"I remembered Lina making a comment about how the official team policy is that players and staffers shouldn't date without HR permission."

A pair of women pass us by, each with a big dog on a leash. Prince Harry goes nuts, and Lucy shushes him.

"That did cross my mind as well." There have been a few relationships between players and employees over the years, but it's not common.

"And I looked it up in the employee handbook, which I happen to have handy since Lina sent it to me when I got here." Lucy looks over at me. She's so pretty with her red hair against the backdrop of the changing autumn leaves.

"So what are we going to do about that?" Last night, I got

home, had dinner with Ava and Bri, then went back to my house to text Lucy. It's felt like we've had one long conversation, starting with when I stopped by her office to bring up fake dating.

"Well, I can talk to Lina on Monday. And... we might have to go to talk to HR."

I groan.

"There might be a loophole because I'm only a contractor. Maybe they won't care since I'm only here for one season."

"Just one season because..."

"I'm trying to get a job with a soccer team in England. My dream job, really."

"Oh, well, fingers crossed you get it." I point to a root on the ground so Lucy sees it. She's cute. And funny. And easy to talk to in an unguarded sort of way. Definitely most likely to trip on a tree root.

"We'll just need to be really convincing to make people believe we'd go through all this trouble for a temporary relationship." Prince Harry darts ahead and barks wildly at a bird. Lucy tugs him back to her side.

"This doesn't bode well for when we meet the mountain lion."

"It does not. Prince Harry, hush!" Lucy unsuccessfully shushes her dog.

"Let's talk logistics," I say when the barking dies down. "If the objective here in Fort Collins is to get Savannah and Paul to think we're happily dating, we obviously need to *show* them we're dating, and not just with a HR meeting."

"Uh-huh."

"I think we can accomplish that with a few key sightings."

"Sightings?" Lucy asks, her voice full of amusement.

"Yeah. You know. Events that they see us together, being... couple-y."

"Right."

"There's a fall festival on October 12, two weeks from now. Costumes, apple cider donuts, haunted house, you know, that kind of thing. It's a fundraiser for a youth sports nonprofit." I point to a particularly colorful line of autumn trees.

"That sounds fun. I did a lot of volunteer work with youth sports back in D.C."

"Yeah?"

"I loved coaching little kid soccer."

Something clicks in my brain. Atticus's comment about Lucy coaching back in D.C. But no way am I mentioning that now. Even if he did bring up a good point about Lucy being trustworthy because she's his sister, and *I* trust *him*, and *he* trusts *her*...

"I miss it already. I would volunteer to coach elementary age teams at the school I went to growing up, or wherever I was needed. Normally by now we'd be in the middle of the season."

Lucy pauses and glances at me, but I keep my head trained to the trail ahead of us.

"Atticus told me your daughter's team needs a coach."

Shit. I finally look at her, and she's staring at me with wide, hopeful green eyes.

"Lucy." It's not a good idea, right? But then I picture Ava staring at me with similarly wide eyes asking if *I* could coach her team.

"Can I help?" There's a tinge of desperation in her voice. "Seriously. It would really help me too. Get me out of Atticus's apartment and into the community."

I make a murmuring sound and realize I'm softening. I could solve Ava's soccer coach problem and make Lucy —my new fake girlfriend—happy. Plus, getting to know her a bit more wouldn't be the worst thing.

"We are in need of a coach." I watch Lucy's face break out in a large smile. "The dad who was coaching had to have unexpected surgery, and since then, random parents have been stepping in. It's been a mess. More than the mess you'd expect from kindergarten soccer players. So... the help would be great."

"Awesome!" Lucy skips a step, and I look over to see her

smiling from ear to ear. "It'll also give me something else to think about besides... well, besides all the things I don't want to think about."

"Okay then. They practice on Wednesday evenings and have games on Saturday mornings, except for today. I'll send you the information."

I wonder what Bri will have to say about this, because it's not like I can not tell her that I 1) got a fake girlfriend and 2) asked that fake girlfriend to be our daughter's soccer coach. But I remind myself this is Atticus's sister, not some random woman I met at a bar. Still, Bri is super protective of our daughter. Maybe not quite as protective as I am.

I hope I don't regret this.

"Anyway." I want to move us on from Lucy as Ava's soccer coach. "For the fall festival, Paul is always there. It's a good media opportunity for the team. I'm assuming you'd already be going to that, so that could be one."

"That's one." She nods.

"Another could be the Blizzard retreat in November." I point ahead of us on the narrow trail and at more prominent tree roots. "Careful there. So the entire team and administration, including you, gets on a bus and drives to a ranch in Wyoming for a team building weekend two weeks before Thanksgiving when we have a break between games."

It's a really fun trip, even though we all grumble about having to go and bond with each other. As if we don't bond all the time? Like every day at practice, in the gym, at games, locker room, when we travel, etc.

But there are hot springs pools and plenty of drinking time, and Coach doesn't give us a curfew or alcohol limit.

"That works." Lucy slows her stride and pulls out her phone. "But that won't be until mid-November."

"Yeah. So we probably need one before that, especially given the fall festival isn't for another two weeks."

"Right."

The sound of water over rocks hits us. "The waterfall is just ahead." A minute later, we turn a corner to the pretty sight of water flowing between two giant rocky mounds into a crystal-clear pool at the bottom.

"Gorgeous," Lucy murmurs. She wanders over to the edge and squats down to run her hand in the water. Prince Harry runs next to her and leans down to drink.

I settle down on a dry, flat rock to the side and watch Lucy as she takes in the scene. She pushes a clump of auburn curls off her forehead. I desperately want to touch her hair and feel if the curls are as soft as they look.

Weird. Inappropriate. I clearly won't let myself do that.

There's a noise in the trees and Prince Harry twists his head to look behind me, then pulls the leash out of Lucy's hand and leaps onto my lap, licking my face.

"Hey! Prince Harry! Down!" I push him away, but when I open my mouth to speak, he licks my lips.

Lucy spins around and laughs at the sight of us before grabbing Prince Harry's leash to pull him off me.

"Sorry about that," she says.

"No worries, I guess." The sun has warmed the air, so I pull off my hoodie and wipe my face clean of Prince Harry's slobber. "I think I technically just made out with him."

Lucy laughs. "I don't think he likes this name."

"Time for a new one?"

"Prince Harry didn't last long, but yeah." She nods, a serious look on her face.

"How about..." I glance around. "Lion?" I pretend to look worried.

"What??" Lucy spins her head around.

"Kidding. There's no lion."

"You're an ass."

I stand and wipe my jeans off, a grin on my face.

"Bear?"

Lucy frowns and rubs her neck. "Not bad." She turns to her dog. "What do you think? Bear?"

Bear wags his tail and gives a short yip.

"Bear it is."

"That dog will never learn his name."

Lucy shrugs. "Meh. Names are overrated."

"What about nicknames?"

"Those are not overrated at all." Lucy pulls out her phone and snaps a picture of him. "I always text my friends when he gets a new name." Lucy gives Bear a pat on the head.

"Should we go swimming?" I nod to the beautiful waterfall.

"Um, no? I didn't bring a bathing suit. And it's warmer out now, but the water is freezing."

"Thought I'd ask." I shrug casually, but I'm really picturing us stripping down and walking into the cold waterfall. I nod toward the trail, and we continue walking.

"I'm not sure how Atticus will react to our plan," Lucy says.

"I'm going to talk to him tonight, we're hanging out at your apartment, actually."

She whips her head toward me. "Tonight? Okay. Maybe I'll let you talk to him first. He might take it better from you—I've probably embarrassed him enough already. He's lectured me ten times on the layout of that hallway since the locker room incident."

I laugh, remembering how freaking adorable Lucy was that day. Her face was redder than it is right now.

She groans. "And I already told him that I'm not at all interested in hockey players. Hanging out or dating."

"What? Why aren't you interested in hockey players?" I'm definitely offended.

"It's not just hockey players. It's... all men." Lucy sneaks a glance at me. "I just feel like I can't trust that people are who they appear to be, if that makes sense. With Ron—my ex—I was so sure things were amazing, but they really weren't. I couldn't see it."

"Sorry. He sounds like an asshole."

"Yup." She attempts a smile, then trips on a rock.

"Careful." I hold out my arm to her, and she slips her hand in the crook of my elbow like it's the most natural thing in the world.

"Then again, Atticus might end up being on board with this. He's got bigger issues with our father than I do. Once he knew how things went down with our mother, he basically hated him. And after I went to college, he refused to spend time with him. Now he only sees Richard occasionally when he's in the D.C. area and with me."

"He doesn't really talk about it that much." I knew Atticus wasn't close to his father, but I didn't know the details.

"Atticus pretends he doesn't care, but I know it hurts him."

We weave our way through a rocky part of the trail, and I'm careful to continue scanning the area ahead of us. I was mostly kidding about the mountain lion thing. It's not common to see them on the more popular trails, but we're in the mountains of Colorado, so you have to be ready for anything.

So when I spot the rattlesnake, I know just what to do.

Unfortunately, we didn't go over snake protocol.

At first, Lucy doesn't notice it.

CHAPTER 11

Fake Dates

LUCY

"After you talk to him, I will."

The more I think about it, the more I realize Atticus will get it. He really will. I bet he'll be completely on Team Piss Off Dad.

"Lucy." Kellen holds his arm out, and I bump right into it.

"Wait, do you think we should do it together?"

Atticus will probably hate it at first, but we can win him over. I know it. Just have to come up with the right pitch.

"Shhh." Kellen doesn't move his arm out of my way.

"What?" I swing my head to him, about to make a comment about shushing me, but he's looking around us intently.

"There." He points to the ground.

I follow the line of his finger, and my eyes land on a snake.

A rattlesnake.

Nestled partly in the brush, it's curled in a neat little pile, its head in the center poking up and pointing right at us, its shaker upright and making that noise.

Am I snake expert? No, no I'm not. But this snake is holding up its damn tail and *rattling*, so I know it's a rattlesnake.

And we're about three feet from it. By the looks of it, the snake is not impressed with our arrival. I bend down and scoop up Bear.

"Good thinking," Kellen says quietly. "Now don't let that dog out of your arms."

"I'm trying not to." My teeth are clenched, my voice shaky, and Bear is squirmy. "Are we going to getting eaten by a poisonous snake?"

"Venomous."

"What?"

"Back up slowly. We're too close." Kellen's voice is calm and steady.

"Too close for what?" I whisper. Oh my god. Too close as in we're going to get eaten by a poisonous—venomous—snake. Why am I in Colorado again??

I take a step back, but Kellen doesn't move.

"Get right behind me."

I do, tucking myself against his back, Bear safely wedged between us.

"Another step back, Lucy." This time we step in unison.

Another step. And another.

"Are we far enough away yet so I can panic?" I whisper.

"A few more."

Suddenly, the rattling stops. I poke my head around Kellen to see that the snake is still there, its cold, beady little eyes fixed on us, but the shaker is blessedly quiet. I breathe out in relief.

"That was terrifying—" A bird swoops down in front of us and Bear starts barking like crazy. He twists his body so hard I lose my grip, and he tumbles to the ground, lunging at the bird, who is halfway back to the rattlesnake.

"No!" I shriek, but I can't grab the leash in time. I picture what's about to happen. He'll either accidentally tumble onto the damn rattlesnake because he didn't see it, or he'll see it and decide to tackle it anyway. Then the snake will bite him or maybe wrap its slithering snaky body around my soft fluffy dog and squeeze and squeeze and squeeze—

But faster than I can imagine moving, Kellen dives down and grabs the leash, pulling Bear back before he gets within striking distance.

"Fuck, come here, Bear!" Kellen growls and grabs my dog off the ground. He turns to me. "Let's get out of here."

I don't need to be told twice, so I spin and lead the way down the path away from the snake.

"Won't it follow us? Stalk us?" I toss a look over my shoulder.

"It's a snake, not a tiger, Lucy. It won't hunt us. We'll just head back down the trail for a minute and then take a big loop around the snake to keep going."

My heart's still racing, but the sight of Bear happily snuggled into Kellen's chest distracts me. Not that it does much to slow my heart down.

"Holy crap. We almost died." I breathe out once we're far enough back down the trail.

"I mean, that's a bit of an exaggeration." Kellen chuckles.

I smile, but I'm suddenly overheated by everything. The exercise, the excitement, and the hot man holding my dog.

"What's the difference between poisonous and venomous?" I ask, remembering Kellen's correction.

"Snakes are venomous if they bite you and you get sick. Poisonous means if *you* bite *it*, you get sick. And most people don't bite snakes."

"Interesting clarification."

Kellen stops and points off trail. "Let's head that way and circle back around past the spot with the snake."

"Or—and hear me out—we can just go back to the car." I'm embarrassingly hopeful he'll say yes.

Kellen watches me for a few seconds. "Sorry. I didn't even ask. Are you okay? We can go back if you want to. If we keep going, there's a lake about fifteen minutes ahead, and then the trail comes back around to the parking lot. It'll take us another forty-five minutes total."

I consider and almost choose to bail, but then Bear gives me his legit puppy dog eyes from Kellen's arms.

"Let's keep going." My heartbeat's almost returned to normal, and I would like to spend more time outside on this beautiful fall day.

"Yeah?" Kellen nods. "If you're sure."

"I'm sweating though, so give me a second." I pull my hoodie over my head and squat to unzip my backpack and shove it in. I feel much better in the tank top. "The whole life or death thing kind of got me fired up." I zip up my bag and stand, swinging it over my shoulder.

"Again, not sure it was quite life or death." Kellen's gaze drifts down my body, then fixes back on my eyes.

"Still." I swallow. "And... thanks for saving us."

"No problem." He absently strokes Bear's head, and the dog stares up at him with adoring eyes.

"Bear likes you. You don't happen to want a dog, do you?"

But even as I say it, my heart gives a little squeeze. I never particularly wanted a dog, but the little weirdo has grown on me. It'll be hard to leave him when I go to England.

If I go to England. I need to get the job first.

"I travel too much for a pet, much to Ava's disappointment." Kellen puts Bear on the ground and keeps hold of the leash. "Follow me. I'll go ahead since it's off path. I can keep an eye out for other woodland creatures."

"How likely do you think that is? That we'll see other animals?" My eyes dart around the forest, almost ominous despite the bright sun and colorful autumn leaves.

Kellen shrugs. I am not reassured.

"Let's go back to fake dating. We have the fall festival and the team retreat." Kellen runs a hand through his hair. He's not sweaty or flustered. I bet his heart's not racing, either.

"The other day when I first met Paul, I was with Atticus in the coffee shop." I appreciate the crunching leaves beneath my feet, and keep my eyes trained on the ground so I don't trip. "Atticus said Paul and Savannah live around the corner and come in almost every day. Maybe we could run into them at the coffee shop for our first public sighting?"

"That's a good idea."

"Oh!" I bump into Kellen, who I'm clearly walking too close to. My face bounces off his back. He spins around. "I'm okay." I hold my hands up.

"Glad to hear it." Kellen's mouth quirks as he turns back to the not-trail.

My feet are starting to hurt. Kellen was right. New boots were probably not the best idea, and I definitely have blisters forming at the back of my heels and maybe on my little toes.

I distract myself by staring at Kellen's backside in his hiking pants, which are loose except for how they tuck right against his butt. The form-fitting gray t-shirt he's wearing probably cost hundreds to look that casual and good on him. His biceps bulge out of the sleeves, and his shoulder and neck muscles shift as he walks and *good lord I need to get a grip.*

"We've talked a lot about Atticus... do you have siblings?"

"An older sister." Kellen glances over his shoulder. "She doesn't live around here, although I do have a house waiting for her next door."

"You just, have a house ready for your sister?" Lordy. Hockey players.

"Yeah." He shrugs. "It's furnished and everything for when she comes to visit. Ava's mom is on the other side of me. We're a good family unit."

My chest warms. A man who co-parents with his daughter's mother well enough to live next door, plus saving a house for his sister? It's a parade of green flags.

"Do you also have a house for your parents?"

"No," Kellen says shortly. "My dad passed away when I was a baby."

"Shoot, I'm sorry." And here I am complaining about my father. I'm the worst.

"It's alright." Kellen turns his mouth down. "My mom remarried when I was thirteen and Kara was sixteen. I didn't think he was a great guy, but Mom seemed happy-ish. When I hit high school, he was overly interested in my hockey career, without being a real hockey fan. He kept talking about becoming a manager or an agent. But he knew nothing about hockey, and I already had a mentor helping advise us."

Sounds like this isn't going anywhere good. I stay quiet as Kellen takes a noisy breath and lets it out loudly.

"Once I got to college, Mom convinced me to trust my stepfather to manage some of my sponsorships. It wasn't a lot of money. A local business. A clothing brand deal. A few other small ones. But when I eventually asked him about the money, he got real cagey. I figured out he'd spent it all on booze and drugs. He claimed it was payment for his management services." Kellen scoffed.

"That's awful."

"The worst part is that my mother took his side. I haven't talked to her in over a decade."

"Oh my gosh." My stomach drops. My father is an asshole, but at least he didn't steal from me. And I'm lucky to have such a great mom in my life. I don't know what I'd do without her support and love.

Kellen shrugs and glances over at me. "It's old news. But it's because of my family that I need to stay in Fort Collins. Playing for the Blizzard. I've hopefully got a few more good years of hockey, but I don't want to live somewhere else, and I don't want to move them."

"I can understand that."

Bear pulls ahead to get to a pile of leaves, and Kellen turns his eyes to me as he extends the leash and stops walking.

"Ava's had serious health issues. We want to keep her near her doctors in Denver."

"Oh." I'm not sure what to say, but there's a tightness in my chest thinking of his daughter being sick. I cross my arms tightly.

"There are pretty intensive follow ups, and if anything else goes wrong, we want to be here."

I nod, a lump lodged in my throat, and follow his lead when he resumes walking. That's a lot for one person to take. His father gone, his mother not supportive, and Ava with a troubled health history. No wonder he's protective. We resume walking and step back onto the main trail a minute later, passing through the woods in silence until we reach a clearing and a large, still, beautiful lake.

"Wow," I say. I can feel Kellen's eyes on the side of my face. "Gorgeous."

"I know the perfect spot, come on." Kellen looks back at me and nods his head, so I follow him and Bear. He leads us a minute past the clearing through a thicket of trees to a sandy shore.

"Ahh, perfect." I sink down on a low boulder and untie my boots. "I need to get these off."

"You might regret that when you have to put them back on." Kellen watches me make bad choices.

"This feels heavenly." I ignore him and strip my boots and socks off. "I'm going to soak my feet—they're killing me." I struggle to roll my jeans halfway to my knees and stretch my toes, rejoicing at the freedom. Kellen steps to me and holds out a hand. I take it and he pulls me to my feet, dropping my hand as soon as I'm upright. Which makes perfect sense, because why would he keep holding my hand?

I step past him and toward the gloriously cold lake.

"So you didn't want to swim in the waterfall, but you want to put your feet in this freezing cold lake?"

"Yes, exactly—" I gasp at the first touch of frigid water and dig my toes into the soft, wet sand. "It's perfect, despite the numbness, which makes my heels feel better, actually. Come on, get in here, live a little."

He shakes his head but finds a rock to wedge Bear's leash in between and takes off his boots and socks.

"That is very cold," he says when his feet meet the water. He easily folds up his pants—clearly I shouldn't have worn jeans—and comes my way, stopping next to me.

The water is murkier further out. I don't know why this bit isn't muddy and gross, but I don't question it.

Bear barks from the shoreline, startling me, and I spin to face him, fully expecting to see a black bear or mountain lion about to eat him. Or us.

It's nothing.

"Maybe we should head back?" I say. I take a step toward the shoreline, but my other foot has sunk too far in the sand, and I lose my balance. My arms flail wildly, and I see the disaster unfolding as if I'm hovering above my body.

With horror, I realize there's no fixing this.

I can't get myself upright. I'm going to fall and get soaking wet in six inches of water. Kellen moves to catch me, and I reach for him and grab his arms, but it's too late.

I twist and the sand releases my foot, allowing me to land with a splash and a thud on my back in the icy cold Colorado lake. Water immediately soaks the back of my tank top, and a split second before I comprehend what just happened, Kellen is falling right on top of me.

He thrusts his hands out on either side of my shoulders, splashing water onto my face but stopping himself before he lands flush against me.

"Oh my god," I gasp. Kellen's face is about twelve inches from mine, his warm torso hovering above my chest, his bottom half sprawled out on mine.

The cold registers quickly, and my breath catches. I'm an ice cube on my back half and on fire on my front.

Kellen pauses for a second more than is strictly necessary, and I feel every bit of him that's touching me. His hard knees digging into my shins. The heavy weight of his pelvis that makes me want to pull him down even further, take his face in my hands and bring it to mine. There are all sorts of feelings rushing through my body. Warm ones. Cold ones. Wet ones. Ones where I want to strip off all my clothes.

A laugh bubbles up and out of me.

"Shit!" Kellen leaps onto his feet, then leans down to swoop his hands under my torso, lifting me out of the water as if I'm a child. "Are you okay?"

Dripping and laughing, I stare at him, not sure if I should cry or scream or continue laughing. I probably look like a wet dog. Speaking of dogs, Bear is barking like crazy, about to rip his leash out from between the rocks.

"I'm so sorry," I manage after the giggles fade, shaking my hands and spraying water on the ground. "I'm the clumsiest human being on the face of this planet." Water drips down my back, but the front of me has stayed mostly dry aside from the splattering of water when Kellen's hands hit the lake. Kellen isn't in as bad shape, but his pants are half wet from the knee down.

"You are very wet," he states, his eyes roaming down my body in a way that feels way more sexual than it should. It shouldn't at all, of course.

"You are also not very dry. Sorry, sorry, sorry." I reach up and touch my dripping hair, which is spotted with patches of rough grains of sand. I'm an absolute mess.

"It's no problem. My pants will dry fast. Your jeans, however..." Kellen's smile is bright and sweet, like I didn't just ruin the hike by dragging him into the cold lake. "So you really did want to go swimming. I knew it."

I attempt to shake sand out of my curls, but it's hopeless. Add this to the list of ways I've embarrassed myself in front of Kellen Bassey.

"At least our shoes are dry?"

"At least." Kellen grabs my hand and pulls me to shore. I let him lead me out of the water. His hand on mine feels so lovely and warm and right.

I can't stop smiling.

CHAPTER 12

Fake Dating Planning Committee

KELLEN

I settle on the loveseat in Atticus's apartment. Harley and Lachlan are already camped out on the longer couch.

Lucy's not here, but I know she's going to get home in a bit.

"So what did you want to talk about?" Atticus tosses Harley a water bottle and opens three beers for the rest of us.

"Remember yesterday afternoon, when you guys were trying to get me to find a girlfriend?"

"Or a fake girlfriend," Lachlan chimes in.

"Well. I took your advice."

"What?" Atticus laughs and hands me my beer. "Already?"

"No time like the present?" My smile falters as I brace myself to tell my teammate I'm going to pretend to date his sister.

Atticus sits on the single chair, and they all look at me expectantly.

"I found the perfect person to fake date."

They all continue to stare at me.

"Spit it out, mate." Lachlan waves a hand in the air.

"Lucy." I watch Atticus for his reaction.

He doesn't disappoint.

"What??" Atticus stands, his eyes comically wide.

Lachlan bursts out laughing.

"No way. I can't get behind that." Atticus shakes his head violently and points the neck of his bottle at me. "That is not what I meant! Find someone *else* to fake date!"

"Yes, you can get behind it," Harley says calmly before sipping from his water bottle. "It's smart. We know we can trust Lucy because she's your sister. And we need Kellen to keep his ass in Fort Collins on the Blizzard."

"And Lucy says she wants help showing her father—your father—that she's doing perfectly fine away from her old life," I say.

"Get my sister's name out of your mouth." Atticus narrows his eyes at me, but the other guys just laugh.

"Oh, come on." Lachlan props his feet up on the coffee table and then lays his arm across the back of the couch. "This is brilliant. You hate that man. How can you resist the opportunity to piss him off?"

Atticus swings his head to me again. "I hate this idea." There's a hint of a whine in his voice, but his objections have already lost steam.

"So you're vetoing the plan?" Harley asks.

Atticus growls and empties his beer.

"Atter? Answer the question." Harley calmly stares at Atticus. There's a brief silence.

"No." Atticus sighs, trying to drink out of his empty bottle.

Relief cascades through me. I might laugh about it, but I don't want to upset him.

"Could be worse. *I* could be fake dating her." Lachlan winks.

"Christ. That would be so much worse," Atticus mutters.

"Listen." I drink my beer, the only one I'll have tonight. We all keep alcohol to an absolute minimum during the season. Except for the team retreat. "We'll keep this above board. It's all pretend."

"And how, exactly, are you planning on keeping this above board?"

"Well, during our hike this morning, we talked about a few events we'd be seen at together."

"Your hike? Now you're hiking with her??"

"We were doing media training." I shrug.

"Bullshit. You don't need media training." Atticus calls me out immediately.

"And making a fake dating plan."

Lachlan slams his hand on the coffee table, and everyone jumps.

"The fuck?" Atticus glares at him.

"This is amazing." Lachlan stands and clears his throat. "I want to officially kick off the first meeting of the Fake Dating Planning Committee."

"No fucking way." I shake my head.

"Yeah fucking way," he says. "You will absolutely need help with this. And I'm sure Atticus will want to be able to offer input on the plan."

I look at the ceiling, praying for it to fall down on our heads and end this.

"Go on," Harley says, biting back a grin. Atticus growls at us and springs up to pace back and forth in the kitchen.

"Agenda item number one!" Lachlan practically sings and plops back down on the coach. "Official appearances of Lucy and Kellen. Kellie? Tell us what you discussed."

"Alright." I twist the bottle in my hand. "We talked about three times we'll *pretend* to be a couple in front of Paul and Savannah." I look pointedly at Atticus, who rolls his eyes.

"Lellen? Kucy?" Lachlan cocks his head and looks at Harley. "Hmm, nothing really rolls off the tongue."

"Lullen?" Harley suggests.

"Kellcy?" Atticus says, then scowls and appears to hate himself.

"Oh!" Lachlan points in the air. "That's it! Kellen and Lucy are now officially Kellcy."

"That is ridiculous. And I thought you didn't approve of this." I growl at Atticus. "Why are you helping?"

"What? I like to be creative." Atticus finally stops pacing and settles back into the single chair. "In another life I might have worked in marketing. Or written a novel."

Lachlan scoffs. "You don't have a novel in you."

"I might!"

"No." Lachlan laughs and shakes his head.

"Whatever," I say, trying to end the stupidest argument ever. "The first public appearance—"

But before I can finish my sentence, a key jangles in the lock and all four of us move our gazes to the front door. Lachlan cackles with glee.

"That'll be my fake girlfriend," I say. Nerves jump around in my stomach. We'd agreed she'd show up and talk to Atticus at some point, but I didn't think it'd be till later.

The door swings open to reveal Lucy, curls down and wild around her face, long legs bare below athletic shorts, a tight sports tank, and her phone held out in front of her.

She's laughing and looking at the screen, and voices project from her mobile.

I swear my stupid heart leaps at the sight of her. My cock is also more than interested. I tell both to shut the fuck up.

Lucy freezes when she finally looks up and sees the four of us watching her. The door slams behind her.

"Shit," she says. "I didn't think you guys were coming till later."

"Hello? Lulu?" a voice comes from the phone. "You look like you've seen a ghost."

"Not a ghost," she says and turns the phone around. "Raleigh, January, say hi to Atticus, Harley, Lachlan, and Kellen."

One woman yelps and the other giggles uncontrollably as Lucy scans the phone around the room.

"Are those your friends?" Lachlan asks, more than interested.

"Yes." Lucy meets my gaze and presses her lips together. "I thought you guys were coming over at eight?"

"Seven. Sorry."

"Glad you're here, Lucy!" Lachlan says. "Ladies on Lucy's mobile, we're having a planning meeting for this fake dating situation. Want to join?"

"Yes!" they both scream at the same time as Lucy says "No!"

She looks across the room at Atticus, who shrugs.

"In case you were wondering, you are now officially Kellcy." Atticus grabs a water bottle for himself, but I'm betting he wishes it was alcohol instead.

"That is perfection," a voice squeals from Lucy's phone.

"You... okay with this?" Lucy looks at her brother with a scrunched-up nose.

"Whatever," he says.

"Okay, then. I just need a minute." My fake girlfriend scoots across the room toward the hallway leading to Atticus's spare bedroom. But as she passes, Atticus reaches out and grabs her phone.

"I'll keep Raleigh and January. We'll wait."

Lucy disappears down the hall.

"Hello, ladies. How are you? How's divorce number two treating you, Raleigh?"

"It's fantastic," Raleigh deadpans.

"She's almost free," January insists.

"And how's London, January?"

"Excellent. I just got back from the pub. This is the perfect ending to my Saturday night."

This was not how I planned on spending *my* Saturday night. But there are worse ways.

Lucy comes back into the family room in a hoodie, hair pinned back in a messy bun. Lachlan throws his legs over the empty cushion between him and Harley, so Lucy is forced to sit next to me.

"Alright." Atticus props Lucy's phone up in the middle of the coffee table against a stray twenty-five-pound dumbbell. "So what's the plan?"

I look over at Lucy sitting so close to me, but when her wide green eyes meet mine, she shakes her head.

"Go ahead." Lucy waves a hand. "You explain the plan. Please."

"It's simple," I say. "We have three events: the fall festival in October, the retreat in November, and some kind of coffee shop date next week."

"Right," Atticus says, nodding slowly. "I always see Paul and Savannah at Deep Roots Cafe on weekday mornings. Like eight o'clock or so on the days I stop by on the way to the arena."

"We can show up before then." I glance back at Lucy, who nods.

"And do what?" Lachlan asks, eyebrows raised, a fake innocent look on his face.

"Have coffee? Say hello to them?"

"If you do that, they'll just think you're cooperating with the sponsorship project, like Paul demanded of all of us. Of *you*." Harley's the calmest person in the room.

"You will need to kiss." Lachlan rubs his hands together. He's our resident fucking chaos director.

Lucy gasps, Lachlan laughs, there are squeals from the phone, and Atticus shouts.

"I don't think that's necessary, do you?" Lucy looks at me, then the rest of the group. Her wide eyes are mildly panicked.

"Totally necessary to convince them you have a thing going on." Lachlan says it like an irrefutable fact. "We'll be away at a few preseason games this week. What day were you thinking?"

"Hang on." I look over at Lucy, who is white as a sheet. "You okay?"

"This is ridiculous," she says to me, voice wobbly but with a sprinkling of amusement, like she's holding back nervous giggles. "It's not what we planned."

"I mean, I know," I say quietly. "But he's kind of right?" My traitorous eyes dart down to her lips. Red and full and shiny, like she just put lip gloss on. I bet they taste fucking amazing. I lower my voice to a whisper. "Okay, sweet potato?"

Lucy cracks up, which was my intention.

"Fine, puppy dog." It's just for me to hear.

I grin.

"Kellen!" Atticus says. "Stop whispering with my sister! And you will not be making out with her."

There are shouts and laughs coming from the phone. Atticus calmly reaches down and lowers the volume on Lucy's friends.

"He will be," Harley says. "And you know it."

Lucy grabs her phone and increases the volume.

"I agree, Lucy. You probably need to do something like that to convince them it's real," her blonde friend says, practically bouncing on the screen.

"Absolutely." The one in London nods enthusiastically. "Kissing is necessary."

"And hand holding," Lachlan adds.

"Lach." I attempt my stern father voice.

"Long, lingering looks," blonde friend says.

"Raleigh Durham." Lucy shakes her head.

"Back massages," London friend adds.

"Enough!" Atticus shouts.

I'm trying to hold in the laughter, because as stupid as this all is, I'm having more fun on a Saturday night than I have in ages. Even Lucy is laughing now.

"Everyone has one vote. This is the official first meeting of the

Kellcy Fake Dating Planning Committee, and we are the founding members." Lachlan stands again.

Her friends cheer.

"Who votes they kiss?" Lachlan yells, raising his hand.

Harley puts his arm in the air. Raleigh and January both shout yes from the phone.

Lucy and I don't move a muscle. Neither does Atticus.

"Four to three. It's settled. This week—they kiss!"

Cheers erupt all around the room.

"We'll be back late Wednesday." I check on Lucy again. "How about Thursday morning?"

"I guess so," Lucy says with a half-smile. "Thursday morning. Deep Roots Cafe. Meet you there at seven forty-five?" I nod. "One kiss. In front of Paul and Savannah."

"What about tongue?" Lachlan says, his face a mask of fake innocence.

"Shut up, Lachlan," I warn, but my insides shift. The idea of kissing this woman? I'll enjoy it too much.

"But I'll see you Wednesday at Ava's soccer practice, right?" Lucy says.

"What's this now?" Atticus asks.

"Oh, I'm helping Kellen's daughter's soccer team... why are you guys looking at me like that?"

Harley and Lachlan stare at her with wide eyes.

"You're coaching the Snowballs?" Lachlan cocks his head.

"Yes, she is," I say. "Don't be dramatic."

"Chill, guys, Lucy did this all the time back in D.C. Right, Luce?" Atticus says, but he knows it's a big deal for me to let someone hang out with my daughter. He looks intently at me, and then at Lucy. I wonder what he's thinking. The coach thing was his idea, after all.

"Wednesday night. Yup." I turn to Lucy.

"And we should plan the breakup," Lucy says. "After the

retreat but before Christmas. That should be enough time to get them off your back."

I blink hard, remembering that the whole purpose of this is to convince Paul I'm not interested in Savannah. "Sure. Will it be enough time for you? To give your old life a big ole' fuck you?"

She nods.

"I think we'll need to meet again as the Kellcy Fake Dating Planning Committee. Including your friends." Harley gestures to the phone, where both women shout in agreement.

"When? If we don't agree to a time now, they'll try to wiggle out of it," Raleigh says.

"Good point." Atticus nods. "How about after the fall festival?"

"So maybe Sunday, October 13?" Lachlan stares down at his phone. "Kellen? Lucy?" Lachlan looks over at us. I give him a nod.

"Sure?" Lucy says.

"Then it's set." Lachlan stands. "Who wants another drink?"

"No one," Harley says. "At least no one who plays hockey."

We have some kind of plan, no matter how ridiculous it is.

And next week, I get to kiss Lucy.

CHAPTER 13

Permission Granted

Tuesday, October 1

"This might be a career-limiting decision." I glance over at Kellen, who's walking down the hall with me to the head of HR's office. I'm ridiculously nervous to face this woman.

"For whom?"

"Me?" I squeeze my hands together.

"Nah. It'll be fine." Kellen is too relaxed, like we're grabbing a casual coffee instead of to the head of Blizzard human resources to declare ourselves a couple. "Didn't I tell you that over text a hundred times yesterday?"

When I got to work Monday morning, I talked to Lina about my relationship with Kellen. She thought I was messing with her. I don't blame her. Just a week ago, I'd reassured her that I'm not going to date anyone.

Yet here we are.

So she said I'd have to go to HR to get the sign off, then gave me a really funny look.

"Yeah, well, they're not going to kick you off the team because you're dating a staffer. They might fire me."

"You're a contractor. They're not going to fire you."

"I'm hoping that this little monster will be a good enough distraction." I nod to Bear, snuggled in Kellen's arms, blissfully happy.

"Maybe." Kellen rubs his head.

In a last-minute decision, I'd brought Bear to the office this morning. I heard that the woman we're meeting with is a huge dog person, so maybe this'll help soften her up to us.

"Want to go over the story again?" After Monday, when Lina made me make an appointment with HR, Kellen and I have been texting a lot to get our story straight. After all, it was only a week ago that Lina mentioned the team policy, and I said *that won't be a problem, I promise.* And that *I'm not into hockey players.*

Sigh.

"No ma'am. I got it. And hey..." Kellen slows to a stop, and I do the same. "Thanks for doing this. I know I get a lot more out of it than you."

"I wouldn't just do this to be nice. There are lots of benefits for me besides the thing with my father."

"Yeah?" Kellen cocks his head. "Like what?" We got an early meeting before his workout and practice, so Kellen's in athletic shorts and a Blizzard t-shirt.

"Well, we didn't add pure entertainment to the list." I hold two fingers up. "So that's two. And distraction from my personal drama." A third finger. "And something to do besides stare at the walls of Atticus's guest room while I'm not working. And—"

"Okay, okay, got it." Kellen grins and I lower my fingers. "Let's go."

I knock on the door, and we enter when Claire Morgansten calls us in. She stands and when she sees Bear, her eyes widen.

"Oh, hold on—" but before she can get another word out, a

small ball of fur and fury shoots out from next to her desk and leaps up at Bear, who's still nestled in Kellen's arms.

Bear reacts by barking wildly and wiggling so much that Kellen struggles to keep ahold of him.

"Shoot! Oh no!"

"Can you put him back in your office?" Claire shouts over the din of two barking dogs.

We back out the door as Claire chases her dog around her desk.

"Shit. I'll just go run and put him back," I say, wide-eyed.

"No, I'll do it." Kellen's barely holding in laughter.

"Fine. Hurry!" I don't know how he's so calm, but he trots down the hall, and I turn back to the open door.

Well. That wasn't a good start.

"I'm so sorry about that," I say when I re-enter the room. Claire's put her tiny dog into a giant crate that contains a fuzzy blanket, food and water, and a pile of dog toys.

"It was unexpected." She hooks the crate closed and turns to me, looking decidedly annoyed. "Chihuahuas are really protective. She's fine with people—sort of—but other dogs really make her crazy."

Lordy. I'm already making a mess of my new life in Colorado. I'm about to lie to the head of HR.

"Sit, sit. How are you settling in?" Claire waves at one of the seats in front of her desk and settles into her office chair, her mask of composure back in place. She gives a meaningful look out the door. "Well, I'm guessing."

"Yeah, pretty well." I let out a nervous chuckle. "The work is good so far. Lina's great, and I'm enjoying the change of working for a hockey team."

"Wonderful." Claire smiles at me. "I knew you'd be a good fit for the Blizzard. Lina's said great things so far."

Ugh. Now I feel worse about lying.

"Hey," Kellen says as he pops back into Claire's office. "Bear is happily waiting in your office for your return, Lucy."

"Thank you," I say.

"So, let's get down to it, as I'm sure you have to get to the gym, Kellen. Why don't you both tell me what's going on?"

"Well—" Kellen and I say at the same time, then look at each other and laugh.

"Why don't you go ahead, buttercup?"

I bite back a laugh as Claire's eyes widen.

"Sure." My mind blanks, and I can't think of one nickname to call him. The only animal names that come to mind are farm animal ones that are decidedly not cute: goat, sheep, horse, cow...

"Lucy?" Claire says, concern etched in her brow.

"Right. I started with the Blizzard just over three weeks ago, and Kellen and I immediately clicked." I swallow and reach my hand over and place it on his knee, palm up. He takes it right away. "Kellen was at my brother's apartment a lot, so we got to spend time together... and here we are." Yup. Just me and Kelley Bassey, holding hands and lying about dating.

"Okay. That's it?"

"Yes. And we just want to be above board with all this. I don't want anyone to get in trouble." Like me. Mostly me.

Claire sighs. "Alright. Fine. I'm glad you came to me. I have a quick paper for you to fill out." She slides a sheet of paper to Kellen, who immediately signs his name without reading, then passes it to me.

I skim and it's a short document officially disclosing our relationship. There's nothing romantic or anything indicated, just recognizing the connection.

"Anything else?" Kellen says, arms perched on the sides of the chair, ready to stand.

"Just... keep it professional. Paul is really focused on ensuring the Blizzard has a great reputation, so any time we get coverage in the hockey tabloids, he's not a fan."

"I understand," I say. "This job is important to me."

She gives me a funny look as if to say, then why are you doing this?

"Got it. Absolutely. I, too, am very concerned with the Blizzard reputation." Kellen leans forward. "As the team captain."

Claire nods and finally looks convinced. After another minute of small talk, we leave her office, closing the door behind us.

"Buttercup, really?" I whisper, laughing.

"I'm deeply disappointed I didn't get called a cute animal name." Kellen puts his hand on the small of my back and leads me down the hall back toward my office.

"I couldn't think of one! The only thing that came to mind were farm animals. Like chicken. Ohhh, that would've been cute! I'm saving it for another time."

We stop in front of my office.

"That was fun, Lucy Knox."

"Glad I entertain you."

"You always do. See you tomorrow at soccer?"

I nod, and with that, Kellen heads down the hall and disappears into the players' gym.

CHAPTER 14

Coach Lucy

KELLEN

Wednesday, October 2

Soccer practice is in full swing when I approach Bri on the side of the field. Ava and her nine teammates are running around chasing a soccer ball like a swarm of bees—maybe scrimmaging?—and absolutely tripping all over each other. I'm not sure they even realize there are two distinct teams.

I've been smiling all day thinking of the meeting with Claire yesterday. How were we supposed to know she had an attack Chihuahua loose in her office?

"Hey," I say to Bri, who's watching the kids with her arms crossed loosely.

"I have so many opinions on this situation," she says without looking my way or including a greeting.

"Yeah? You met Lucy?"

"Sure did. I'm just confused as to why she would volunteer to step in as coach for a bunch of five-year-old kids she doesn't know." She shakes her head. "They are cute but have literally no idea how to play soccer."

"Because she's a nice person? She misses coaching kids, like she did back in D.C., remember?" I watch Lucy as she gently positions children in the correct spots on the field, her curls secured in a ponytail. "She needs something to do to keep her mind off her cheating ex and overbearing father?"

Bri turns to stare at me.

Lucy squats down next to Ava and says something that makes my daughter laugh, then Lucy points to one of the other players. Ava nods and appears to be paying attention.

"She's really good with them. With Ava." I gesture to the field and Bri turns back to watch Lucy.

"Yeah, she is."

"I know we don't usually invite people to hang out with our kid like this."

"True."

"But she's Atticus's sister. She's been background checked recently. And she even provided a reference to the elementary school where she coached last." The head of recreation at Ava's school had called Lucy's last team, and they did nothing but rave about her.

"You already convinced me." Bri huffs out a chuckle. "And you need to do whatever you have to do to convince Paul Harrison you're not interested in his wife. Like maybe never look at that woman again."

I groan. I agree, but it's easier said than done.

On Sunday, I stopped by Bri's house and told her all about the fake dating plan. She was surprisingly chill about everything, mostly because she's just as worried about me getting traded as I am. It affects all of us.

Lucy blows a whistle and tells the kids to take a water break. Ava sprints in our direction.

"Daddy! You're here!"

I squat down and give her a giant hug.

"I needed to make sure your first practice with Coach Lucy is going okay."

"It's going amazing! She showed us pictures of her dog. His name is Bear now!" Ava cracks up.

"Drink some water, girly." Bri hands Ava her water bottle.

"Glad you're having fun."

"SO much fun. Coach Lucy is way better than Bella's dad." Ava loudly whispers this last part. "Bye!"

I chuckle as Ava turns and sprints back across the field, jumping onto Lucy's back. I cringe, but Lucy easily grabs her legs and spins around in a circle, laughing.

"I'm not sure she could be more of a hit with our daughter, actually." Bri raises her eyebrows and watches the other kids attach themselves to Lucy's legs. Lucy tries to walk and then falls to the ground dramatically, giggling with the girls as they pile on her.

Thirty minutes later, the practice is over and there's a line of parents talking to Lucy, thanking her for taking over.

Bri leaves with Ava, but I wait my turn.

"Wow," I say when the last mom heads to the parking lot with her daughter. "That was impressive."

Lucy smiles widely. Her cheeks are flushed, and she lets out a breathless laugh.

"That was a lot of fun. I didn't realize quite how much I'd miss coaching when I left D.C."

There are so many curls that have escaped her ponytail, and I want to push them back from her face.

"You have a knack for it."

Lucy's an adorable coach, wearing a team t-shirt declaring the Kindergarten Snowballs—it's a little snug, which I don't mind—paired with black athletic shorts. Plus she threw on shin guards and soccer socks. She looks legit.

"With little kids, yes. I'm not sure I'd want to coach older kids. Definitely not adults."

"Well, thank you, everyone is grateful."

"No worries. Really."

A brief silence falls between us as we stare at each other. The last car pulls out of the parking lot.

"Ava is so sweet."

"Clearly she loves you. Having a cute dog is definitely in your favor."

"I probably should've brought him to butter the kids up, but knowing Bear, he'd cause chaos. Probably by running around looking for Chihuahuas to fight."

I laugh. "That was deeply entertaining yesterday."

"I guess you could call it that." But she's smiling too.

"Ready for tomorrow morning?"

"Yes." She nods. "See you in the square at seven forty-five, right?"

"Then we'll head to Deep Roots Cafe."

Now *that's* when I'll get to kiss her.

"Looking forward to it." Lucy laughs with what might be a tinge of nerves.

"Me too. Let me help you clean up." I glance around at the balls and cones.

When we're done, I walk Lucy to her car and make sure she pulls away safely from the parking lot.

I drive home with a giant smile on my face.

CHAPTER 15

Almost Definitely a Fake Kiss

LUCY

Thursday, October 3

Kellen sits on the edge of the fountain in Old Town Square—the heart of Fort Collins—looking down at Ava, who's shoving a chocolate sprinkle donut in her mouth. I feel like a bit of a voyeur stopping to watch them, but I can't help myself. Bear sits at my feet, for once not being a menace to society.

We're meeting up before heading to Deep Roots Cafe for our first public moment in front of Paul and Savannah.

The moment when we're supposed to kiss.

Which we agreed to do by committee vote last weekend.

The idea of kissing this man is freaking me out. It's got my pulse racing a bit faster than it should, and I brushed my teeth for more than the required two minutes this morning.

Here we go.

I approach Kellen and Ava, and when she sees me, she squeals.

"Coach Lucy!" She drops her donut on a napkin and jumps up, then spots Bear and gasps dramatically. "Your dog!!"

I nod down to Bear. "He's super friendly. Go on and pet him if you want to."

Ava drops to her knees and holds her hands out to Bear, who licks her enthusiastically. Kellen's daughter is so darn cute. She's an exact mix of Kellen and her mom, and the little girl is super friendly and sweet.

"I love the name Bear! But Daddy told me he used to be Waffles?" Ava looks up at me with big blue eyes.

"It was Waffles when I first got here, but he wasn't listening very well."

Kellen scoffs gleefully behind Ava, and I shoot him a dirty look.

"Since then he's been Zeus, Taco, Harry, Prince Harry, and now Bear. But I don't think he likes the name Bear." I stop myself from revealing that her father suggested his current name.

"That's so funny!"

"I'm still trying to find the right name for him. But he keeps changing his mind."

"Really?" Ava stares with wide eyes. Bear sits and gazes lovingly up at the little girl. "How do you know if he likes the name?"

"Well. If he responds to it. If he seems happy when I say it. I'll show you." I clear my throat. "Bear, roll over."

He doesn't react to my voice.

"Bear. Do you like your name?" Nothing. "Hello?"

At that, Bear turns to look at me.

Ava bursts into giggles.

"Do you have any good name ideas?"

"You want me to name him?" Ava's eyes widen, and she looks at me, completely serious.

"I'd love it." That's not exactly what I meant, but we're gonna go with it. A bunch of adults have not managed to successfully rename my dog. How much worse could it be if a five-year-old girl did it?

"Lucy? You might regret this," Kellen says.

"Nah."

"I'm gonna come up with the best name." Ava's face scrunches into a determined mask.

"Let me know when you figure it out."

"I will." Ava nods solemnly.

"Did you have fun at practice last night?"

"Yes, so much fun!"

"Good morning." A younger woman walks up, and Ava jumps to hug her. The woman takes the backpack from Kellen's outstretched hand.

"Lucy, this is Grace, Ava's nanny."

"Nice to meet you," Grace says.

"You too."

"Lucy works at the Blizzard."

Grace smiles at me and then leans down to touch Ava's shoulder.

"Time to go, Ava. Let's get you to school."

"Awww." Ava leans over and kisses Bear's head, and he leans into it.

"He likes you." I stand. I don't say that Bear pretty much likes everyone, and I'm glad, because the smile on Ava's face is worth it.

"Say goodbye to me, Aves."

"Bye, Daddy!" She leaps into Kellen's arms and kisses his cheek.

"Did you just kiss me with the same lips you kissed that dog?"

"Yup!" Ava jumps down from Kellen's arms and walks away with Grace. "Bye, Coach Lucy! Bye, Bear!"

"She's such a cutie," I say, aware of Kellen's eyes on me as I wave goodbye to Ava before turning to him.

"Sure is." Kellen sticks his hands in his jeans pockets. He's wearing a Blizzard t-shirt that's fitted around his chest and loose around his waist. "You're good with her. And the other girls."

I shrug. "I love kids. I'm grateful you suggested I help out with the Snowballs." Even though I'm pretty sure I begged him to let me help.

"I should be thanking you. Let's turn this season around for that team."

I laugh. "I'll do my best. But they don't keep score in kindergarten soccer."

"Fair enough." Kellen chuckles. "But honestly, telling Ava she can rename Bear wasn't the smartest move. She definitely loves you now though."

"I'm sure it'll be fine." I squat down and give Bear's head a pat. He attempts to slime me with his long tongue.

"Hey. Just so you know, I'm not going to tell Ava we're dating. Especially since you're also coaching her."

I look up at Kellen, and he's got a furrowed brow.

"Of course not." I nod and stand. "I wouldn't expect you to."

An awkward silence settles between us.

"Should we go—" Kellen's eyes flit down to my shirt, and he groans. It's a DC FC jersey. "Are you wearing a soccer jersey?"

"Yeah?"

"You work for a hockey team. Your brother plays for a hockey team. You are dating a hockey player. Please get some hockey apparel. Preferably Blizzard."

I laugh. "*Fake* dating, and yeah, I know. I'll work on it."

"Let's go." Kellen shakes his head and huffs with (probably) fake annoyance. "Paul and Savannah are supposed to be at the cafe in fifteen minutes."

I nod and fall into step next to Kellen.

"I hope you're not offended that I'm not telling Ava. It's not personal."

"I'm not offended." He's being a good dad protecting his young daughter. I get it. And it makes him that much more attractive.

"I don't want to introduce her to people I date just to have things end." Kellen turns his body to shield me from a trio of men in suits talking and not paying attention to where they're walking. "There was one woman I dated a year ago." He glances at me. "We dated casually for a few months, but she had a painfully hard time interacting with Ava and Bri."

If meeting Ava and Bri was a test, I think I passed. At least with Ava. And last night, Bri was friendly enough when I introduced myself to her and the other parents at practice.

"After I ended it, she shared all these pictures and details about our life with a hockey gossip website."

"That's awful." How could someone do something like that? It's one thing to be mad at a man for hurting you—I totally relate to that—but to do something to harm his child? Unimaginable.

Kellen shrugs. "So I'm very cautious. Especially when it comes to Ava."

"I appreciate you trusting me with her."

"Well, you did pass that background check."

I laugh and gently elbow him in the arm.

A few minutes later, I'm waiting at a table at Deep Roots Cafe while Kellen gets us coffees.

My heart races in anticipation of our kiss.

"You feeling okay about this?" Kellen places a covered cup in front of me along with a jumbo slice of crumb cake.

"I guess so."

"Did I get your coffee right?" Kellen glances at the cup. "Vanilla oat milk latte?"

"Perfect." I nod.

"The crumb cake is really good here." Kellen sits down right next to me. "So are the muffins."

"Macarons are my favorite baked good. Not that you asked." I wish I could control my tendency to offer too much information.

"Yeah? What flavors?"

"All the flavors?" I smile. "But if I had to choose: chocolate, pistachio, and salted caramel." I tick them off my fingers.

"That's good information to have about my fake girlfriend."

Kellen unwraps the crumb cake and breaks it in half, pushing a section to me.

"Holy, that is so good," I say as I bite into the dense, rich crumbs.

"Right?" Kellen pops the entire piece into his mouth, then casually lays his hand on the table, palm up. "Should we hold hands?"

"That was quite the transition."

He grins. "Rip the Band-Aid off, I suppose."

"Makes sense." I move my hand towards his, and my body seems to go in slow motion. The sounds of the coffee shop fade around us, and all I can focus on is reaching across the table.

The feel of our hands touching is a lot to take in. He slowly entwines his warm and rough fingers with mine, like he's taking his time, learning the shape of me.

My heartbeat has not slowed down one bit.

I'm going to have to pull it together, or I'll blow this whole thing, for me and for Kellen.

"Tell me a story while we wait. Distract me." Kellen's voice has the slightest shake, like he's nervous too. Which I must be imagining, because would one fake kiss really make Kellen nervous?

"Okay." I try to think, hard, but I keep losing my train of thought as I look into Kellen's blue eyes. The dark swoops of hair on his forehead. The way his thumb is slowly moving on the back of my hand. Does he know he's doing it?

"I'm not a great soccer player."

Kellen laughs. "Really?"

"Yeah. Really. I got on all the good soccer teams growing up because of my father. I'd be on this top team and clearly the weakest player." The memories of those games are not great. I truly loved being with the team but always felt a degree of shame at not carrying my weight on the field. I would've been much happier on a lower team. Richard took that opportunity away from me by giving me what he thought of as a better one.

"Oh no."

"It finally ended after high school. I refused to even try to play college soccer. Not that I would've been able to. Dad was so disappointed. I know everything about the game, and I loved working for a soccer team. I like to watch. Coach kids. Not play."

"What about Atticus? Did he ever play?"

"He was a great soccer player. But he loved hockey far more. Pissed our father off. To this day, Richard is not supportive of Atticus, which I know you know." I shake my head.

There were so many fights growing up. Atticus and our father never got along.

"So by being here, you're basically taking Atticus's side."

"I guess." I glance down at our hands. I can't ignore the sensation of us touching, and the way his thumb is still gently moving against my skin. It feels warm and comforting. Natural.

"They're here." Kellen looks over my shoulder at the door.

"Okay."

Time slows and I take a deep breath. We lock eyes and everything fades away, including Paul and Savannah's presence.

"Are you ready?"

"Yeah." I nod and swallow.

"Alright, Lucy. I'm going to kiss you now."

My name out of his mouth washes over me like that first step into a hot tub. I nod.

Kellen reaches his other hand over and slides it along my jaw and behind my head, so gently. Tingles burst from where he's touching me, and I melt into his palm.

I glance down at his mouth as he closes the distance between us. I think my heart is going to beat right out of my chest and explode in the middle of this cafe.

Then our lips touch.

It's soft and sweet, and I forget to breathe while our mouths are pressed together. The voices around us dim, and romantic music floats through the cafe. Someone throws rose petals. A dove flies elegantly by. A narrator says something like and *there it is, ladies and gentlemen, the infamous first kiss.*

And then it's over, and Kellen leans back, letting his hand linger on my neck for a second longer than is required, his eyes still locked with mine.

I unintentionally let out a deep, whimsical sigh, and force myself to sit back. *Pull it together. It was just a fake kiss.*

"You okay?" he asks, his voice with a slight rasp. "Was that too much?"

Too much? No way. It wasn't enough… not by a long shot.

"It was—" I search for an appropriate word. "—nice." I lean back in the chair, desperate to project nonchalance. I can't take my eyes off Kellen, and he's got a soft smile on his face.

He glances at the door, raising a hand. "They're leaving, Savannah just waved. They must've called their drinks in ahead of time."

Right, we did that for Paul and Savannah's sake. I might have forgotten all about them.

"Oh, great." I look over my shoulder and catch Savannah raising a hand back at Kellen. Once outside, she jogs to catch up to Paul and whispers something in his ear.

"They're talking about us," I note.

"Probably. Then again, we're HR official now, so it's basically public record."

Any chance this man liked that kiss as much as I did?

"Well, nice working with you."

"You too," Kellen says. Then we both crack up.

We are the most awkward humans on the planet. Kellen runs his hands through his dark hair and pulls his phone out of his pocket.

"I gotta run to practice. You headed to the arena?"

I shake my head. "I'm heading home before dropping Bear at the Delightful Doggy Palace."

"I'll walk you back to Atticus's apartment." Kellen stands. I follow him out the door, and we walk in silence to my brother's place.

"Next Saturday, right?" I ask, like I don't have our next fake date engraved on my soul.

"Yup. The fall festival."

I pause with my key in the lock and watch him walk away.

I liked that kiss way more than I thought I would.

I like Kellen more than I thought I would.

This is unexpectedly confusing.

CHAPTER 16

No Kiss Necessary

KELLEN

Saturday, October 12

I missed Ava's soccer game last weekend because we were en route back from our last preseason game, and we were at our first regular season away game during this past Wednesday's soccer practice.

But I saw Coach Lucy at Ava's game this morning, in all her glory coaching five- and six-year-old girls.

It was adorable, and hilarious, and I couldn't stop smiling. I'm also happy to say that the Snowballs are now on a two-game winning streak—score being kept or not—thanks to Coach Lucy's strategies. The main one being to remember which way to kick the ball.

Seeing Lucy coach Ava's team did something to me. Is it possible I missed her? Maybe. But I definitely can't stop thinking about her. The way she makes me laugh. The easy way she connects with Ava.

And that soft kiss that I've been reliving multiple times a day.

My phone buzzes.

LUCY

On my way, be there in ten

ME

Ok no problem

LUCY

I was busy celebrating over a few drinks with my winning soccer team

ME

1) The game was eight hours ago, 2) No you weren't, unless it was with chocolate milk or Capri Sun, and 3) they're a bunch of kindergarteners so I don't think that's appropriate

LUCY

Don't be jealous because I didn't invite you

I grin and slip my phone back in my pocket.

I've been looking forward to tonight, and it's got nothing to do with s'mores or pumpkins.

"Hey." Lucy appears in front of me dressed as a soccer player for Halloween. She's wearing her DC FC jersey, short athletic shorts, high socks, and sneakers.

"Are you kidding me?" I fake scoff at her. I'm not in costume but instead wearing my Blizzard jersey working next to Harley, handing out s'mores kits to kids. "What did we talk about with the soccer gear?"

Every year, a bunch of guys on the team work different booths at the fall festival. Some years we're away at a game and miss it, but we got back late last night after three days on the road.

We played two away games and won both. Atticus, Harley, and I managed to score against Chicago securing a 3-2 victory on Wednesday night. Nashville wasn't as close—we walked away with a 4-1 victory.

Paul didn't travel with us.

"What? I didn't have much to work with." Lucy looks down at her soccer outfit.

I shake my head. "Give me about two minutes to finish up."

"Whatever you say, roo."

I stop and look at her. "Roo?"

"You know, as in a shortened version of kangaroo?" My eyes widen, and she bites her lip. "No? Doesn't work?" Lucy sighs. "I'm having a hard time coming up with pet names for you. I feel like after puppy and kitten, it's kind of weird."

I laugh and go back to stacking graham crackers and chunks of chocolate on plates. "It's definitely weird. Luckily, there are endless options that involve food, my little cream puff."

"Damn, that does sound better."

"Here you go," I say to a young girl, who adds an extra marshmallow to the plate I hand her. "Have fun!"

"Yay!" The girl takes her mother's hand and walks away.

When I look back at Lucy, she's staring at me with a warm smile on her face. And I swear her gaze flits quickly from my eyes to my lips.

"Want to make a s'more?" I wonder if she's been thinking about me as much as I've been thinking about her.

"Of course I want to make a s'more."

"I can handle this, Kellie. Go on," Harley says. "Help your little cream puff make a s'more."

"Christ," I grumble and grab supplies. "Stop eavesdropping."

Lucy laughs and follows me to the bonfire. Her red curls are loose around her head, and I take a moment to absorb her. She's gorgeous. I thought so from that first moment on the ice only a month ago, when I handed her Waffles. But each time I've seen her, she gets prettier.

Even in a soccer uniform.

Or maybe it's just how I'm seeing her that's evolving.

We sit on an empty hay bale, and Lucy stabs a giant marshmallow onto the skewer. She looks at me questioningly.

"Roast my marshmallow for me? Honestly, I'll probably fall into the fire, or my hair will go up in flames."

I laugh and take the skewer, stepping close to the fire.

"I'm kind of an expert at this."

"You're a big s'mores household?"

"Sure am. I have a built-in fire pit in the backyard and always have s'mores ingredients on hand. We switch it up sometimes and use peanut butter cups or caramel chocolate." I glance at Lucy.

"Sounds amazing." Lucy licks her lips, and I almost drop the skewer into the fire. "How's Ava feeling after this morning? She did a great job out there."

"She was so happy. She can't stop talking about Coach Lucy and Bear on the sidelines." Honestly, the girl loves Lucy. Even Bri has been impressed.

"I'm so glad she had fun." Lucy gives me a giant smile. "Hurry with the s'more, roo, I'm starved."

I turn back to the roasting marshmallow. "The key to a perfect s'more is patience. Low and even heat over hot coals, no catching fire. The marshmallow or you." Lucy giggles, and I twist the marshmallow, perfectly browning each side. "Got that chocolate on the graham cracker?"

"Yes, chef."

I turn and carefully place the gooey, brown marshmallow on top of the chocolate she's set on one of the graham crackers, then sandwich it in with another and gently pull the skewer out.

"There. Let the chocolate melt for a second."

"It's beautiful." Lucy takes a big, messy bite and moans as the s'more breaks apart in her teeth, sending crumbs all over the place. I settle next to her on the hay bale as she finishes every last bite.

She attempts to lick the chocolate off her lips, and I try not to stare.

"You've still got chocolate all over your face." I sigh and pull a napkin out of my pocket. "No wonder Ava likes you. She eats s'mores the same way."

"Hey," Lucy starts, but stops when I run the napkin below her lip, then touch the corners of her mouth gently.

"There. You're good." I swallow.

She's good, but am I?

"Thanks." Lucy presses her lips together, suppressing a smile.

"Ready to stroll?"

Lucy nods. I hold out my hand and she slips hers into mine, letting me pull her up off the bale.

"Did you see Paul when you got here? I've been behind the booth for two hours."

She nods. "Yeah, he was over by the drinks tent with Savannah."

"Well, let's get a drink." I don't let go of her hand. No way I'm gonna do that tonight, when I have the perfect excuse to act like her boyfriend. Besides, her hand fits perfectly in mine. Might as well leave it there.

"Ava with Bri tonight?" Lucy steps closer to me to let a group of kids in knight costumes run by, and her body presses against my side.

"At a birthday party. Bri brought her earlier, and she shoved her face with s'mores. Just like you."

"Hey." Lucy squeezes my biceps with her free hand.

"Ouch! You're strong for a soccer player."

Lucy laughs and relaxes her grip on my arm.

"Bri likes you, you know," I say.

"Thank goodness." I feel her look my way. "Were you guys married? Together long?"

"No." I glance back at Lucy. "The short story is that Bri was in town for a weekend. She'd been broken up with her boyfriend for a month. We just had a one-night thing but then she realized she was pregnant a few months later. She did the math and knew it was mine."

"Wow."

"Showed up at my house six months pregnant. And never

left." My complicated life with Bri is one of the reasons I've never wanted to deal with dating. I have too much on my plate, and I don't want to be with someone who will end up jealous or not understand how our co-parenting relationship works.

"You didn't think about getting back together?" Lucy's voice sounds curious, not jealous.

"No. We were never together to begin with, and we just focused on Ava once she got here. We're family now."

I love Bri like family. She *is* family. We work well as co-parents. I don't want anything more with her and she feels the same.

"Oh, mulled wine!" Lucy exclaims and pulls me to the right. Lachlan's working the drink table, and he raises his eyebrows when we approach.

"Well, there's Kellcy, looking cozy."

"Hush. Can we get two mulled wines?" I hand him cash and look around the crowded tent. "Is Paul around?"

"Just walked out." Lachlan points out the other side of the tent to a group of people standing around high tables.

"Ready for this?" I look down at Lucy, who nods.

"Let's do it." She accepts a steaming cup of mulled wine from Lachlan and takes a sip. "Wait." She looks back and forth between me and Lachlan. "Are we kissing?"

"Abso-fucking-lutely," Lachlan immediately replies.

"Only if necessary," I say, because I can't read Lucy.

"Help me, help you, mate," Lachlan says with a giant eye roll and Lucy giggles.

"Fuck off." But I'm not really mad, because Lachlan at least made Lucy laugh.

"If you don't do it, I can." The Aussie tucks a blonde curl behind his ear, hair loose from his usual man bun.

Lucy takes a deep breath. "Okay."

"Okay *I* can do it? Or Kellen?" Lachlan plasters an innocent look on his face.

"Kellen, if it comes to that." She bites her lip, and I follow her out, avoiding Lachlan's knowing smile.

I take her hand and follow her lead. The crowd of people at the table has thinned, and Paul and Savannah are standing by themselves. They haven't spotted us yet.

"Let's go." Lucy drags me right over to their table. I'm too stunned to question her methods—I'd have needed to gather the nerve to approach them.

"Hello, Lucy," Paul says. His eyes flick to me, then down to our linked hands. "Kellen."

"Soccer player? That's brave of you." Savannah tilts her head and smiles at Lucy. Paul watches the interaction.

"I guess I'm a soccer girl at heart." Lucy squeezes my hand.

Savannah looks at me, then back at Lucy, calculating. Not unkindly. I bet she's thinking of the cafe kiss she witnessed.

"How is your father?" Paul asks Lucy, who shrugs.

"Haven't talked to him recently."

"Things going well with the work here?" Paul looks like he's taking mental notes.

"It's going great," Lucy says too enthusiastically. Savannah raises her eyebrows.

An older man calls Paul's name, and he holds up a finger.

"We have to go. Enjoy your evening." Paul nods his head at us.

"Bye, have fun tonight." Savannah follows Paul but looks over her shoulder as they walk away. There's an interested look on her face.

Shit. I should've kissed Lucy before we walked up to Paul and Savannah. Should I kiss her now? Savannah's no longer watching. They're long gone.

"Um, did our plan work already?" Lucy asks.

A panic rises in my belly at the idea of us achieving our fake dating goals too early and ending this delightful charade.

"Nah. It'll take more than two appearances to convince them for sure."

"You think?" A pair of kids dressed as minions runs past us, and Lucy smiles and watches them. "Even with the HR paperwork we signed?"

"Yeah. Did you see that look she gave us?" I feel like an asshole immediately. It wasn't a mean or vengeful look. If anything, it was a wistful one, like she'd rather hang out with us than talk to another old dude.

"I guess you're right. Maybe we should have kissed in front of them."

I swing my head to look at her, eyes wide. She's got a corner of her mouth turned up. I consider suggesting a practice kiss but totally chicken out. *Would* she let me kiss her right now?

How had Lucy's idiot ex cheated on her? I take the last sip of my mulled wine and place the empty cup on the table just as my phone buzzes.

It's a text from Savannah.

SAVANNAH

Can we meet up for a drink? I don't think Paul even remembers the whole NHL Tea picture thing

I flash the text to Lucy, relief washing over me. Relief that Savannah is not yet off my back.

What is wrong with me?

"Look," I say, ignoring my inner thoughts. "It's not working well enough yet."

"Oh." Lucy smiles after reading the text. Is she relieved as well? Because I feel like this—whatever it is we're doing that's possibly not only fake dating—is just getting started.

"Want to go on a hay ride?" My phone buzzes again in my hand, and I glance down.

SAVANNAH
You seem happy with the PR woman. Glad
for you

I don't show Lucy the second text.

"Sure," she says.

I slip my phone in my pocket and pull her against me, leaving an arm around her shoulders. Lucy snuggles into my side and looks up with wide eyes and a smiling, tempting mouth.

I could fake date this woman all day long.

CHAPTER 17

Kissing by Committee

LUCY

Sunday, October 13

I cannot believe my dating life is being run by committee.

Raleigh and January are on Atticus's screen, and he's perched on the single chair in his living room. Harley and Lachlan are on the big couch. Kellen is sitting next to me on the love seat. Same setup as last time.

I feel like I'm on some kind of reality show, and we're about to go into the hot seat with shark hosts about our relationship.

"As you all know, we're here to discuss the progress of Kellen and Lucy's fake relationship," Atticus starts.

"Kellcy," Lachlan sings.

"Kellcy." Atticus nods solemnly, but I know he's supportive of me fake dating Kellen. When Kellen asked me—or maybe let me invite myself—to coach his daughter's soccer team, Atticus was happy that his teammate was helping me stay busy and also impressed that Kellen let me get involved with the Snowballs, even though it was my brother's suggestion to begin with.

He told me exactly that one morning over coffee.

"First agenda item is to find out how the fall festival went.

Lucy, care to summarize?" January's voice rings from the mobile phone propped on the coffee table.

Traitor.

My friends are getting way too much enjoyment out of me fake dating Kellen. And they're totally in cahoots with the hockey boys on these damn meetings.

"It went well. The s'mores were delicious, as was the mulled wine," I say, watching my friends roll their eyes in their little video call squares.

"We talked to Paul and Savannah." Kellen shifts next to me. "Not for long, but then Savannah texted me afterwards asking to hang out."

"What did you say back?" Lachlan asks.

"Nothing." Kellen shrugs. "I feel like any texting with her is a bad thing, including her texting me without me answering back. Makes it look like we're meeting up anyway but not documenting it."

"So our job here is not yet done." Lachlan nods and runs his hand over his blond beard. "Right, Harley?"

"Yes, correct."

"I think the big problem yesterday was the lack of kissing," Raleigh pipes in.

I groan. Although... I did notice that we didn't get to kiss again. We were prepared to, but then the moment swiftly passed after we talked to Paul and Savannah. It's okay. It wasn't needed. We're not going to just randomly make out. And the night was a lot of fun anyway.

"I can't believe you didn't kiss her, mate." Lachlan shakes his head. "There was an obvious opening."

My cheeks warm, and I avoid looking at Kellen.

"But let's make sure to keep it PC," Atticus says in a stern voice. "Kiss her like you'd kiss your sister."

"Gross, dude." Kellen groans.

"Exactly."

"Hello? *Her* is right here." But they all ignore me.

"The next event is a big one," Lachlan says. "The retreat. You'll have all weekend to prove to them you're really together. Or at least banging."

Oh my god. It's seriously like I'm not even present for this meeting.

"Lachlan!" Atticus throws a remote control at the Aussie.

"Whatever." Lachlan easily catches it. "You know what I mean. Try harder."

"What does that mean?" Kellen shakes his head.

"It means we need to get you and Lucy in a compromising situation where Savannah can see it and report back to her husband. Because you know Paul won't be hanging out with the team. He goes to whatever cold dark place he retreats to when he's not harassing hockey players." Lachlan swigs from a beer. "That's what I mean."

"Stop drinking." Kellen waves a finger at Lachlan. "We have four games this week."

"This is my only one. See? What would I do without you, mate? Hence why we're all so interested in keeping you on the Blizzard." Lachlan slides his beer onto the coffee table.

Kellen grumbles something and leans back, resting his arm across the back of the couch behind me.

"How about progress with your father, Lucy?" Harley asks.

"I haven't heard from my dad, so I'm not sure. Paul asked about him the other night though, so I'm guessing they'll talk at some point."

"I haven't heard from Richard either, if anyone cares," Atticus says. "But I have an idea for how to make sure he knows about Kellcy."

"Go on," I say to my brother.

"I'm warning you, it'd be a baller move," Atticus says to me and scoots forward on the single couch. "Thanksgiving."

"Huh?" But I almost instantly understand.

"Kellen should come with us to Mom's. Richard always wants to meet for a late dinner on Thanksgiving. If Kellen comes, it'll cement the idea that you're happy with a professional hockey player and working for a NHL team. Not in D.C. Not working for DC FC. Not with that fuckwhit who he refused to fire."

"And you'll go to dinner too?" I furrow my brow. Atticus usually won't meet up with our father, and I don't blame him.

"Yup. I'll want to witness this firsthand."

Everyone nods, including Raleigh and January on the video call.

"You hate him that much, Atter?" Lachlan says to Atticus, mostly kidding, but also serious. "You went from *how dare you fake date my sister* to *bring him home for the holidays* pretty smoothly."

"I do hate him that much." Atticus's voice sounds like a sharp bark, but to me, he's more a kicked puppy than a vicious dog.

Makes *me* hate our father even more.

"Well, it's Bri's year with Ava," Kellen says. "Usually, we all get together anyway, but she's planning to take Ava to her parents' house in Pueblo, which is the absolute last place I want to be, ever. So I was going to stay in FoCo anyway."

"Come with us. Mom's a great cook. You won't regret having Thanksgiving at her house," Atticus says.

"Lucy?" Kellen gently nudges me with his elbow. "What do you think?"

I look at him and press my lips together. "I'm game if you are."

This all feels unreal. In a parallel universe, I'm bringing Ron to Mom's for Thanksgiving, and we're wedding planning. But in this one, I'm bringing a fake boyfriend home—I'll have to fill Mom in on everything—and most likely upsetting my father by moving on from the man he so wants me to be with. A man more like him than I want to admit.

"Sure." Kellen smiles broadly and it's like the rising sun after the darkest night.

My stomach gently turns over when I think about bringing Kellen home. Even though it's fake, it hits differently. It's so personal.

"Any other concerns?" Harley says.

"I have one more topic." Lachlan raises his hand.

"Of course you do," Kellen mutters.

"And it involves adding another event."

"But we just added one," Kellen says.

"This is a democracy, not a dictatorship," Harley says. "Let Lachlan speak."

"For fuck's sake," Kellen says under his breath, and I laugh quietly. He rewards me with a sweet smile.

"The retreat is a month away." Lachlan points at Kellen. "Thanksgiving is more than that. That's too long."

"So what are you suggesting?" Atticus asks.

"Home game. Lucy in Kellie's jersey." Lachlan grins.

The group *oooos* and *ahhhhhs*.

"I guess." Kellen turns to me. "What do you think?"

"I'm okay with that," I say. It'd be a huge thing to be in that setting as Kellen's girlfriend. So public.

"And overall? Just do better," Lachlan says. "More making out."

"No, don't touch my sister." Atticus growls at Kellen.

"I think this plan specifically dictates I should touch her. Remember? We voted on it." Kellen slowly lowers his arm from the couch to around my shoulders.

Atticus groans and shuts his eyes. Everyone else laughs, including me, but I love the feel of Kellen's arm around me. I want to scoot closer, but I don't.

And I don't want to ask for a vote on it.

Even though we're fake dating by committee, if I close my eyes and feel his arm around my shoulders, and remember the way he cleaned chocolate off my face, the way he held my hand, sat close to me on the hay ride... it almost feels real.

CHAPTER 18

A Hot Mess

KELLEN

Thursday, October 17

My shoulder crashes into the boards. I straighten and skate back into position quickly, ignoring the pain radiating down my arm.

This game feels out of control.

We're in Dallas and getting our butts kicked. Score is only 1-0, but it's pure luck it's not much worse. The first intermission can't come soon enough so we can regroup.

The other team is playing aggressively, and I can't keep my head in the game. Normally, I can compartmentalize my thoughts while I'm playing. My mind is a house. I can shove stray thoughts in different bedrooms and lock the doors. They're still there in the background, but I can focus on what's happening in the main part of the house.

But right now, all I can think of is Ava and tomorrow's oncology appointments.

Over the years, the sharp fear about Ava's health has faded into a constant dull ache. I'm sure all parents feel this to a point, but being the parent of a cancer survivor is a whole other ball game. It's the lack of control over my daughter's future, and by extension, myself. If something happened to her—if she got sick again—I can't fix it. Not money nor prayers nor the best doctors can assure me everything will be okay.

I've trained myself to live in the moment with her. Live for today. Not worry about the future.

But sometimes that training slips.

Especially leading up to her appointments.

The whistle blows, and we head to the visitor locker room for what I imagine will be an intense lecture by Coach Jackson.

I barely hear Coach talk to us about the mistakes we made, getting our heads back in the game, staying strong against the provocation of the other team. When his five-minute team speech is over, he leaves us to our individual intermission routines—everyone hydrates, stretches, and some meditate, listen to music, chat with each other, anything to reset and refocus. He pulls aside a few players for individual talks.

I close my eyes and lean against a locker, trying to push my wayward thoughts into their assigned rooms so I can get my head in the game.

Underneath my worries about Ava, there's a nervous excitement about the situation with Lucy. Her as Ava's soccer coach. Our moments at the fall festival. The upcoming retreat in Wyoming and Thanksgiving together in D.C.

Before I manage to ground myself back in hockey, Coach is calling our attention for the last minute's pep talk.

I don't feel any better skating back onto the ice for the second period.

And it shows.

One of the Dallas Stars' forwards keeps attempting to provoke me with trash talk, but joke's on him as I can't focus on his jabs.

But Lachlan can.

I can hear him growling behind me. He can have a temper on

the ice, so hearing him getting pissed off actually helps bring me to the present.

The other team scores. Our line is swapped with Finn, Armas, and Rhys. Lachlan heads off with the other defenseman and a new pair skates on.

"You've gotta keep it together, Lach." I attempt to diffuse the situation, but he just glares at me.

My line heads back on the ice, and Lachlan's joins us in defense a minute later.

It can't be more than thirty seconds later that Lachlan is shoving the Stars' forward into the boards and throwing a punch at his helmet.

Shiiiiit.

The crowd screams in encouragement and astonishment—this is what the hockey audience often wants—but from our perspective, fighting is only a bad thing. I pull Lachlan off the Stars player and the ref sends our best defenseman off but lets the other team keep their player, even though he's the one who started the fight.

The Stars are pushing us hard during their power play and the puck stays in our zone. Fuck! Ref should've sent the other guy off. Asshole was looking for this exact thing to happen, and now he's got a smug look on his face that I want to punch off.

I won't, of course.

I'm usually the one stopping the fights, not starting them.

The other team scores twice during the period.

During the second intermission, Coach gives us a longer than usual speech about team integrity and player accountability, then he pulls Lachlan aside.

This time, I focus intensely on my mental exercises. Taking all my distracting thoughts and pushing them to where they belong while I'm on the ice. Then heading back to the main room of my house. The hockey room.

At the end of the intermission, Coach leads us in a five-minute meditation and focus session, and the energy in the locker room shifts noticeably.

Finally, I feel calm.

Everything clicks into place—the bedroom doors are all locked in my house—and instead of distractions, my mind is a ticker tape of plays, strategy, positions, and control. Lachlan looks better as we skate onto the ice, that fury gone from his eyes, replaced by grim determination.

We pull our act together in the last period and Harley and Atticus both score, but we still lose 3-2.

On the bus to our team plane, I read a flirty text from Lucy, but my heart's not into responding to it. Instead, I text Bri and confirm our plans for the morning. It's always like this around Ava's appointments. I'm withdrawn and distracted and forget to give myself a bit of a break.

I put in my AirPods and don't interact with my team on the flight home. They know what's coming up, and they understand to leave me alone.

I just gotta get my family through tomorrow.

CHAPTER 19

Immune to the Charms of Hockey Players

LUCY

Friday, October 18

"Do we need to meet again?" Lachlan says, starting to unbutton his collared shirt.

"I think we got what I need. Thanks."

"Bye for now, Lucy." Lachlan, shirt half open and with an armful of clothes draped over his forearm, bows and grins charmingly before heading out of the conference room where I've been camped out for photo sessions.

The Australian is a huge flirt, but also polite and gentlemanly whenever I'm around him. And anyway, I'm immune to the charms of hockey players.

The photographer packs up, but leaves the green screen set up because it belongs to the Blizzard. I thank him, and he disappears into the hallway. We're doing a supplemental photo shoot with all the players. There was a media day last month, but Lina and I agreed we could make use of additional photos of the players to pitch different sponsorships. So this photo shoot is about adding to the catalogue of great photos we already have of all the players.

Kellen's the only one who didn't show.

I sit and look at our text messages from earlier.

KELLEN

I might be late to the photo session—at an appointment with Ava that could run over

ME

No problem, good luck

I didn't bother him when his appointment time came and went. Then, an hour ago, I sent one more text, which has gone unanswered.

ME

Hey, hope all is okay. Are you going to be able to come by for the photo session?

I sink into one of the conference table chairs and close my eyes. I shouldn't have mentioned the dumb photo shoot. It's so not important. My phone buzzes with a text and I jump.

It's from Lina.

LINA

How'd it go today?

ME

Good. All done

LINA

Great! Sorry I couldn't be there

I'm so glad Lina and I have a positive relationship. We have weekly one on ones, and we've gone for coffee a few times. She's invested in helping me get the Winchester FC job in England. She tells me all the time how great I'm doing here, which is refreshing after not getting much feedback from my boss at DC FC or my boss's boss, who happened to be my father.

At the Blizzard, it's delightful to know my chain of command doesn't include Richard.

The door to the conference room swings open and I flinch, almost dropping my phone. In walks Kellen Bassey, a wardrobe bag hooked over his shoulder.

"Kellen." I sit up straight in the chair.

"I'm so sorry about missing my appointment. And not responding to your text." He looks around the empty room and shuts his eyes. "Shit. The photographer's gone."

"Yeah, they packed up a bit ago." I stand and the office chair rolls back against the conference room table.

Kellen's squinting his eyes shut. He takes a deep breath and lets it out slowly. The vibes I'm getting from this man right now are so different than the usual casual, warm ones.

"Hey, you okay?"

Kellen hadn't specified what the appointment was for with Ava. Given his current mood, I'm terrified it wasn't a good one.

Kellen opens his eyes. "Yeah." He's a step through the doorway, one hand clenched at his side, the other still gripping the wardrobe bag. He's wearing a white t-shirt and open flannel button down that projects perfect Colorado casual.

Something is definitely wrong.

The stupidest idea crashes into my mind but I run with it, like Bear with one of Atticus's shoes.

"You know what? I can take some pictures on my phone. Or I can at least include them as placeholders until we can reschedule the session."

What in the actual hell am I talking about?

"Yeah?" Kellen raises an eyebrow.

"I took some photography classes in college." I did not. "And I took pictures of players sometimes for my job at DC FC." Lies.

Kellen's mouth quirks on one side. "Alright. Let's do it."

I press my lips together. I'm such an idiot.

"Great! We can start with what you're wearing, then change to your suit, then the jersey. Okay?"

"Sure."

"I've been watching the photographer do this all afternoon, so I know what poses he's looking for." My voice is overly cheerful, and Kellen seems temporarily distracted from whatever his problems are.

What would be helpful right now is the photographer's lights, professional camera, and, you know, overall training and job skills.

Like a lunatic, I gesture to the stool in front of the green background. Kellen lays his wardrobe bag over the back of a chair and takes a seat in front of the screen.

"How do you want me?" He's got a hint of a smirk on his face, like he knows I'm completely full of shit. It's much better than the anxious expression he had when he first walked in.

How do I want him? So many ways.

What am I doing? I have no idea.

Will I text the photographer and say *hey do you think these cell phone photos are good enough for a professional portfolio?*

Obviously not.

So what, exactly, is my plan here?

There's a fluttering in my chest. I want to do anything I can to make Kellen feel better. Get him to smile. To laugh. And maybe my plan is to spend time with this man, which is something I happen to enjoy. Too much.

Maybe it's because when he looks at me, I sense something between us.

Something decidedly not fake.

I swallow and goosebumps tingle on my arms.

I'm probably imagining it. Or in the very least, it's just one-sided. He can't feel the same for me. And even if he told me he did, how could I believe him? I'm clearly a terrible judge of character. I thought Ron loved me. I thought he wanted to be with me forever. Instead, he'd been looking elsewhere all along.

But right now, I want to live in the moment and enjoy spending time with Kellen. Is that such a bad idea?

"Be natural. I'll snap a few." My voice is shaky, and I chastise myself for being such a sucker for this man.

Kellen leans forward, elbows on his knees, and stares at me as I lift my phone. Good lord. I don't think it'd be an exaggeration to say he's freaking gorgeous. I steady my hand and snap a few pictures. They come out crooked, so I try again.

I'm a thirty-three-year-old woman. Why do I feel so fluttery around this man?

I'm not interested in a relationship. Not even a casual one.

I'm not interested in the way I always feel like I'm not good enough.

But somehow, when I'm with Kellen, I don't feel like that. Maybe that feeling is coming. Waiting in the rafters. Maybe he's a really good actor, even better than Ron, but Kellen doesn't treat me like I'm not good enough to be with him. Even if it's fake. When we're together, he treats me like we're really dating. An actual couple.

"Can you smile?" I lower my phone. "Like you're happy to be here?"

"I am happy to be here." Kellen sits back, hands on his thighs, and smiles. It lights the room.

"That's perfect," I say, not meaning to say it out loud.

"Do any of those work?"

"Yeah. Yes. They'll work." I breathe in but don't look at my phone.

"What's next? Suit?" Kellen nods toward the chair with his wardrobe bag but keeps his gaze locked on me.

I swallow and nod, my eyes darting to the privacy screen that we set up for changing purposes. He grabs his clothes and disappears behind the screen. I try not to picture him taking off his flannel shirt, his t-shirt, his pants, and his shoes. Standing there in his boxers, chest on display. Does he have more than a six pack? How many can a man possibly pack? All of those.

"Ava's appointment today was with her oncologist," he says from behind the screen.

The air freezes in my lungs. "Everything okay?" I manage to get out.

"It's why I was late." He pauses and the silence is intense. "Her appointment was in Denver. A routine annual checkup. It went well. I thought I'd be back in time for the photo session, but they were running behind."

I swallow a lump in my throat. I'm fake dating Kellen for petty revenge on my father, and he's fake dating to keep his family in Fort Collins near his daughter's trusted doctors.

We are not the same.

Kellen steps out from behind the screen, and my heart skips a few beats. He's got his suit pants on, a shirt buttoned halfway up, and a loose tie hung around his neck. The top of chiseled pecs peeks out along with a scattering of chest hair. He lays the wardrobe bag back on the chair.

"I'm so glad she's okay. I've been thinking of you guys all day. I kind of thought it might be an important doctor's appointment for you to miss practice and her to miss school." I breathe in through my noise. "That must all be so hard."

"I trust the children's hospital in Denver." He closes his eyes for a beat. "Her doctors. The specialists. I know there are good doctors everywhere, but I want to stay here. *We* want to stay."

We being his family unit: Ava and Bri.

"I can understand that." But do I? How can I understand something I've never been a part of? That kind of strong family anchor. Sure, I love my brother to bits, and my mom and I are close. But the determination to keep everyone together, even amidst a split or divorce... that's different.

"I know if I got traded and had to move, they could stay here. I'd visit as much as possible." Kellen's gaze drifts to the ground.

"But after what we lived through, I can't do it. I couldn't live with myself being away from Ava more than absolutely necessary."

My gut twists for Kellen. It's so intense. Having gone through something like that with your own child? It's heart breaking.

Energy surges through me. I have to make sure this works for Kellen. That we really convince Paul he's not a threat and deserves to stay on the Blizzard. I can't bear it if Kellen were to be separated from his daughter. It's so much more important than me proving something to my father.

I don't understand what Kellen's going through, but I know what it's like to feel a little lost. With me, it's about proving I'm good enough to do things on my own, to achieve things without the unwanted help of men in my life.

"All that to say, sorry I missed the real photographer."

"You don't think I'm a real photographer?" I attempt to smile, but he just stares at me, all serious. "Sorry, not a joking time. You don't have to explain."

"Thank you." He nods.

"And you can trust that I'm not going to freak out about something so minor. As your fake girlfriend, of course."

His throat ripples as he swallows.

Kellen runs his hand through his wavy hair, and instead of messing it up for the pictures, he manages to make himself look even hotter, if not slightly rumpled. He's now a handful of steps away. My eyes fall to his tie and the three remaining buttons of his shirt. This man is throwing me completely off-kilter. Why? Because he's hot?

Feeling moved by the emotion in Kellen's voice, I close the gap between us and lift my hands.

I'm *not* falling for the hot guy.

But I also don't have a heart of stone, and this man is struggling right now. I want to be there for him.

"May I?"

He nods, and I touch the button that hits mid-chest. My

fingers brush his skin, and his chest rises with a breath. I keep my eyes focused but can feel the heat of his stare on my face.

One button done.

I swallow, and I'm sure he hears it. I move to the second button and fumble, my fingers touching his bare skin again, this time at the section of his chest where his collarbones meet. It's a hard, smooth spot, warm to the touch, and my traitorous brain imagines kissing it.

Second button done.

At the top, I'm touching his neck. There's no way I'm imagining that his breath is speeding up, or that mine is.

Third button done.

I look up at him, and our eyes meet. I reach for the tie and tug it until it's the correct length on either side to knot. I cross one end over the other. Slowly, because my hands are shaking again.

"You're a great dad. A good person. Not that you need me to tell you that."

There's a buzzing between us. In this room. The hum of electricity, building up to something, a generator shaking with energy, about to sputter and explode.

Kellen lifts a hand and pushes an escaped curl off my forehead, letting his fingertips skim my skin, but doesn't say anything back.

I meet his eyes.

He looks at my lips, and my heart stutters.

I don't even know what I'm doing with the tie anymore. Am I trying to braid it? Turn it into a friendship bracelet? His hand is gently pulling on the curl, then moves down my hair, not quite touching me, not letting go.

"I have to start over." I unloop the tie and let the ends lay flat, smoothing the silky fabric down with my hands. My palms freeze against his chest in a position that's much too intimate. I stare at my fingers splayed on his shirt, trying to steady myself, because I'm not sure I can meet him in the eye again without my knees giving out.

"Lucy." Kellen reaches up and wraps his hands around the tops of my wrists, and the touch causes my insides to flutter. I stare at where our skin is together, marveling at how it feels to be connected to him in a circle like this. Heat spreads across my skin.

I look up.

I know he's waiting for me to do so.

Our eyes meet, and we're close. His gaze flits down to my lips and a rush of desire roars inside me.

No one is watching. There's no purpose to us touching right now. To whatever is about to happen. It's pure want.

Kellen's got tiny lines branching out from the corners of his eyes. Thick eyelashes. Those dark blue irises. The shadow of facial hair along his jaw. His lips. His mouth.

I don't think any more, I just do it.

I go up on my tippy-toes and tug down on his tie, gently bringing him toward me.

I kiss him.

He's expecting it, and I suspect that if I hadn't done it, he would have.

The kiss is soft and sweet, our mouths coming together gently, lips closed. I savor the touch. The burning feeling it ignites inside me.

I want Kellen.

We lean back for a beat and lock eyes, but I need much more than what I just got. I need more than I got at the coffee shop a few weeks ago. This time, we come together more intensely, and I release the tie and slide my wrists out of his palms, moving my hands up and around his neck, pushing my fingers into the hair at the base of his neck. His hands drop and tiptoe around my waist, not pushing or pulling or grabbing. His mouth opens, his tongue swiping carefully between my lips. There's a pulsing in my body. An ache deep inside.

I think I've been pushing the feeling away since I arrived. I'd admitted to myself he was hot and nice, but I truly didn't think he was interested in me in a way other than as his fake girlfriend. I'm just Atticus's older sister. The PR person at work. But as I move my hips forward to meet his, and he breathes in sharply through his nose, I know he wants me back.

We kiss and it's sweet and slow and hot. I could do this all day. His hands drift down but stop abruptly before they go below the curve of my waist.

His hands stopping is like pressing the pause button, and facts flash through my mind. The conference room door is unlocked. The lights on the ceiling are too bright. Kellen's a hockey player. I'm working for the team. My little brother is his teammate. The Winchester FC job. My painful breakup with Ron.

How nothing I do is good enough.

How I have to get out of this place, this country, as far from my old life as possible.

I pull back, and in the split second before his eyes fly open, I see him. Cheeks flushed. Hair mussed. Swollen lips. Kellen in the raw.

He blinks and the rawness fades.

"Sorry. I got carried away." Kellen steps back. I ignore his apology.

"Let me reschedule the shoot. Cell phone pictures are probably not going to be good enough." I take a step back as well.

The spot between his eyes furrows and a flash of something—maybe hurt—crosses his face.

"Right. Okay."

What would happen if I told him I liked him? And not just as a fake boyfriend? That everything feels right when he touches me?

But I know he's not interested, even if his body is. He's had trust issues with women—and everyone—in his past, and he doesn't want a relationship. He wants to be a good dad. Keep his spot on the team. Stay in Fort Collins with his family. He's so cautious about who he lets in.

Me liking him would change nothing and only complicate his life.

I don't want a relationship either.

"Let me know when it is." He picks up the rest of his things from the table and heads to the conference room door, pulling it open. "Thanks, Lucy."

"For what?" I ask, but he's already gone.

Hasn't he already let me in?

CHAPTER 20

The Right Jersey

KELLEN

Saturday, October 26

I haven't stopped thinking about the kiss at the photo shoot. Not for one minute.

That afternoon, I arrived deflated, raw, and vulnerable, which is usually how I feel after taking Ava to her oncology visits. She's doing amazing. But I can't forget the trauma of her diagnosis and her treatment. That shit was scary as fuck.

Kissing Lucy made the pain fade.

She brings something out in me. Something good and strong. Protective, and not just about my family. Because when I watch her with Ava, she looks like she *is* family.

It's a crazy thought.

It scares me.

Maybe we shouldn't have kissed. Probably. Definitely? I'm assuming she agrees because we haven't talked about it once in our approximately one billion text messages back and forth to each other.

Coach Jackson shouts and sends our line back on the ice—me,

Harley, and Atticus. I desperately try to focus, but my mind is on Lucy.

A lot of our messages were pictures of Bear for me to show Ava, or action shots of Ava at soccer practice. My pictures to her have been a different vibe. St. Louis is a cool city, but we're not exactly tourists when we play there, so I didn't have many good photo opportunities.

She's been telling me a lot about her mom to prepare me for Thanksgiving with her family. Honestly, her relationship with her mother sounds sweet and healthy. Her mom's house is a real home for Lucy and Atticus when they're there. I've tried to keep it positive and told her about my sister (we're close but she lives far away), what it was like playing high level hockey in high school (crazy but exciting), and what it was like when Ava was a baby (I changed my first diaper).

Today, we're at home playing the Winnipeg Jets, and one of their players zips through our defense and scores. Fuck. The crowd voices their displeasure, and Harley hits his stick on mine twice. It's his way of indicating the play he wants to execute.

I shake away thoughts of my family and Lucy. Atticus and Harley perform the first passes of the play perfectly and deliver the puck to my stick, and I spin and toss the puck past the goaltender's outstretched hand into the back of the net.

The crowd erupts. We're down 3-2.

Our line skates off, and I collapse on the bench.

Why hasn't Lucy shown up to this game? I haven't heard from her today, which is weird, especially since I sent her a present this morning.

The Kellcy Fake Dating Planning Committee voted that she come to this home game wearing my jersey. I decided to also send her a few other things.

I might have gone overboard.

Paul and Savannah are probably in the corporate sponsorship box, but they have a pretty good view of the seats I got for the game. Bri and Ava are already there, and I managed to secure another ticket for Lucy.

When we were away last week, I went out with Atticus, Lachlan, and Harley after our game. Atticus and Lachlan were hitting on women all night, but it wasn't even a consideration for me.

Because I have a fake girlfriend.

And I just wasn't interested in anyone.

What's worse is that the boys left me alone, whereas they normally push a girl toward me. They seemed to accept the fact that I'm not available. But I am! Everyone is confused. I wonder what would have happened if I'd hit on one of those women? Took her home? Would Atticus have been pissed because of Lucy?

It's getting really muddy.

I feel very much not single, even though it's all an act.

Coach waves our line back on, and I glance up at the seats where Lucy should be sitting next to Ava and Bri as I glide onto the ice.

Lucy's there. Wearing my jersey.

I focus back on the game. I have a ridiculous urge to show off for her. I play for myself, my teammates, and Coach, but right now, I want to play for her.

I shout a word at Atticus and Harley, and we attempt another play.

I weave in and out of the defenders like an Olympic level figure skater, but this time one follows me closely. I get the puck but can't get a shot in, and we end up battling it out behind the net. I get the puck to Atticus on the side of the boards, but he doesn't have a shot. But when I emerge out the other side of the net, he gets me the puck, and I fly it past the goaltender.

I grin and the crowd cheers. But there's no time to bask in glory.

3-3.

I want one more goal.

I want a hat trick in front of Lucy Knox.

Now *that* would be a cause for celebration. I've done it one other time in my time with the Blizzard, but it's been a few seasons since. A handful of other teams have had one this season.

It's our turn. *My* turn.

I grit my teeth down on my mouthguard.

"Don't even fucking try it." One of the forwards from the Jets growls at me during the face-off.

The referee drops the puck, and the Jets player attempts to slap it toward one of his forwards, but I'm faster. I get it to Harley and zip up the rink toward the goal. Harley passes it back to one of our defenders, who snaps it up to me.

And I score.

The crowd goes wild and hats go flying in the stands to celebrate the hat trick.

I pump a hand in the air and the team piles on me, laughing and cheering and almost taking me down. We're winning 4-3.

Coach waves our line off, and I glance up at Lucy, who's smiling and clapping.

We might have been texting a lot, but it's been a week since I've seen her as I was traveling, and Ava didn't have a game this morning. I need to make sure she's not freaked out about the kiss, despite her casual messaging with me.

We crossed a line at the photo shoot.

No, *I* did.

It doesn't matter how good the cafe kiss felt. Sweet and soft.

Our nonstop text message conversations.

Ava's constant chatter about Coach Lucy and her dog.

The way she makes me laugh.

The photo shoot kiss, hot and deep and leaving me wanting so much more.

This was not part of the arrangement.

I need to pull it together.

I'll find her after the game and make sure things are right.

CHAPTER 21

The Suit Hits Just Right

LUCY

"You'll be fine, Bear." I push a curl off my forehead and reach down to scratch my dog's head. He's sitting at my feet in my office. Actually, he's sitting *on* my feet.

Bear turns and licks my hand.

"I'll be back in an hour. You have treats, water, and a dog bed."

Bear seems fine with the whole situation. After all, he's wearing a doggy Blizzard shirt, courtesy of Kellen. He also sent me a hoodie, t-shirt, and car decal, along with his jersey.

I stare back down at my laptop, where I was streaming the pregame while finishing some work I came in to get done.

I paused and gaped when Kellen walked through my screen into the arena, the poster child for hot hockey player. I didn't get to see him fully suited up last Monday... Not the complete picture, anyway, as we kissed before I could even get his tie knotted.

That kiss. I can't get it out of my head.

On the screen, Kellen's smiling as he follows my brother into the building with his tie expertly fastened.

I shut my laptop and breathe out. I don't usually work on Saturdays, but I needed to get a few things done and was too jittery to work at the apartment.

I flash back to the way I could feel Kellen's heart race when I laid my hands on his chest. I kissed him. I did that. And while he didn't exactly hesitate to kiss me back—it was like he'd been waiting for me to do it—he also kept his hands securely on my waist.

I kinda wish he'd have let them wander.

Now *my* heart's racing. I place a hand on my chest and will it to slow.

The kiss wasn't for show. Paul and Savannah weren't anywhere around. We didn't even pretend it was practice.

My neck heats, and I rub it with one hand. I wanted so much more from him, but I'm so glad we stopped before things went too far.

Aren't I?

But it doesn't feel like I'm glad. I haven't even texted him to say thank you for the gifts. I kinda don't trust myself not to cross the line again.

I roll my shoulders back and smooth down the number seven Kellen Bassey jersey I'm wearing. I cracked up when I took it out of the package and saw all the other Blizzard merchandise, including that shirt for Bear.

I pat my dog one final time and pull my office door shut behind me. My phone buzzes, and I pause before pushing into the arena.

> JANUARY
>
> Lulu, You look like 🔥 in Kellen's jersey
>
> RALEIGH
>
> I feel like this is a big deal

I type a response. I'd sent them a quick selfie of me in the jersey.

ME

Bigger than kissing him at a coffee shop? Or holding hands at the fall festival?

JANUARY

Or making out with him in a conference room where no one could see?

ME

JANUARY

That's what I thought, babes

RALEIGH

And it makes this an even bigger deal

JANUARY

Go sleep with him. He'd be a pretty impressive rebound

ME

Janny. I'm not rebounding with Kellen Bassey

JANUARY

Right. Sure

RALEIGH

Why are you calling him by his full name?

JANUARY

I cannot wait to see this in person

ME

You won't. Remember? We'll be fake broken up by then, sis

JANUARY

K

ME

But you can have your pick of hot hockey players then

RALEIGH

A good way to celebrate my divorce being final

I slip the phone into my pocket.

It's been a week since the kiss with Kellen, and a daily topic of conversation with my friends.

Through the arena entrance, the stadium is loud and crowded. I find the seats Kellen directed me toward, right next to Bri and Ava.

"Coach Lucy!" Ava jumps up and throws her arms around me.

"Hey, soccer star, how are you?"

"Amazing. Where's Bear?" Ava asks.

"He wouldn't do well in the arena. Remember what happened when I brought him in here last time?"

"He peed everywhere!" Ava is delighted at the reference.

"Hey, Bri, how are you?" I settle down in the seat next to Bri.

"I'm fine. Ava's been excited to sit with you at the game." Ava's mother looks strikingly like her, with blonde hair, blue eyes, and a Blizzard sweatshirt. Bri's eyes dart down to what I'm wearing. Her daughter's father's jersey.

"Well, I'm excited to sit with you too." I smile at Ava, and she beams back.

"How's... all this going?" Bri waves her hand in the air toward the rink and then me.

"Good, I guess?" This woman must think I'm insane for fake dating Kellen.

"We do what we have to do, right?" Bri says.

I nod.

"Bear's actually in my office having a nap." I lean forward to talk to Ava, who is now playing with a Barbie doll dressed in scrubs. "Or destroying things, it's hard to predict with him."

"Aw, I wish you could've brought him." She pauses for a second, then stands and jumps up and down twice. "Oh! I thought of the best name!"

"Sit, Ava. And I don't think Lucy needs help naming her dog. He already has a name."

Ava sits. "Mommy, Coach Lucy changes his name all the time." Ava glances up at her mom and then back at me.

I nod. "I mean, that's technically true. I'm trying to find the right one for him. One that he really likes."

"Okay. Ava, but don't be upset if she decides not to use the name. Deal?"

"Deal!" Ava squeals.

"What do you got, Ava? What name should we try next?"

"Are you ready?" Ava leaps up again. "Mister Barky McBark-face." The little girl bursts into laughter and slaps her hands on the sides of her face, clearly delighted at her creativity.

There's a roar from the crowd, and my eyes lift up to the ice, but I don't want Ava to think I'm ignoring her, so I look back at her.

"I think that's absolutely ridiculous, and amazing, just like Bear himself." I purse my lips, like I'm really thinking about the name. "Mister Barky McBarkface. It's perfect. I'll test it out on him after the game."

"Really? Hooray!!"

"But honestly, when he gets a new owner, they might change his name anyway." As soon as the words are out of my mouth, I wish I hadn't voiced them. Why would I say something like that? In front of a five-year-old who's in love with my dog?

This is exactly why Kellen probably doesn't want to bring women around his daughter. It's confusing and they all end up disappointing him and her.

The crowd roars again and we all turn to watch Kellen make a breakaway, shooting neatly past the final defenseman and goaltender to score.

Everyone cheers, but I just about hear what Ava whispers to Bri.

"Mommy? Can I be the new owner of Mister Barky McBarkface?"

I press my lips together at her sweet words, pretending not to have heard them. Ava would be the perfect person to love that dog forever.

As Kellen skates back to center, he veers to the side of the rink and heads directly our way. To see his daughter, obviously. He blows a kiss in our direction, and Ava squeals and waves.

Then he winks. At me.

I glance behind me up at the corporate sponsorship box, where Savannah and Paul are supposed to be. I don't see them, and they certainly aren't watching us.

The rest of the game, I keep my eyes on the game in between chatting with Ava and Bri. Kellen scores a hat trick, and the arena goes crazy for him.

Ava gives me a giant, warm hug before she and Bri leave. I promise to give her a full report at soccer on Wednesday of how Mister Barky McBarkface likes his new name.

The team is all smiles when they skate through the team exit. Kellen looks right up at me as he passes and grins brightly. This time, there's no confusion about who the smile is meant for. His daughter is gone.

It's all for me.

I head back toward the double doors in the arena that lead to the players' gym, locker room, and administrative hallway so I can fetch Mister Barky McBarkface.

My insides are swirling. We checked the box of me wearing his jersey to a game, but I don't know if Paul and Savannah even saw.

I scan my badge, and the noise of the arena fades as the doors click shut behind me. I stride down the hall to my office. I can't believe I agreed to rename my dog Mister Barky McBarkface. It even takes a long time to think it.

I open the door and call to him with his new name. Immediately, a flash of white and brown darts toward me and jumps on my legs, barking.

"I guess you like it?" I laugh and make the mistake of not shutting the door behind me right away. Mister Barky McBarkface zips through my legs and down the hall, his purple and yellow Blizzard shirt acting like a superdog cape.

"Shit! Hey!" His new name immediately flies from my brain. "Bear! Taco! Waffles!!"

I dart out the door and turn to follow him toward the arena, but Kellen is standing at the end of the hall holding my dog. He's wearing a tight Blizzard t-shirt and athletic shorts, and Mister Barky McBarkface is snuggling into his chest.

Kellen strolls toward me, cradling my dog, who stares up at him adoringly.

I can relate to the feeling. I'm as frozen as the ice in the arena. He stops a few feet away but makes no move to hand over the dog.

"I feel like we've done this before. Me capturing your escaped dog."

"Thank you for that. And for his new shirt. Also, his new name is Mister Barky McBarkface, courtesy of your daughter."

Kellen bursts out laughing, and I love the sound of it. I want to run my hand over the stubble on his chin. Feel that mouth on mine again. His laugh relieves some of the tension in the air, and I grin as his chuckles taper off.

"Of course she did. You know you don't have to actually call him that?"

"That's what Bri said." I shrug. Maybe my friends are right. *Do I need to sleep with a hot hockey player? Specifically this one?* "We'll see how he likes it."

Kellen's staring at me with a slight smile lingering on his face.

"How's it going? Did you enjoy the game?" His eyes dart down to my lips and back up. Tingles run up my spine and a single, intense beat of desire pulses in the bottom of my stomach.

"It was a good game. Congrats on the hat trick. And thank you for the jersey. And the shirt. And the hoodie. And the decal? It was a bit over the top."

Kellen's mouth quirks into a smile. He steps forward. So many things zip through my mind, the most prominent one being a wish that he'd grab me by the waist and kiss me.

"I wanted to apologize about what happened at the photo shoot," he says in a low voice. "In person. I know we've been texting since then, but I really feel like I crossed a line."

"You don't have to apologize." I curl my toes.

"I do. I wasn't in my right mind that afternoon. And I don't often feel comfortable talking about Ava's past issues."

Did he forget that I'm the one who kissed him?

"No worries. I've barely thought about it." But I can't help the stupid grin that's on my face. Damn, I am not subtle.

"Yeah, me neither." He presses his lips together and holds out Mister Barky McBarkface. "Here's your dog. I have to get to the post-game yoga session, or I'll catch a lot of shit."

"Of course." I accept the squirming canine bundle. "Have fun with your downward facing dog."

I imagine the Blizzard doing yoga together. It's a delightfully wholesome picture.

"My favorite is the cobra."

I tilt my head in question.

"You know, lay on your belly and press down on the ground with your hands and arch up off the floor. Stretches your back." Kellen lifts his chin up and curves his back to demonstrate. "Just picture the rattlesnake we saw on our hike."

I laugh. "I got it now."

"See you around, Lucy." Kellen's gaze lingers for a second more, then he turns and walks away.

"Bye."

I watch Kellen retreat and wish I wasn't so focused on how

broad his shoulders are, so strong and capable. I wish I wasn't thinking about how kind he is and observant to how I'm feeling, like a big, sweet, gooey cinnamon roll that I could sink my teeth into.

I'm in so much trouble.

CHAPTER 22

A Swing and a Miss

KELLEN

Friday, November 15

The Blizzard has been on the road a lot over the past three weeks, and Lucy's been busy with work. But it hardly feels like we've been apart.

It's probably the constant texting.

And Ava's last soccer game, where the whole team—especially my daughter—was devastated for it to end and to say goodbye to Coach Lucy.

I had my rescheduled photo shoot, this time with lots of supervision and no kissing. Last weekend, a few of us hung out at Atticus's apartment on Saturday night, but she was out for a drink with some women from work. Lucy even attended another home game and sat in Atticus's seats, this time wearing the Blizzard hoodie I got her.

A few days ago, I dropped off a box of macarons and got a squealing thank you text, impressed that I remembered her favorite flavors from our conversation six weeks ago. Salted caramel, pistachio, and chocolate.

But we haven't been alone together.

I miss her, even though I have no right to.

And now we're on the bus to Wyoming for the team retreat. There's a Kellcy Fake Dating Planning Committee group text chain popping off. I'm going to act offended, but I'm really damn eager to get to spend a few days pretending to be Lucy's boyfriend.

LACHLAN

Welcome to the Kellcy Fake Dating Planning Committee text chain

ME

Really, Lach?

LACHLAN

Really, Kellie. I won't forgive myself for not creating this sooner

ME

Fine then. Hello, Lucy's friends

RALEIGH

Thanks for including us!

LACHLAN

We're about to head to Wyoming for the retreat. There will be hot springs pools

JANUARY

I want to go to hot springs pools in Wyoming! Which are not words I ever thought would come out of my mouth

HARLEY

Howdy

LUCY

Is a group text really necessary?

LACHLAN

You're lucky I didn't keep the original name, which was Kellen & Lucy Pretend to Bang

ATTICUS

I'm going to kick your ass

I bite back a grin.

Fake dating Lucy Knox hasn't really worked out like I thought it would.

For instance, I don't think I should be fantasizing about my fake girlfriend day and night, reliving each time we've touched. Including the conference room kiss. *Especially* the conference room kiss.

I didn't expect to miss her when I'm not around her.

Lucy's ten rows ahead of me, sitting with a woman from accounting. I'd kind of hoped we'd sit together, but instead, I stick in my AirPods and turn on the true crime podcast I've been following.

Two and a half hours later, the bus pulls up to the luxury ranch resort. Saratoga, Wyoming, feels like it's on a different planet from Fort Collins. It's remote and rustic and charming. Not that FoCo isn't beautiful, but this is different.

The annual retreat is purely a bonding event, with the requirement being that we get in some kind of workout every day—a low-key but tailored workout agenda was assigned to each player by the team trainers—and attend the team activities. Every year we play laser tag, and it gets super competitive. The resort also has paintball and other more intense activities, but it's in our contracts not to participate in extreme sports. Is paintball really extreme?

The Blizzard rents out the entire place for three nights. The resort has a series of connected one-bedroom cabins—rustic in their decor, but expertly decorated and full of luxury touches. Each has its own private lounging area and hot springs pool. The pools are supposedly filled with water from the hot springs, but it's filtered and chemically treated so it's really just like a giant hot tub. There are also normal hotel rooms in the main lodge for the more junior ranking players.

I hop off the bus, and Lucy's off to the side with her boss, the accounting woman, and the social media manager. She briefly glances my way, and I wave—I actually fucking wave—and she turns back to gawk at the scenery with the other women.

I am such a dork.

A sleek black Ferrari pulls up. Paul and Savannah. Everything is going according to plan.

"Here to ruin the fun," Atticus says under his breath from next to me.

I shrug. He's right, but they're also the reason I get to fake date Lucy Knox, so it's a bit of a toss-up. I follow Atticus into the lobby to get our keys.

I'm feeling bad about cutting Savannah off completely and also making her seem like the bad guy. But what else should I do? Risk my future to be her friend? Do something else that'll end up on the NHL Tea hockey gossip site?

I've gotta protect my family.

* * *

Later that evening, we're all hanging out around the resort. In the front of the main building, there's a fire pit surrounded by rocks perfectly shaped for sitting. A few groupings of wooden chairs are on the long, covered porch attached to the lodge. And around back are secluded lounging areas.

The night is cool but still comfortable, and most of the guys are wearing hoodies or long-sleeved t-shirts, warmed by the fire. Mid-November can go either way in this part of the country. It could be freezing or still warm.

I'm sitting with a bunch of my teammates around the firepit, including Atticus and Harley. Savannah is with us, along with a handful of staffers. Lachlan and a few other guys are off to the side in a circle of chairs with Lucy and another woman. He looks over at me and raises his eyebrows, then pulls out his phone. Mine buzzes a few seconds later with a string of texts to just me.

LACHLAN

Mate. Get your ass over here and hang out with your girlfriend. Before someone else snatches her up and I have to kick a rookie's ass

ME

1) fake girlfriend

ME

2) they wouldn't dare

LACHLAN

That's it. I'm going to the Kellcy Fake Dating Planning Committee text chain

ME

NO

For a beat, I think about how Lachlan would normally threaten to snatch Lucy up himself like he did at the fall festival, but I'm then distracted when a string of texts buzz into the Kellcy Fake Dating Planning Committee text chain.

LACHLAN

Hello, Team Kellcy. It's time our lovebirds act like a couple

JANUARY

Take this seriously, Lulu! What are you doing? Lachlan, I give you permission to forcibly push them together

LACHLAN

Working on it

As I'm considering a response, a picture from Bri of Ava with Mister Barky McBarkface pops up on my screen. My daughter was thrilled that Bri agreed to dog sit while we're at the retreat.

And this picture is a perfect excuse to approach Lucy.

But halfway over, a hand wraps itself around my biceps. I turn. Savannah.

"Hey, Kellie. How are you?" She's wearing tight workout gear, and her hair is pulled back into a bouncy ponytail. Her makeup is minimal, and she looks genuinely pretty.

But no relationship—even just friendship—is worth it with this woman. Not with the trouble it's already gotten me in.

"Hi, Savannah."

She drops her hand from my arm. I look around to find Paul, but he's not out here, thankfully. Lucy's staring at us, and she nudges Lachlan, who rolls his eyes at me and shakes his head, as if to say *that's what you get for waiting.*

"I thought I'd update you on my plans for the bar exam. It's been so long since we've gotten to catch up."

"Yeah, I know, sorry." I turn back to Savannah. "I've been really busy."

I wouldn't mind being Savannah's friend under normal circumstances. I want to encourage her to find her own thing to do that will give her some kind of purpose outside of following Paul around and hanging out with Blizzard players.

But I bite my tongue.

"Busy with hockey? And your daughter?" She leaves the question hanging.

"And my girlfriend." The perfect opening. "Lucy Knox. You've met her."

"Right. I saw you guys together at the cafe. And the fall festival. And the game." She smiles. "I guess it's obvious you two are together."

"Yeah, I suppose." And this was the entire point of all this. Relief cascades through me. It really worked. "I believe Paul knows her father."

"Now that I think about it, I remember talking to Paul about you two." Her forehead crinkles. "I just forgot." Savannah shrugs.

This couldn't have worked better.

"She's really pretty. Girl-next-door pretty."

My gaze drifts to Lucy, and I catch her smiling at something Lachlan says. I nod because Savannah is exactly right.

"I'm happy for you," Savannah says.

With perfect timing, one of Paul's staff walks over and asks Savannah about a holiday charity event. I take that opportunity to escape further conversation.

I practically run toward Lucy, who stands and smiles.

"You okay?"

"Yeah, of course." I'm okay now that I'm next to her. Appearance wise, Lucy's about as far from Savannah as possible. Her hair is a bit crazy, curls tumbling out of the low ponytail. Her freckles stand out on her pale skin, and her green eyes reflect the dancing orange flames of the bonfire. She's not nearly as put together. But who really wants put together? I want real.

"What'd she say to you?"

"I told her we were dating." Actually, I think I said that Lucy was my girlfriend.

"You did? What'd she say?" Lucy presses her lips together. That little smile is fucking adorable.

Savannah said she's happy for me. The woman absolutely believes Lucy and I are dating. Plus, she literally talked to Paul about it.

But I can't say that to Lucy.

Because if I do, then it'll be like this fake dating charade doesn't need to go on any longer, at least from my side. And if Lucy thinks that's true, then maybe she'll decide we should back off tonight.

"Nothing, really. But regardless, she's not going anywhere. She needs to find another focus besides me."

Half truth, half lie.

"True." Lucy scrunches her mouth to one side. Is she thinking about how we might not need to pretend to date?

"Hey, look at this picture I just got." I tap on my phone and flash the picture of Ava with her cheek pressed against Mister Barky McBarkface's cheek, his tongue out and making contact with my daughter's chin, a contagious smile on her face. Lucy takes a step closer to me and puts her hand on the phone, brushing against my fingers.

It feels stupidly good to have contact with her again.

"Oh my god, that is the cutest thing I've ever seen."

"Yup. As usual, your dog is a big hit."

"Gosh, I miss coaching Ava's team! I can't believe how fast the season flew by. Those girls are so sweet. Especially your daughter." Lucy looks up at me with her big green eyes and smiles.

"Well, we'll have to find a reason for you to see her again. Because she asks about Coach Lucy and Mister Barky McBarkface all the time. Dog sitting him is basically the highlight of her entire year."

Lucy chuckles and drops her hand from my phone. "I'm so glad you brought up that her team needed a coach. Between that and helping with the Thanksgiving food drive for the Blizzard, I feel like I'm actually doing something good."

"You're also helping me out, don't forget."

"I'm happy to help with the Kellen Bassey charity as well."

We stare at each other, both with goofy smiles.

"Can you thank Bri again for dog sitting? I don't think Mister Barky McBarkface would do great in a kennel."

"Yup, on it." I type out a text to Bri.

"And can you send that picture to me? It's adorable."

I nod and text it to her immediately.

As soon as I press send, I realize I just voluntarily shared a picture of my daughter with someone not in my little inner circle. I should be freaking out about it.

But I'm not.

Probably because Lucy already has many pictures of Ava on her phone from soccer practice and games. And it hasn't bothered me one bit. I have no fear that Lucy would share private pictures of my daughter with anyone.

"Done."

"Great. I'm thinking it might be useful when trying to place him in a new family. You know, great with kids and all. I'd completely block out Ava's face, of course."

My stomach twists, and Lucy's smile fades.

"Of course." I clear my throat and pocket my phone. What a freaking bummer. Just another reminder that Lucy is leaving. I clear my throat after an awkward pause. "This weekend we need to work hard to convince Savannah this is really happening. You and me. It's our last big chance."

"Yeah. Okay." Lucy's throat ripples as she swallows. She crosses her arms, her thin sweater stretching across her arms. Does she even believe our charade anymore? "What do we do tonight?"

"I think we make a show of leaving here. Together."

"Okay." Lucy nods. "And go where?"

To my room? But I don't say that.

"I know a place with the absolute best views of the stars. Want to see?"

"Let's go." A blush creeps up her face as I reach for her hand. She lets me take it, entwining her fingers with mine immediately.

Not sure why I think an isolated spot behind the hotel is the best place to show everyone we're dating. Not just an isolated spot —one of the most romantic places I can think of.

But I know why.

I like her.

I slowly lead Lucy to the dimly lit sidewalk that goes around the main lodge, giving the people we're walking away from time to observe us. Do they? I have no idea. I don't really care if Savannah is watching, because she's already a believer.

It's quiet behind the hotel, and I point to cushioned lounge chairs out on a gravelly area a way back from the building. We walk on the stone pathway until we get to them and settle in, both of us laying back on the reclined chairs and staring up at the sky. It's much darker out here away from the hotel, so the stars absolutely pop against the black sky.

"Did they see us?" she asks.

"Who? See what?"

"Everyone back there."

I turn to look at Lucy's profile.

"When we walked away from the group." Lucy shifts her head to meet my eyes.

"Oh, yeah, probably."

Lucy folds her hands on her stomach and turns back to star gazing. It's a perfectly clear night and the sky is carpeted with stars, like Ava took a giant bottle of glitter and threw it over a black poster board.

"My god. It's so gorgeous." She takes a deep breath in.

Sitting with Lucy out here feels good. Right. Like she's someone I've known for years.

Maybe we should talk about fake dating right now. What our next steps are. The strategy for tomorrow. But I don't care about any of that at this moment.

"Where have you seen the best stars?" I ask instead. "What's your favorite spot?"

"Besides here?" She huffs. "I vacationed in Maine with my mom and brother as a teenager. It was pretty amazing up there. Not sure if it beats this though."

I sit up slowly, swinging my legs over the side of the lounge chair, watching her profile as she gazes up on her back. It's dark, but the light of the stars is enough.

"I've always wanted to see the northern lights," I say. It's true, but I'm not sure I've ever said those words out loud.

"I want to see them too. I mean, I'm not sure when."

"We could go. Sometime." The words are out before I can stop them, and my eyes widen as she pushes up on her elbows from her sprawled position and looks at me.

"I'd love that." Her eyes are shimmering in the starlight. "This has been a lot of fun, Kellen."

I nod, unable to find the words. I don't want to talk about fake dating. Because I'm convinced that's not what's happening anymore, at least not from my side. I like this woman. I trust this woman. Trust her with my daughter, which is the highest level I can offer someone.

"Hey, you okay?" Lucy sits up completely and faces me, her knees lightly touching mine.

I just want to kiss her. That's all I can think about right now.

"Lucy."

"Yeah?"

"Can I kiss you?" I wish I could say this is lust talking, but it's not only that.

"Practice?" she whispers.

"Something like that."

"Okay. I think I'd like that." Lucy leans toward me, and I'm almost frozen.

Something in my chest is shifting. Something warm and bright.

I close the distance between us and the touch of our lips together is an explosion. Each time we've kissed has been different. The first sweet and soft, the second heavy and hot, and this one... desperate and intense. Her tongue swipes into my mouth and touches mine, teasing me, and I slide my hand back to bury it in her soft curls. I could get lost in them.

In her.

A soft moan escapes her throat. I slip down to my knees and kneel in between her legs, my face at the same height as hers. She pulls me closer, and I slide my hands around her waist and onto her lower back.

I want to keep kissing her, ideally forever.

I slip my hand under her shirt and caress the bare skin on her back, up her spine and back down.

Fuck, I want to be with her. I want to touch her everywhere and show her how amazing she is. Her arms are around my neck, and she arches into me. I'm about lose the little control I have around this woman.

"Lucy," I say between kisses. It's a statement of fact, and she murmurs something in response that I don't quite catch. I kiss her neck, my mouth lingering on the sweet curve of her throat.

A woman's laugh sounds from the lodge, followed by a man's low voice.

Lucy stiffens and turns her head toward the noise. I pause for a beat, my lips hovering above her skin, but soon return to kissing her neck. I slide my hands to her ass and tug her toward me, cupping her round bottom in my palms.

"Fuck 'em," I say against her neck. "They won't see us out here."

She breathes out heavily but straightens her body.

"I think that's my brother." Lucy turns back to me, eyes hooded, just like I imagine mine are.

"Fucking Atticus." I groan and stare at her lips, red with my kisses. She doesn't laugh like I want her to. I slide my hands back to her waist.

Lucy glances back toward the voices. I push curls away from the side of her face and take in her freckles, sweet mouth, and long lashes over moonlit eyes.

"Want to come to my cottage?" The words fall out of my mouth unintentionally, my subconscious speaking for itself.

"I don't think that's a good idea." She looks at me, but her eyes are far away.

I pull it together, nod, and slide my hands off her body, regret running deeply through me.

CHAPTER 23

Death by Orange

LUCY

RALEIGH

You did not send him to his cottage alone. Tell
me that's not what really happened

ME

It was the right thing to do. This is getting too
messy, and I'm not even going to be in
Colorado much longer

RALEIGH

What is wrong with you?? Calling

"Hello?" I'm hiding in a tucked-away bathroom before I
head to the ballroom for lunch. This morning, the
team and staffers were split into groups for the escape
room bonding event. I was with a bunch of women from administration, and it was a lot of fun. We escaped with forty-seven
seconds to spare.

None of the hockey players escaped.

I can't stop thinking about last night and how it ended.

"Lulu! What've we talked about?" Raleigh's voice is chastising,
like she's the teacher and I'm a repeatedly misbehaving student.

I lean against the wall and close my eyes. All I can think about is Kellen on his knees kissing me underneath a beautiful starry Wyoming night sky. The feel of his mouth on mine. The way his hands wandered to the base of my spine, splayed against bare skin. The way he pulled me toward him at the end before we were interrupted. His palms on my ass.

I desperately wanted him to continue.

But then I heard Atticus's voice, and it brought me back to reality.

This is supposed to be fake. Kellen and I have crossed too many lines, and saying no felt like the right thing to do last night.

But this morning? All I've felt is regret.

"I don't remember being a part of the conversation you're referencing, but you and January seem to think I should sleep with Kellen."

"Bingo. He likes you, girly. Why not let yourself have some fun?"

Why not?

I'm not sure anymore. In the moment, there was a whole list of reasons why I needed to walk away.

But right now, the only one that really matters is protecting my heart. Someone like Kellen could stomp all over it. I look at him and can see myself falling for him.

I don't want to do that.

"I'm leaving in a few months."

"Psshhhhtt. That's a lame excuse. A few months is a long time!"

"I'm just worried..."

"Worried about what?"

"I like him, sis."

She's silent for a moment.

"Maybe just trust yourself. Kiss him, sleep with him, whatever. Just don't let yourself fall in love or anything." Raleigh laughs, as if that's not exactly what I'm afraid of happening.

"Raleigh Durham. How on earth do I do that?"

"Just think of him as a hookup. Sure, you like him, but pretend you're using him for sex. He won't mind, trust me." Raleigh laughs. "Not that I'm the expert on casual relationships."

"You've been married two times, so I'd agree that you have a hard time keeping it casual." I chuckle.

Could I do that? Trick myself into not falling for him by focusing only on the physical connection between us?

Ten minutes of a pep talk from Raleigh later, I'm settling at a table with some of the other staffers and poking at a turkey sandwich.

"Listen up!" Coach Jackson shouts from the middle of the large room. "My delightful admin Laurie will be sending out the laser tag team assignments for this afternoon."

A table of players hoots and cheers.

"We'll be mixing the teams with players and staffers, just to keep it fair."

"Just say we're the weakest links," the accounting woman grumbles. We all laugh. We might've kicked hockey player butt in the escape room, but a physical competition is another story altogether.

"There will be four teams of eight people each. Every team will have a color. The objective of the game is to be the team with the last player standing. If you get hit three times by another team, you're dead. You're out. Your laser gun will no longer work, and you must exit the field."

"What do we get if we win?" Lachlan calls out.

"Good question from our resident Aussie." Coach points at Lachlan. "Each player on the winning team gets a $500 bottle of champagne." Cheers erupt from the room, as if these boys can't afford to buy their own damn champagne. "Meet in the laser tag room in one hour to gear up."

My phone pings, along with everyone else's. I'm on the red team with the accounting woman and six players.

Including Kellen.

I snort and the social media manager gives me a look.

"What?" she asks.

I shrug and shake my head. "Nothing. Just thinking of how bad my aim is. Or, I'm assuming it is, since I've never picked up a gun or a laser gun or anything similar."

"Me neither," she groans.

An hour later, we meet in the laser tag room and hotel employees help everyone get geared up with sensors and guns.

"Hey."

I spin around to face Kellen, sensor vest on his wide frame and laser gun slung across a shoulder, looking annoyingly hot and tough. I bet I look like a kid in a Halloween costume.

"Hi." My cheeks heat as every detail of last night flies through my mind, as well as my conversation with Raleigh that has me convinced to take things further with him.

"Having fun today?" His eyes twinkle.

"I'm going to be terrible at this game. I'm sorry you're saddled with me."

Kellen grins. "I'll protect you." He leans forward and nudges my shoulder with his elbow, bending down to reach my height.

"I don't need protecting, moose."

He raises his eyebrows.

"They have moose here in Wyoming, who would've thought? And bison. And grizzly bears." I shudder.

"So I shouldn't protect you?"

"I mean, maybe in this one situation, I might need protecting."

"Well, then stick with me, my little Brussels sprout."

I giggle like a teenager.

Why am I resisting this man? I'm not. Not anymore.

Before I can respond, one of the other players on our team slaps Kellen on the back and nods over to the rest of the people with red guns and vests.

Kellen is not in my plan. I'm in Colorado for one reason, and only for a few more months.

Maybe two reasons.

Secure a great reference for the Winchester FC job.

Prove to my ex-life I can succeed on my own.

But Kellen can be a side quest, can't he?

* * *

Half an hour later, it's me, Kellen, Finn, and Heath still alive on our team.

We're in a giant ballroom that has been completely transformed into an intricate laser tag landscape. Dim lights, roughed-up boards and fake boulders, caves, trees, and four mountains—red, orange, yellow, and green—as home bases for the teams. Clouds of smoke drift along the ground. There's ominous music playing in the background, the kind I imagine war video games would have.

Somewhere in the room, someone screams.

It's a freaking battlefield.

I'm currently huddled with what's left of my team, and we—and by *we* I mean *they*—are formulating a plan. Shouts and high-pitched laughter sound from around us.

I am *so* gonna die. It's remarkable I haven't already as I've been shot twice. I have one life left. I've only gotten this far because Kellen has dragged me along with him. Otherwise, I probably would've just sacrificed myself so I can go sit in the dead player zone.

Kellen's got one life left as well.

The other two lost protecting me.

"Heath and Finn will go after what remains of the green team," Kellen says. "They have the most still alive, I think. Harley, Grayson, and Romeo for sure."

"Savannah too," Heath says.

"You guys get them." Kellen nods. There's no way he's going after Savannah's team. "After you're done with the green team, go after yellow."

"Yes, Captain," Finn says with a smirk and salutes Kellen, who gives him an exaggerated dirty look.

"Lucy and I will target Atticus and the orange team." Kellen looks at each remaining team member in turn, his mouth twitching ever so slightly when he meets my eyes.

"I will follow any order you give me," I say, but then play back my subservient words. My face heats as the group chuckles.

Kellen clears his throat. "Survivors, meet back at the red mountain as soon as possible."

Finn and Heath charge away.

"I didn't mean it like that."

"Mean what?"

"That I'll follow your orders."

"I'm not sure what you're implying, Lucy." Kellen leans against the mountain next to me with a straight face, and for a second, I think he truly doesn't know what I'm talking about. But then he turns fully to me.

"I'm really doing my best not to get inappropriate here." I crack up, and he does the same five seconds later.

"Ready to go shoot your brother?"

"I've never been more ready for anything in my life," I say.

Kellen laughs again, flashing his white teeth, and my insides flutter.

Lordy. The way he knelt before me last night.

"So what's our strategy?" I say.

"Shoot people." He cocks his head.

I raise my eyebrows. "That's it? We each have only one life left." I gesture to the single red bar on his vest.

Kellen shrugs. "This is laser tag. It's just a game."

"Isn't hockey—"

"Hush now." He presses a finger to my lips, and I hold back a laugh.

Shouts from our teammates distract both of us.

"Follow me," he says, and I'm loving the man-in-charge side of Kellen. It's so damn sexy.

I crouch, mimicking Kellen's posture, and creep after him onto the battlefield. It's quiet for a second. Too quiet. We're exposed on our way to the orange mountain to shoot Atticus, but they're nowhere in sight.

Suddenly, my brother's team pours out from behind two large boulders next to their mountain. It was a trap. There are so many of them. Too many. Atticus and two other hockey players I don't know descend on us, all shooting wildly.

"Lucy!" Kellen shouts and throws his body on top of mine.

I'm laughing, half squished and half turned on by his show of over-the-top protectiveness.

Atticus cackles maniacally.

"Kellen! I can't breathe," I say between giggles, demonstrating that I can, in fact, breathe.

"I'm so sorry." Kellen rolls off and turns to me with a concerned look on his face. "Are you okay?"

I sit up and can't stop laughing. Tears stream down my cheeks.

"Lucy! Are you hurt?" He kneels next to me and touches my face. "Are you crying?"

"I'm fine." I get the words out between giggles.

"You're laughing? I just died for you, and you think it's funny?" He's indignant but smiling as I get tagged from multiple sides. The light on my vest fades to nothing.

I'm dead.

"If you weren't laughing so hard, we might have at least saved *you*." Kellen shakes his head. "My sacrifice would've been worth it."

"I'm touched. But like I suggested, your *shoot people* plan didn't work."

"Let's get out of here." Kellen sighs deeply and pulls me to my feet for the second time in ten minutes. "Crouch low and run to the side."

"Why run? We're already dead."

"Lucy. You'd be a terrible soldier." Kellen shakes his head.

"Good thing I have no plans to be one," I whisper-scream and follow him toward the dead player zone, which is just a wall on one side of the ballroom.

Thirty seconds later, I sink to the floor next to him.

"I'm exhausted. And I think I'm gonna be sore, which is frankly embarrassing."

"A hot springs pool will fix everything." Kellen strips off his vest and pushes dark hair off his forehead.

"A hot springs pool sounds delightful."

There are two big common pools on the property and smaller private pools for each of the one-bedroom cottages.

Like Kellen's.

Which is part of tonight's plan.

Tonight, we won't be alone. We'll be playing a part in front of Savannah and other people.

"Have you been keeping up with the Kellcy Fake Dating Planning Committee text chain?"

I snort.

"Kellen, I try my very best not to."

He chuckles, and his eyes drift over my face, like he's deeply curious about me.

I feel like he's actually seeing me.

How much can he see?

A cheer rises up, and my brother's voice is loudest.

"Shit. Your brother's team won."

"He's gonna be insufferable later."

Later. When we're all in the hot springs pool, where Kellen and I have to put on a performance.

In bathing suits.
All wet.
My heart beats just a bit faster.

CHAPTER 24

Really Hot Springs
LUCY

The group is laughing and drinking around the fire pits like last night, with more than a few of the hockey players getting tipsy. I'm standing along the edge of the group, watching Atticus and Lachlan perform gymnastics in an open space and get rated by their audience.

Savannah is off to the side talking to someone I don't know, but she's watching the theatrics. From what I've seen of her, she actually seems nice. Maybe a bit over eager, but I don't see her purposely hitting on any of the players, and she's been perfectly friendly to me.

Maybe it's just her husband who's the asshole.

I can see that.

My brother does a graceful cartwheel. Cheers go up and there are shouts of nine and ten.

"Three," Kellen calls with a stony face from the other side of the circle around the gymnasts. "Lachlan did it better."

My brother swings his head to the source of the low score, then sprints toward Kellen and takes him down at the waist, rugby style.

"Stop!" Coach Jackson yells. "Your contracts say no extreme

sports!" The sound of laughter fills the area, but the coach looks dead serious.

Which makes everyone laugh harder.

"What is wrong with my brother?" I say to myself, chuckling at his antics.

Kellen pushes off Atticus and both men hop to their feet.

"Sorry, Coach." Kellen brushes off his jogging pants.

"Why don't you show us your cartwheel, Bassey?" Atticus, with red cheeks and our wild hair, faces Kellen. He doesn't even acknowledge Coach Jackson, the man who at least partially controls his hockey career.

My brother is trashed.

Thinking Kellen will ignore the challenge, I almost turn away.

"I'm mostly sober, don't worry," Kellen says to his coach before casually striding into the circle and performing a perfect ten cartwheel, like a wagon wheel turning with exact precision. The group cheers. Coach Jackson covers his eyes.

Kellen bows and retreats to the side of the circle where Savannah is standing with Atticus and Lachlan, then he turns my way and winks. My traitorous body has a visceral reaction to the acknowledgement.

Alcohol is probably not a great idea tonight, but I'm nervous about the plan we have later, so I finish the bottle of beer in my hand.

Any minute now, some of the group will start heading back toward Kellen's pool.

I've got a bikini on underneath my sweatpants, tank top, and zip-up sweatshirt, and I guess it won't be long before I strip down.

My phone buzzes.

LACHLAN

It's time for action. Places, everyone!

RALEIGH

I am so jealous

JANUARY

Me too. I'm up for an early run along the
Thames, but I'd rather be partying in Wyoming!

KELLEN

Meet you guys at mine

I look up and Kellen's slipping his phone in his pocket. He glances my way and nods to the pathway, waiting for me to fall into step beside him.

"Cartwheels, huh?" I steal a look at him.

"When your brother challenges, I can't back down." Kellen throws his hands up. "I'm incapable."

"He's feeling cocky after distributing glasses of his $500 bottle of champagne," I say. Atticus has been hilariously painful to be around this evening. He was so proud to have taken Kellen down in laser tag. It's good to know my almost thirty-year-old brother is just as goofy as he was in college.

"I was sure I had a better cartwheel than him. I do them with Ava all the time."

"She is very good at cartwheels." I smile, delighted at the image of Kellen and his daughter cartwheeling together. I saw plenty of Ava's gymnastic moves during soccer season. "The Snowballs had a distracting habit of doing them on the field in the middle of games."

"Yup. I tried to tell her to keep it to a minimum, but there's only so much I can do."

I chuckle. We stop with the others when we get to the pool outside of Kellen's cottage.

"Why is your pool so much bigger than mine?" Atticus says.

"That doesn't even need a response." Kellen reaches behind his neck and pulls his t-shirt off in one swift move, revealing chiseled abs, and throws it on a lounge chair. "I'm going to get drinks." Kellen slips into his cottage, and Atticus and Lachlan strip to their swim trunks and jump in, both yelping about the heat. Lachlan shakes his blond curls like a golden retriever drying off.

Across the pool, Savannah pulls off her short dress and slips gracefully into the water. She looks over at me and waves, and it takes me a second to realize she's encouraging me to get in.

"I can't be the only woman in the pool, please," she calls and smiles. It's disarming. She's really pretty with her blonde waves and picture-perfect body, but it's the friendly look on her face that takes me aback. I'm always expecting her to be kind of a monster.

For a second, I wonder what we're trying to prove to her. Does she even care? Does Paul? But I shake the thought out of my head. What's important is Kellen gets to keep his family in Fort Collins. So we'll do whatever it takes to make sure that happens.

"Working on it," I say back to her. I pull off my sweatshirt and tank and adjust my bikini top. Kellen comes back out of his cottage, a bucket of beer bottles in his hand.

He looks over at me and does a double take before he kicks off his joggers and slips into the water, breathing out in pleasure and staring at me.

Two more women who I vaguely recognize as hotel employees show up, followed by two other players. I'm thankful none of the staffers are here—Atticus and Lachlan were going to try to keep them away so I didn't feel even more uncomfortable.

"You made it," Lachlan calls to them.

I shimmy down my light pants and try to be causal, but Kellen is still watching, leaning his elbows on the concrete outside of the pool, swigging from a bottle. I slide down to sit on the edge of the pool a few feet away from him, my legs hanging in the delightfully warm water. Not as warm as a hot tub, but perfect for the cool November night.

Kellen scoots over, wet hair sticking to his forehead and droplets of water clinging to his cheeks. He looks up at me.

Well, crap.

I know I've always said I'm not a hockey player kind of

woman, but looking at Kellen with those rippling shoulders and gorgeous blue eyes? I guess anyone could become one.

Or maybe I'm just a Kellen kind of woman.

Either way, there's an ache in my center as he leans next to me at the pool's edge, his forearm lightly against my thigh.

"Ready for this?" His voice is low and there's a slight wobble. Is he nervous? Nah, can't be.

I nod. "But remind me what we're doing, exactly?" Damn, *I'm* nervous. Nervous and frozen to the side of this pool.

"First, you have to get in."

"And then?" My chest thumps as Kellen turns to me, stepping casually between my knees, my thighs opening automatically to accommodate him. He puts a hand on either side of me.

Holy—

"Get in, Lucy."

My mouth opens, but no words come out.

"Get in or I pull you in."

A shiver runs up my back.

Kellen slips his hands under my knees and tugs.

I squeal. "Fine! Fine. I'm coming." He lets go, so I scoot down and slide into the water right in between his arms. Kellen doesn't move, and now we're standing a foot apart, and I'm looking up at him. My breath catches... at the temperature of the pool. "Oh my god. That's so warm." The water heats my skin, and I can't tell if I'm flushing from Kellen's proximity or the hot springs.

"Second part of the plan is to look like we're a couple."

"Okay. How do we do that?" Maybe by my heart racing a hundred miles a minute. Because that's what's happening right now.

"Stay close to me. Like a couple would do."

"Like this?" I say, my gaze locked with his. "Because we're pretty close."

He nods.

"Okay," I breathe out. "What else?"

"Couples touch each other." Kellen takes my hands—hanging uselessly by my side—and pulls them to his chest. "Like this." He slides his hands to my waist. "And this."

The feel of his bare skin under my hands is so unlike the brief brushes as I buttoned his shirt at the photo shoot. Our bodies almost touch from the waist down, and I move an imperceptible bit forward to get him to be flush against me. He intakes a sharp breath, and that reminds me to breathe. All the blood rushes between my legs and the heat from the steamy pool is melting me.

"Is she watching us?" Kellen asks.

"Who?" As soon as I say it, I realize. "Oh, right, Savannah." I glance over Kellen's shoulder, and he moves his hands a few inches along my skin toward my back. "Yes. She's watching. Sort of."

Across the pool, Savannah glances our way and raises her eyebrows, but she goes back to chatting with Lachlan and the women from the hotel, who are sitting on the side with their legs dangling like I was a minute ago.

"Good."

Atticus jumps out of the pool and helps one of the women stand. I hear him suggest his superior pool to her. My brother makes eye contact with me and shakes his head in disgust, then stifles a fake gag. I huff a laugh as he disappears down the pathway with the woman. The other one hops to her feet.

"They're getting out. Atticus is gone, thank god."

Kellen slides his hands fully around to my back, slowly moving them up until his fingers sweep the bottom of my bikini top. I suck in a breath and hold it. His fingers feel like rods of fire against my skin.

"I hope I'm not making you uncomfortable." Kellen's hands move back down to the top hem of my bikini bottom. I wish he'd push all his weight against me.

"No, of course not," I squeak. I try to contain a moan and don't look at him, keeping my eyes on the departing group. "Savannah is now out of the pool." There are still two hockey players in the water, Lachlan stands at the edge, and the remaining hotel woman lingers by the pathway.

"Oy, on to Atter's." Lachlan stops on the path and waits for the last guys to exit the water and walk ahead of him. He stands patiently while Savannah casts a last glance at us. She literally shrugs and turns to Lachlan, linking her arm in his and laughing about something as they walk away.

And then they're all gone, their voices fading to nothing.

Kellen moves a step back from me, breaking contact.

My eyes dart to his.

"Was that too much?" His brow is furrowed. I'm almost cold in the hot pool without him touching me.

He was acting. Of course he was. My stomach drops.

"No." What's my move here? He's ready to walk away. I rejected him last night. He doesn't know about my conversation with Raleigh. He doesn't know that I want to do this with him. My hands—no longer on his chest—shake at my sides. Do I have the nerve to make it happen?

Kellen looks over his shoulder, and I just know he's about to walk away.

So I reach out my hands and pull him to me by his waist. He looks back at me with sharp surprise etched in his raised eyebrows and lets me close the gap between us, but doesn't touch me. His hands clench and unclench at his sides.

"Last night..." I start.

"It's okay. It was too much."

"No." I shake my head. "I want this to happen."

Kellen blinks at me, then moves a hand to the side of my neck, moving it up until he's cupping my jaw. I lean into him with my eyes shut.

"Lucy. Look at me."

Our eyes meet, and it's fire. I'm not going to hold back with this man right now. I deserve this. I need this.

"Kiss me, Kellen."

And he does.

The hot water around me is nothing compared to the molten blood rushing through my veins as he presses his mouth against mine, first softly, then bringing the kiss deeper. I could kiss him all night. It does something to my soul. It fills me. It's so right and perfect. Kellen pulls me harder against him and buries a hand in my curls. His tongue swipes into my mouth, and I open wider, giving him full access. Now he's pressing himself against me, and I feel his desire on my stomach. I'm pulsing for him.

Kellen pulls away.

"I really like you, Lucy. I want you to know that." He's breathing heavily.

I absorb his words. They're not words of obligation, are they? He's not drunk. Neither am I.

"I like you too." I move my hands up his wet chest, memorizing the feel of every muscle and line, trying to build a protective wall around my heart so I can be with him physically.

Maybe telling him I like him doesn't go with the idea of only being physical.

But then he kisses me again, and I don't care.

Our bodies spark against each other, and I press against him as he moves his hands down my body lightly, over the curves of my ass, until he touches bare skin where my bikini bottom ends. Then he stops again.

"In another universe, you're not just my fake girlfriend."

I swallow. *Oh, shit.* Not sure those walls can handle this kind of talk. "What does that universe look like?"

We're on seriously dangerous ground now, but I can't stop myself.

"It's a universe where you're here permanently. Where we have coffee every morning. You coach my daughter's soccer team. We get to touch each other all the time. We laugh, hang out, hike, fight off wild animals, and spend a lot of time naked."

I smile, and he kisses me again.

"That sounds perfect," I say, but the words are lost in our kiss.

I continue in my head. It's a universe where he can trust people. A universe where I can believe I'm enough.

The water slides against my skin as he pushes my bikini bottoms down to access the skin beneath. I'm throbbing between my legs, and I want his hands everywhere.

"Can we go somewhere more private?" I whisper as I press harder against him. Because as amazing as this is, I'm not into risking the hockey boys coming back this way.

We've already shown the public what they need to see.

This? This is just for us.

Kellen tugs my suit back up and lifts me out of the pool, then practically leaps up next to me. He pulls me onto my feet and toward the door to his cottage, where there's a private lounge area hidden from view completely.

I tug him to a lounge chair and sink onto my back, pulling him down on top of me. I don't want to be deprived of his touch for one more second.

He buries his head in my neck and slides a hand down my stomach and to my aching front. I practically purr as he touches me. Finally. Stroking. Touching. Pressing. Fire is burning inside me, and it's not just in my between my legs.

It's in my chest. And that's a problem.

I feel like I'm floating, and I arch against him. I'm dripping pool water and should be freezing in the cool Wyoming night, but his lips are setting me on fire.

He moves his mouth down my neck and my chest until he wraps his lips around a nipple through my bathing suit, his fingers still stroking so softly between my legs that I might die. I'm a rag doll in his arms, destroyed by the sensations of his fingers, his mouth, his body.

"You're perfect," he says. "This is all I've been thinking about. You're driving me crazy, Lucy, with your curls and your lips and your laugh…"

"Kellen," I whisper, burying my hands in his hair as he pushes my bikini top down and takes my exposed breast in his mouth.

This time, I can't hold back the moan.

I'm floating with his touch, but I want more. I want everything.

He swoops me up and locks my legs around his waist.

"You deserve a bed, Lucy." So he backs me up into his cottage and slides the door shut with one hand, then lowers my feet onto the floor. "We need to get out of these clothes so the bed doesn't get soaked."

I raise my eyebrows at him, and he has such a wicked look in his eyes that my body practically explodes on the spot. He disappears for a second and returns to toss a condom on the nightstand.

Kellen pushes my bikini bottoms down while keeping intense eye contact. I want him to touch me, but instead, he slowly picks at the back of my top, pulling the tie loose and nudging the fabric off my shoulders until I'm standing in front of him naked.

After he pushes his bathing suit down—holy hell—he lets his eyes roam my body. Then he gently backs me up until the bed hits the back of my knees, and he's scooping me up and laying me down on the scratchy comforter. He leans down and places light kisses on the inside of my thighs, creeping his mouth closer and closer to my core.

I throw my head back and breathe out as his mouth finds my center. He wastes no time exploring with his tongue, pausing only to pull me down further to him.

"You're so good at this," I whisper. My mind is at odds with my body. This is exactly what I want. What I need. But it's more than that.

It feels *right*.

Kellen moans and wraps his arms around my thighs, resting them on his shoulders.

"Oh god, Kellen." I bury my hands in my hair as my orgasm builds with him buried in between my thighs. The world turns black around me, and I ride on intense pleasurable waves. He stays between my legs until my shoulders fall and all the tension releases from my body.

I collapse back onto the bed, my legs jelly, my heart racing. Kellen climbs up and lays next to me.

"Kellen?"

He turns his head to me. "Yeah, Lucy?"

"That was amazing."

"You're amazing."

My heart skips a beat.

Why is this so confusing? First we tell each other we like each other, now he tells me I'm amazing?

We're just banging this out. Not starting a whole thing. But I can't bring myself to say that to him, because the way he's looking at me hints toward it not being that simple.

"Hey," he says. I turn my head to look at him, my breathing slowing down.

"Hey." I bite my lip. Kellen's eyes are still hooded with desire. I run my hand down his chest and abdomen, and he breathes in sharply when I wrap my hand around his length.

"Lucy," he says. I wait for him to continue, but he doesn't. He just reaches next to him to grab the condom, nudging my hand aside and gently crawling on top of me.

He pushes inside me slowly, keeping eye contact, looking at me like I'm more than just a quick lay. It's too much for my soul to take, and I shut my eyes as he fills me.

This is supposed to be just physical, so I thrust against him and concentrate on the rhythmic movement between us, in sync and like we're one and the same person. We come together moments later. I chuckle and stare wide-eyed at the ceiling. Some kind of euphoria fills me, and I want to laugh and dance around the room.

"What?"

"I can't believe we did that." I shut my eyes and let the warm feelings envelop me. Purely physical feelings, of course. Not warm from the inside. Not warm at having done this with Kellen specifically.

"I can," he says. I turn my head and Kellen's staring at me. "I've wanted to do that for a while now."

"Really?"

"Really," he says. "And I'd like to do it again in a little bit."

Kellen reaches over and takes my hand, weaving my fingers with his. It takes my breath away just a little. We lay on our backs like that for a while, until our heartbeats are more in control.

Eventually, Kellen starts running kisses down my neck again.

In the morning, I'm going to have to accept the fact that this thing with Kellen is no longer fake. If it was fake, we would've only had sex, not said all those things.

If it was fake, I wouldn't be feeling this way about him.

I think I'm screwing this up.

CHAPTER 25

She's Probably Already Convinced

KELLEN

Saturday, November 23

"Is this meeting really necessary?" Lucy says as Harley and Lachlan settle on the long couch in Atticus's apartment. I'm next to her on the love seat, like last time, and Atticus is in the single chair clutching a beer. Raleigh is on Atticus's phone, but no January as she's seven hours ahead in London.

The adrenaline is pumping through my veins at being this close to Lucy.

After spending last Saturday night together at the retreat, we've continued to text daily. Little things about our days.

I told her about Ava's new ballet class, where they're learning a little kid version of the Nutcracker. She said she wished she was a ballet instructor as well as a soccer coach so she could spend more time with Ava, and my chest expanded uncomfortably with affection.

She told me about getting Mister Barky McBarkface a new collar, and how she considered getting him a name tag but isn't ready to commit to his new name yet.

As if she's not going to give her dog away.

As if she's not probably moving thousands of miles from here in a few months.

As if what happened last weekend wasn't a huge deal that changed everything.

There's a knock on the door.

"Come in!" Atticus shouts.

The door swings open and Finn, Heath, and Romeo walk in.

"The fuck are you guys doing here?" I say.

"We're here for the Kellcy Fake Dating Planning Committee meeting, obviously." Finn heads to the kitchen. "Drinks in the fridge?"

"How the hell did you know about this?" These guys are a welcome distraction from my nerves, but really, why the fuck are they here?

"Lachlan spilled it all last Saturday night at the retreat when we ran into him after he left you and your fake girlfriend—hi, Lucy— in your pool. We're all caught up." Romeo smooths back strands of hair that escaped his curly ponytail—which we all mercilessly make fun of him for, not that he cares, and accepts a can of sparkling water from Finn. "Don't worry, we won't get in your way. We just want to be included, you know?"

No one knows Lucy and I slept together last weekend. When the boys all walked away from my hot springs pool, I was barely touching her. I even stepped away once they were gone. I wanted to respect her rejection from the night before.

But she'd changed her mind.

This isn't fake anymore, but it sure is messy.

And maybe—just maybe—the boys suspect something. After all, we didn't rejoin the group after they left us in the pool.

The newcomers scoot onto the kitchen stools and appear to wait for something. Heath doesn't say anything. He's a quiet guy, but Finn and Romeo do plenty of talking for the three of them.

"So you were telling me the truth?" Lucy looks at Atticus.

"You guys really don't go out partying on Saturday nights?" There's a desperate edge to her voice.

Everyone's heads swing toward her. Romeo stops mid-sip with a confused look on his face.

"Why would you think that?" Harley asks, dead serious. "We hardly ever go out partying."

"My body is a temple, man. I cannot keep this in shape—" Romeo runs his hand over his chest and down his abdomen. "—if I'm drinking all the time. Also, I need a full eight hours of sleep." He swigs noisily from his can before placing it on the counter in front of him. "But sometimes we meet for book club."

"We're reading a psychological thriller next month," Finn adds. He's a pretty short guy for a hockey player, but stocky and built like a brick wall. Makes him a force when his line swaps with ours on the ice. "Hey—" He looks at Lucy. "You should buddy read with Kellen."

"For fuck's sake," I say under my breath.

"I don't know. We'll have to see if there's an opening in the book club." Atticus shakes his head at his sister. "It's very exclusive."

"In what world is our book club exclusive?" Lachlan laughs.

"I need *something* of my own, okay?" Atticus says with a whine in his voice. "Do you have to invite my sister to everything?"

"Yes, Atticus, we're going to invite your sister and her hot friends to everything." Lachlan rolls his eyes.

"How do you know they're hot? I'm the only one who's even met them in person," Atticus grumbles.

"Hello? I'm right here!" Raleigh says. Her face is red, but she's clearly holding back laughter.

"We know," Lachlan says. "They both have sexy voices. And we can see their faces on video. Hot." He waves to Raleigh on the phone screen.

Raleigh giggles and Lucy snorts.

"As entertaining as this is, can we move on?" Lucy says. "To whatever this meeting is about?"

I sneak a look next to me. I can't get a read on her tonight. Our thighs are just six inches apart. Her hand twitches in her lap. Her back is straight, and so is mine, like we're a couple on an awkward first date.

I'd fantasized all week about sneaking away with her. Grabbing kisses in her office. Sharing intense looks across the arena.

But the team was away for three nights, and when I got back, she was busy helping to organize the Thanksgiving food and coat drive that the Blizzard is hosting to benefit FoCo families.

I stopped by with a case of yams. I managed to pull her into a dark hallway and kiss her until neither of us could breathe. She laughed and buried her hands in my hair. I leaned down and pressed my forehead against hers.

That was two days ago.

This is all too much. I don't have time for a real girlfriend. It was never supposed to turn into this. This warm, full feeling in my chest.

"Of course. Let's get started. We have a lot to cover." Lachlan nods solemnly.

"We do?" I ask. "What on earth do we have to talk—"

"Agenda item number one," Lachlan interrupts. "Let's review the recent events."

"Let's not," Lucy whispers, just for me, and bumps her thigh on mine. I turn to her and crack a grin, and she's got humor dancing in her eyes as she gives me a side glance, her cheeks turning pink.

"How did the retreat go?" Lachlan cocks his head to me, and I rip my gaze from Lucy.

I could say a lot of things right now. That we hooked up in the pool, on the lounge chair, and in the bed. That she confused me. That it felt right when she fell asleep nestled on my chest.

That it wasn't just sex.

"It went as planned. Which you know, because you were there, orchestrating the whole thing." I attempt to sound indignant and press my lips together. Harley and Atticus laugh.

"I talked to Savannah at the fire pit," I say, because everyone is waiting for me to say more. "After I kicked Atticus's ass at cartwheels."

"Like fuck you did!" Atticus growls. I ignore him.

"At that point, I didn't think Savannah was buying me and Lucy being together." I'm doubling down on this lie, I suppose. For a second, I feel bad about depicting Savannah as the bad guy. I mentally shake that thought out.

"And then?" Finn prompts.

I give Atticus a dirty look and wave a hand at Finn, Heath, and Romeo, who are watching the meeting like we're putting on a performance. "Seriously, what are these guys doing here?"

There's another knock on the door.

"Come in!" yells Lachlan.

"Who the hell is that?" I ask, just as Bri walks in.

"You invited Bri?" I look at Lachlan with a huff.

"Bri deserves to be involved in things that affect her and Ava's life," Lach condescends to me.

I groan and roll my eyes.

"Who's watching Ava?" I ask.

"Relax," Bri shrugs with a smile. "She loves when the high school girl down the street comes to babysit."

I groan as Bri drops onto the couch between Harley and Lachlan, who each scoot a smidge to the sides.

"Hi, Lucy." Bri lifts a hand.

"Hey! Welcome, I guess." Lucy smiles at Bri.

What's going on here? But a laugh bubbles up inside me, and I shake my head.

Bri waves to Raleigh on the phone.

"Hi! Are you Lucy's friend?" she asks.

"Yes, she is," Lucy says. "Raleigh, meet Bri. Raleigh's one of my best friends, my old college roommate. Bri is Ava's mom."

"Hi!" Bri and Raleigh say at the same time.

"This is a complete circus," Lucy whispers. I chuckle and nudge her leg like she did before.

"Go on," Lachlan says to me.

"Since Savannah was still doubtful, we went with the original plan and made sure we convinced her in the pool later. With your help. Remember, Lach?" Now my face is burning as an audience of people stare at me: Harley, Lachlan, Heath, Romeo, Finn, Bri, Raleigh.

And Lucy.

"Hmm, I do, mate, I do."

I wait for Lachlan to push more, but he doesn't.

"Satisfied?" I ask.

"Sure." Lachlan shrugs.

"Agenda item number two," Harley says, saving us, I guess? "Do you think Savannah bought it? Did she tell Paul?" He sips from a bottle of water.

"I think Savannah is a believer now." I definitely won't be sharing that she was already a believer going into the retreat. That detail would help no one.

"She didn't even mention you when we were chatting walking away from the pool," Lachlan says with raised eyebrows. "No comments or questions. I'm not sure she gives a fuck about your love life, mate."

"Great news." Harley looks at Atticus, and then Lucy. "And how about your father, Lucy?"

Lucy shrugs. "I haven't heard anything from my father or my ex. So I'm not sure."

"Me neither," Atticus adds, running a hand through his red waves. "Not that my father would ever think to call or text *me*."

"Hmm." Harley nods thoughtfully. "You three leave this week for D.C., right? What's the plan?"

"We fly out Wednesday afternoon, spend the night and most of Thanksgiving Day with my mom, then meet up with my father later that evening." Lucy pushes back a chunk of red curls. "We fly back early on Friday morning since you guys have a home game that night."

"Should be fun." Atticus rubs his hands together and grins.

"You just want to piss off Dad." Lucy rolls her eyes at her brother.

"Yup, sure do."

"I'm not as worried about my father these days," Lucy says. "As long as we've convinced Savannah and Paul. That's more important."

My breath catches in my throat, and I turn to her.

"Convincing your father is important too, Lucy," I say quietly.

"No, it's not," she says and shakes her head. "Truly. I care more about Ava."

I nod and swallow a lump in my throat. Everyone's watching and listening.

"We'll finish the job in D.C. and convince Richard." I keep my eyes on Lucy. Side conversations pop up around us.

"It'll work." Her eyes go to my lips, and I wonder if we can slip away together. "And thank you."

"For what?"

"I guess for helping me piss off my father, but really for distracting me for the past few months. And making me realize what's actually important in life. And spoiler alert, it's not pissing off my father."

"Lucy..." I swallow a lump in my throat. I'm glad no one's listening to us right now.

"Seriously. Your focus on your daughter and your family and your team is so sweet. It's been lovely to get to know you all." A sad smile comes over her face, and something in me sparks and glows.

"One last agenda item," Lachlan calls and the conversations die down. Lucy and I look over at Lachlan. "It's a sad one."

"The breakup," Harley says.

"Awwww," Raleigh says from the phone.

"Mid-December, right?" I look over at Lucy, and she nods.

"I'll go to a home game and talk to Savannah about how we broke up," Lucy says.

"You can't be devastated. Nonchalant would be best," Harley says. "You don't want Paul reporting back to your father that you're sad."

"You don't think she'll be devastated to break up with me? I'm hurt." I grin, but *I'm* hurting inside. Hurting from the idea of a breakup with my fake girlfriend.

Who is not really fake.

Lucy huffs a laugh and pulls at her hair. "I understand the assignment."

"Well, I think that's the whole agenda." Lachlan claps his hands together.

Talking and laughter erupts in the room, and I turn to Lucy. "You okay?"

"I'm good," she says, her cheeks still flushed.

Lucy twists her body to face me. I'm so happy to be in her orbit again. She's warm and sweet, and I would do just about anything to kiss those lips.

"Kellen?"

"Yeah?" I'm staring at her mouth.

"I—" she starts, but her phone vibrates next to her and Raleigh's name pops up. "I'm gonna take this in my room."

She jumps off the couch and disappears down the hallway to the guest bedroom. I'm deeply disappointed but don't have time to dwell as Bri plops down next to me.

"So," Bri says.

"So." I raise my eyebrows.

"I had some thoughts." She glances to where Lucy just walked off. "About Lucy."

"Okay, what now? And since when did you join the Kellcy Fake Dating Planning Committee?"

"First of all, that name is perfect. I'm glad you're embracing it and all of this. I can't believe I wasn't invited to the other meetings." Bri pouts her lips.

I sigh and look up at the ceiling, praying for this conversation to be over.

"Seriously though. I think that this thing you have going on with Lucy is something."

My stomach twists. She's correct. At least from my side. Am I that obvious? Am I even trying to hide it?

"Why would you say that?" I attempt to protest.

"These days, you spend a lot of time staring at your phone with a goofy smile." Bri cocks her head. "And you practically skipped over to my house the other day. And told Ava another story about that dog."

"She loves dogs!"

"Listen. I know she's leaving. And I know you have issues with trusting people. Women."

I make a noncommittal sound as all the words stick in my throat.

"But don't hold yourself back from something good because of me and Ava," Bri says. "Don't worry about the future for now. Go to D.C. and let yourself go a little, okay? Have some fun."

Shit. I'd love to, but I can't change the plan now. We did what we needed to do. It's almost all done. It's supposed to be over.

"It doesn't have to be love, Kellen, or permanent, or long-term. See where this goes." Bri's voice is gentle.

"It's not love." Of course it's not love. I shake my head, trying to convince myself more than anyone else, but Bri is already getting off the couch.

I stay seated by myself, thinking about what she said.

What if I did let myself go a little with Lucy? Let myself have fun with her in D.C., really play up the part of her boyfriend in front of her father? See how it goes?

It wouldn't hurt anyone. Like Bri said, I'll just not think about the fact that she's trying to move to England. Hell, who knows if that's even happening still? She doesn't talk about it much.

Maybe she's changing her mind.

I feel like I can trust Lucy, which probably means I should run screaming.

I already decided I shouldn't trust anyone in my life besides my tiny inner circle of people. Even my own mother betrayed me.

But maybe Lucy is different.

I stand and slip down the hallway toward Atticus's guest bedroom. Lucy's room. I knock the back of my knuckle gently on the door and it opens a second later.

Lucy's eyes widen in surprise to see me in her doorway.

"Get over here," she says with a grin when she recovers, and pulls me in by my shirt.

I kiss her and feel her smile on my mouth. I push the door shut behind me.

It's only kisses, and even if they notice we're both gone, so what?

Sneaking around with Lucy, kissing her in hidden corners and secret rooms... I don't want to be anywhere else.

CHAPTER 26

(Not In) the Mile High Club

LUCY

Wednesday, November 27

Atticus ended up between me and Kellen on the plane. We're in first class—thanks, hockey player salaries. They chatted, I stared out the window.

Since the last Kellcy Fake Dating Planning Committee meeting on Saturday, it's been a busy week for all of us. The team traveled, then returned to Fort Collins for a home game. I was wrapping up the Blizzard food and coat drive, which was a huge success thanks to the players dropping off cases of canned goods and brand-new jackets.

Tuesday morning, there was a vanilla oat milk latte and a piece of crumb cake waiting on my desk with a note: *Good luck with your interview -K*

The video interview with Winchester FC went really well. I probably won't hear for a few weeks, and I'll be busy enough that hopefully I won't keep thinking about it. I hardly had time to recover when Kellen walked in to check how it went and ask what he should wear to dinner with my father on Thanksgiving. It was a good distraction, especially when he shut the door to my office and pushed me up against the wall.

Then he left to get ready for the home game that night.

Between that kiss and the stolen one at the KFDPC meeting on Saturday, I'm embarrassingly desperate to get him alone again. I couldn't have him spend the night on Saturday because we've not revealed to anyone that our fake dating has turned decidedly real. We haven't even directly acknowledged it to each other.

We arrive at Mom's house at nine o'clock at night, and she's waiting at the front door with the biggest smile on her face.

"Hi, Mom." I wrap her in a giant hug.

"Hello sweetheart, welcome home." Mom's voice is muffled against my shoulder.

Even though I never lived at the vineyard full-time, it's always felt like home. To me, my mom is home.

"Atticus." Mom envelops my brother in a long embrace. She gets so angry when my father ignores him, dismisses his accomplishments, overlooks the man he's become. Atticus melts into her arms and looks more like a little boy than a hulking hockey player.

Kellen lingers behind us. We told him earlier that our mother is in on the fake dating scheme. In fact, when I told her, she giggled in delight.

Mom leans back and releases Atticus.

"Mom, this is Kellen." I almost finish with *my fake boyfriend*, but I can't say that out loud any more.

"I've heard all about you and how wonderful you are. Come here for a hug." She pulls Kellen in and gives him her special mom hug. He's stiff for a second but then relaxes his shoulders. "It's lovely to meet you."

Lordy, Mom. My face heats.

"Mom. Not sure I called him wonderful?" *Did I?* I didn't tell her that this thing between me and Kellen is turning more than fake, at least not directly. But I'm sure she caught the idea when I explained all the things we were doing to convince the team owner that we're together.

"Thank you for having me." Kellen stands up straight when Mom releases him. He's got a sweet blush creeping up his neck.

"Well. Happy you're here. And I was absolutely delighted when I heard of this plan to stick it to my asshole ex." Mom smiles at each of us. "Come on, come in, drop your stuff in your bedrooms and let's have a glass of wine."

We follow Mom into her house. She waves down one hallway and looks at Kellen.

"Kellen, there's a spare bedroom next to Lucy's. She can show you." Mom looks at me and winks.

I give her a warning glare.

"Come on." I wave Kellen to follow. Atticus heads down the other hallway. His bedroom is near our mom's on her side of the house.

"Do you feel weird about this?" I ask Kellen as he grabs my bag from my hand. The thing is, it doesn't feel weird to me. It feels normal. Like one of Atticus's friends coming home for Thanksgiving, or January, or Raleigh. Not some stranger.

"Nope. I don't feel weird." Kellen stops right behind me when we get to the two open doors. "And your mom seems great."

"Yeah, she is pretty wonderful. We're lucky." I turn to face him, but as soon as those words are out of my mouth, I remember Kellen's story about his mother and stepfather. How terrible he was, and how his mother took the stepfather's side. *Shoot.*

"You are lucky."

"Was that insensitive?" I swallow hard. "Sorry, I forgot for a second. About your mom."

"Insensitive?" Kellen shifts on his feet, his Blizzard-branded duffel in one hand and my rolling suitcase in the other. "No way. I'm not jealous of other people having good parents. I'm happy to see people loving and supporting their children."

"Like you do," I say.

Kellen locks eyes with me and his mouth twitches. That mouth.

The things he did with that mouth.

I'm happy I made the decision at the retreat to give in to a physical relationship with Kellen. The problem is, I'm not sure I've protected my heart like Raleigh and I discussed I should. I'm afraid it might have a complete mind of its own at this point.

We stare at each other for a second.

"That's your room." I point to the one across from mine, willing my heart to slow its roll in my chest.

Kellen nods. "I'm gonna go call Ava. I'll join you guys in a few." He disappears into his room and shuts the door with a gentle click.

I shut myself in mine. It's not a child's bedroom—I was never a child while Mom's lived here. It's decorated in greens and grays and looks like something out of a Pottery Barn catalogue. I'm not sure why it's even 'my' room.

Because my mom made it that way. I don't thank her enough for being the amazing person that she is. She's kind and welcoming and always on my and Atticus's side. It's easy to forget that not everyone has that.

* * *

Mom refills my wine glass with a fresh bottle of the delicious Merlot from her vineyard. It feels so good to relax and hang out with her, Atticus, and Kellen.

The boys only have one glass each. They have a game Friday night and were all given strict instructions not to party too hard over Thanksgiving or eat too much unhealthy food. But Atticus convinces Kellen to go out for a drink later, my brother mumbling something about me stealing his best friend.

"Did Lucy tell you Ava is obsessed with her dog?" Kellen glances at me.

"Is she? That's so sweet." Mom shakes her head. She's already asked him a hundred questions about his daughter. And Kellen shared a hundred pictures of Ava from his phone.

"She's responsible for his name." Kellen shakes his head. "Again, sorry about that, Lucy."

I shrug and smile, my chest warming at the easy way Mom and Kellen are interacting.

"Mister Barky?" Mom attempts.

"Mister Barky McBarkface." I lift my wine glass up. "Ava wins the best name award for sure. I'll admit it's a bit of a mouthful."

"Seriously, you do not have to keep that name." Kellen chuckles.

"Maybe I'll shorten it to MBM. Or even M. That's a lot easier to say." The second glass of wine is making me feel light and silly.

Mom laughs and shakes her head. "I can't believe you took Ron's dog."

"What was I gonna do?"

"Hmm." Mom narrows her eyes a bit and smiles at me fondly. "Still, Lucy, one of your weirder life choices."

"Maybe."

"She's going through a midlife crisis," Atticus says matter-of-factly.

"I'm only thirty-three."

"A one-third life crisis?"

"You're only a few years behind me, brother."

"Four years! That's a lifetime." Atticus pretends to look deeply offended.

I groan and can't help but laugh.

Kellen watches our banter and chuckles.

After the boys head out for their drink, Mom and I finish up in the kitchen and sit on the couch to chat about the details of our lives. When I'm falling asleep on the soft cushions, she leads me to my room and tucks me in like I'm eight years old again.

I text Kellen from the warm, comfy bed.

ME

Hope you're having fun! Good night

Kellen responds immediately, like he's watching his phone instead of living in the moment with my brother.

KELLEN

Good night, my turkey. Sorry we couldn't hang out tonight

ME

No problem. Have fun with Atticus, chicken

ME

Oh, see that? Yours is a food and mine is an animal but both can be either

KELLEN

I smile and fall asleep with my phone on the pillow next to me.

CHAPTER 27

Gobble Gobble

LUCY

Thursday, November 28

This day has been so good.

We all got up to help Mom cook the Thanksgiving meal, served around noon so we could drive up to northern Virginia to see our father later today. There was way too much food, and Mom had picked up pumpkin, apple, and vanilla creme pies at a bakery in her small town. Kellen stole a kiss in the pantry while Atticus was helping Mom do dishes, and I ran my foot up his leg under the table while we ate dessert. He smirked, and I couldn't stop smiling.

Now we're walking into the restaurant to meet Richard, and I'm filled with dread. Why do I even care what my father thinks? When I left for Colorado, it all seemed so important. But spending time with Kellen and his family made me realize that's what's really important.

Richard already thinks the world revolves around him. By fake dating Kellen just to make him mad, I pretty much confirmed that.

Everything feels different now.

I... don't care what my father thinks of me.

Richard is sitting across the room at a table alone, sipping a glass of amber-colored liquid. Guess his wife didn't feel the need to join us.

Atticus follows the hostess, and I trail behind, with Kellen bringing up the rear. I can feel his stare on my back, and he touches my elbow. Now he can touch me openly because we have an excuse. An audience of my father.

We're putting on another performance.

"Ready for this?" he asks when I slow.

"Sure." I nod, then crinkle my nose. "Actually? No, not really. I kinda wish we'd cancelled." Not cancelled bringing Kellen home to D.C. but cancelled seeing my father.

But that was the whole point.

"It'll be fine. Just hold my hand." Kellen winks at me before grabbing my hand and linking our fingers together. I breathe out a laugh and my anxiety decreases just a tad.

Dad stands at the table and shakes Atticus's hand, then steps forward to embrace me. Unlike my mom's hug, this one is not nearly as warm or loving. More like a stiff, compulsory pat on the back.

"How are you, Lucy darling?" Dad steps back to study my face, ignoring Kellen standing next to me.

He knows who Kellen is. I told him Kellen was joining us for Thanksgiving. That he's a star hockey player. Atticus's teammate.

My boyfriend.

"Great." I step back. "Dad, this is Kellen. My boyfriend."

"Ah. I didn't realize you were bringing someone, Lucy." Richard makes a face, like he truly didn't know.

"Yes, you did. I told you."

"Well. Hello." There's no follow up of an interesting question or a welcome or anything. Dad holds out his hand, and Kellen pumps it a little too hard.

"Where's Carrie?" I look around pointedly, as if she's hiding under a table or behind a plant. Dad's fourth wife is nice enough, but she's not been overly interested in hanging with me, even when I lived in D.C.

"My wife is with her sister this evening. She sends her apologies and greetings."

She probably doesn't want to spend any more time than required with my father.

We settle in our seats. Richard orders another whisky, Kellen orders a bottle of wine, and I pick a bunch of appetizers for the table. No one is particularly hungry after our meal with Mom earlier. Richard glances at the entrance to the restaurant. It's quiet, but there are more people than I'd have thought on Thanksgiving night. I guess not everyone has someone cooking them a delicious meal.

"How are things in Colorado?" Dad turns to me.

"Awesome," I say, a touch too brightly. "Everything is going great."

Dad gives a sidelong glance at Kellen.

"I've heard you've been keeping busy." He emphasizes the word *busy*, as if it's dirty.

I blink. To be fair, I did do a few dirty things.

Atticus snorts.

Dad drains his golden drink.

A server brings his refill plus three glasses and a bottle of Malbec. After Kellen approves the wine, the server pours, and I eagerly grab one and not-gracefully take a large gulp before responding.

I don't have a game tomorrow.

"Work is going great. I love working for the Blizzard, actually. It's a lot of fun. The administrative staff gets included in team building and other activities. It's a really positive vibe." The words pour out of me in a rambling sort of way, and my voice is too high and tinny.

Sigh. Good start.

Richard makes an unimpressed *mmm* sound. "Well, when

you're done playing around over there, your job, and your whole life, is waiting for you in D.C."

What the hell does that mean?

But I know, of course.

Golden boy Ron is probably in Richard's ear, telling my father how he's asked me to come back, and I've said no.

"Dad." I attempt to infuse a warning tone to my voice. "I quit DC FC. And I'm not coming back."

The server returns with a bread basket.

"Listen, Lucy. I know things got rough with you and Ron—"

"Got rough?" I can't help but scoff at my ex's name. I take another gulp of wine.

"—but surely that's not a real reason to give up a great job? A solid future with DC FC? A wedding to—"

"I'm done at DC FC." I cut him off. I don't want to hear about a wedding to Ron. "I love working at the Blizzard." I grab a piece of warm bread and shove it in my mouth. It's too hot, and I almost spit it out but suffer through the burning as punishment for going through with this dinner.

"So you're not applying for that England job anymore?" Richard's voice is calm and collected. He never freaks out. Never raises his voice. He's perfectly logical, like some kind of AI robot.

"Of course I am." Crumbs literally fall out of my mouth.

Kellen huffs a quiet laugh and slides my water closer to me. I take a sip so I can speak with dignity again, then chase the water with wine.

"I'm absolutely applying for the Winchester FC job," I say when my mouth is empty. "I had a video interview yesterday. I'm not staying in Fort Collins."

There's marked silence. Kellen places a hand on my thigh. Everyone at the table watches the motion.

"Lucy and I are really happy together," Kellen says.

Atticus downs his wine and waves at the server for another

bottle. I would enjoy reminding my brother about his game tomorrow, but I'd never do that in front of our father.

"You just heard her, she's not staying," Richard snaps at Kellen, who doesn't react.

I practically gasp, but my breath and my words get stuck in my throat. Kellen's mouth narrows into a thin line.

My father turns to me. "I'd heard all about you and the hockey player from Paul. He called me a few weeks ago."

Wow. Our plan worked for me too. Just as we hoped.

"Everything doesn't have to be forever, Richard." Kellen says, as if my father is engaging in a conversation instead of ignoring him.

Kellen's words linger in the air, then settle down onto my heart in a heavy way.

"And with love, it often is not." My dad agrees, not looking at Kellen.

I don't think that's what Kellen meant. He didn't mean get married four times and continue to trade your wives for younger models. I wonder how long he and Carrie will last. It's about time for the next divorce.

Ugh, I hate that my father makes me think that way.

Kellen subtly squeezes my thigh. Is he doing it for show? Reassuring me that things won't end? Or maybe that it's okay that they will. I slowly twist my wine glass on the white tablecloth.

Either way, I love the weight of his hand on me.

I love *him*.

Shit, no, what? I freeze my hand on the stem of the glass. That can't be true. I shove those three little words into a tiny box to be opened at a much later time. Maybe never.

Because now is not the moment to be questioning if I've let myself fall for my hot hockey player fake boyfriend.

"I've had a great season so far, Richard, in case you were wondering." Atticus leans back in his chair. Our father's jaw clenches. He hates it when Atticus calls him Richard.

They argue back and forth about what defines a great season, and I mostly block them out. Kellen leaves his hand on my thigh, moving it slightly every few minutes.

I turn to Kellen to say something to him—anything—when a movement at the front of the room by the entrance catches my eye.

It's *Ron*.

Ron's here. A desperate squeak escapes my throat.

My ex-fiancé walks up to the hostess stand and talks to the woman before looking around.

"Oh my god," I say. Atticus and Richard stop arguing and everyone looks at me, then follows my gaze.

"Are you fucking kidding me?" Atticus realizes what's got me spooked. He turns back to our father. "You invited *Ron* to join us?"

The waiter comes at that moment and distributes plates of appetizers. Then the man pulls another chair to the table and nods at Richard.

"What did you do, Dad?" I whisper.

"Oh, darling. We can all be mature adults, can't we?" He doesn't look one bit sorry for this situation.

Ron slowly walks our way, eyes locked with mine, looking just as freaked out as I feel. This is not happening. As much as I wanted to show my father and Ron that I'm fine on my own, I never wanted to look at my ex in person again. I broke up with him, and I meant it. It was over when I walked out. I had no intentions of going there ever again.

Kellen leans his lips close to my ear.

"Hey, I'm right here, okay? Don't worry. You don't have to say anything to him if you don't want to." Anger tinges his voice, but his warm breath tickles my neck, and I'm comforted by his presence.

"Hello, Lucy," Ron says, nodding at me. "How are you?" His face is pale, and his voice shaky. He didn't know I was going to be here with Kellen. Or maybe he didn't know I'd be here at all.

As angry as I still am at Ron for what he did during our relationship, this situation is all on my father.

I swallow and attempt to speak, but it's like a whole bag of cotton balls have been shoved down my throat, and I can't get a word out.

"I'm Kellen Bassey." Kellen stares hard at Ron. "Lucy's boyfriend."

Ron blinks at Kellen, then slides his gaze to me. "You have a boyfriend?"

So word *hadn't* gotten back to Ron that I'm dating Kellen. Dad didn't tell him. Of course he didn't. He still wants us to get back together.

Our plan didn't work perfectly after all.

I nod but still can't manage to speak.

"Don't talk to her. After what you did, you don't get to talk to my girlfriend." Kellen clearly emphasizes the word *my* and *girlfriend*, and my breath catches. "You blew your chance with Lucy." He takes his hand off my thigh and entwines his fingers with mine, thumping our hands right on the table, a show for Ron.

Atticus literally laughs out loud.

I turn and stare at Kellen's profile, my heart beating loudly in my chest.

"I was hoping we could talk," Ron says to me. "But clearly this isn't the time. Maybe tomorrow—"

"I'm gonna stop you right there." Kellen rolls his neck and bones crack. "Lucy's not going to talk to you, and her dating life is none of your business. If you have something to say, then go ahead right now. But please keep it civil. It's a holiday. We're trying to enjoy a meal."

I press my lips together and suppress a hysterical giggle. Kellen turns to me and winks. Everyone sees it.

Somewhere at the table Richard is saying something to Ron, then to Kellen, but all I know is that this man next to me is picking a fight with my ex-fiancé to defend my honor.

And it's the hottest thing I've ever seen in my life.

Ron scurries off a minute later, declining Richard's offer to have him join us. The added chair remains empty at the table.

We leave the restaurant after scarfing down the appetizers and engaging in twenty minutes of awkward small talk. Richard briefly shakes Atticus's hand and ignores Kellen. He embraces me before striding quickly away. We don't discuss the Ron incident.

There's mostly silence on the way back to Mom's. I fill her in on all the events and Mom's appropriately shocked and appalled. Atticus crashes early. Kellen goes to talk to Bri and Ava in his room. I change into comfy sweatpants and a tank top and sink onto my bed.

It's been a long day.

I finally have time to think about the three words that popped into my head earlier.

There is no room for me to fall in love.

I lay back on the comforter. I gotta talk myself out of this.

There's a soft knock at my door.

"Come in," I call softly.

Kellen walks into my room. My chest immediately pounds, and I scramble to stand.

"Hey," Kellen says, stopping close to me. "I know it's almost midnight, but I wanted to check on you. Are you okay? After that dinner?" He reaches out and places a hand on each of my biceps. His touch is warm and firm and gentle at the same time.

"Yeah. Thanks for what you did."

"What'd I do?"

"You made me feel like I'm not crazy. You defended me. You put Dad in his place. Told off Ron. Made me feel..." But I don't know how to finish. Kellen's moving his hands slowly down my arms. His fingers leave a tingly trail, and my body warms in response.

"Made you feel what?" His eye are bright. I move forward and wrap my arms around his waist and rest my cheek against his chest.

"You made me feel good."

Kellen's chest is warm, covered with a thin t-shirt. His heart pounds against my cheek.

"Did we do what we needed to?" He wraps his arms around me and kisses the top of my head, letting his lips linger.

"Yeah. We did it."

Kellen rubs my back, and I close my eyes.

I'm falling for Kellen Bassey.

Shit.

I pull back and look up at him, pressing my body against his. I'm suddenly extra aware of the thin layers of clothing between us. Nothing stopping us from being together. A repeat of the night in Wyoming.

But is it really the same?

"Lucy," he says.

"Yes?"

Then Kellen leans his face down and presses his lips to mine, leaving one hand around my waist and moving the other into the back of my hair, burying it in my curls.

It feels like the first kiss, but it's not. Not even close. Electricity runs between us, but we take our time. Small kisses turn into longer ones. Mouths open and our tongues connect. I run my hands up his chest and want there to be less between us.

This. This is everything I need and want. After the day I've had —the year I've had—if it all led up to this moment with Kellen, I'd do it all again.

But there's more.

I want more.

CHAPTER 28

Midnight

KELLEN

Lucy presses her body against mine, and I'm immediately hard. Harder. I was ready the second I saw her standing in her bedroom in that skimpy tank top and sweatpants sitting low on her hips, revealing her soft belly and the curves of her hips. I press her gently against me.

This woman is falling right into my heart.

I could not believe her asshole father invited her dick of an ex-fiancé to dinner. What would've happened if I wasn't there? He would have joined them, and Richard would've continued to push them together?

Over my fucking dead body.

I take my kiss with Lucy deeper and my hands lower, pushing her sweatpants down on her hips so I can feel more of her skin.

It's been almost two weeks since we slept together at the retreat. I've grabbed time with her every chance I've gotten, but it's not enough. It never seems to be enough.

"Kellen, I want you," her voice is a whisper against my mouth.

I could kiss Lucy all night and day, but I also want to be inside her. And the way she's pressing up against me, rubbing her hips against my jogging pants? I don't need her to tell me she wants me.

I move a hand along her waist and to her stomach, then down until my fingers are playing with the waistband of her sweatpants. She presses against my hand, and I smile into our kiss before lowering my fingers along her skin, inside her underwear, and finally onto her hot, slick center.

"Lucy, you're so wet for me."

"Why is this so good?" she asks with a moan as I stroke a finger along her wet opening. Our kisses pause as she breathes heavily into my neck, moving her body against me.

"You deserve to feel amazing. You are incredible. Let me make you feel good." I want to make her feel like no man ever has. I want her to know she's the only one in my life. The only woman I fantasize about when I go to bed each night.

The only one I want to be with.

I shake the thoughts out of my head and focus on the physical. I keep stroking, and she clenches around me. I push harder, faster, until she's moaning my name and coming onto my hand.

I'm harder than I've ever been but this is not about me. I leave my fingers inside her until her breathing steadies.

"God, Kellen." She leans her head against my chest. "We didn't even get our clothes off yet." She laughs and I kiss her head, then push her sweatpants and underwear down around her ankles.

She steps out of them and gives me a wicked smile.

I step back and look down at her. "That's better."

"I'm not naked yet." Lucy pulls off her tank top in one swift motion and there. Now she's naked. Her breasts bounce as she rolls her shoulders back.

She's incredible.

"This feels different with you." Lucy steps forward and runs her hand along my cock though my pants.

"I know," I murmur and cup a breast with my hand. She moves her hand slowly up and down and it's almost too much. I walk her backwards, and she falls back onto the bed.

She's waiting for me. I grab the condom from my pocket and

strip my clothes off before crawling on top of her until I get to her breasts, where I play with her nipples until they harden into peaks in my mouth. I rip the condom open and slide it on without letting her out of my mouth.

"Kellen," she says, like it's a complete sentence. Her hips lift off the bed, and I nudge her thighs apart and let my cock tickle her entrance.

I love my name on her lips. I release a nipple and kiss her mouth slowly. Gently. Reverently. I push the tip into her, and she moans, eyes rolling back in her head. She's warm and wet and a perfect fit for me.

"You make me crazy."

Lucy wiggles down until I'm farther in, and then we're completely together and everything feels right and good, and I can't help but think that this is meant to be, that I am with the woman I'm supposed to be with, no matter how it started. Lucy pushes me off and then she's on top, breathing heavily as she rides me, and I'm transfixed with the way she throws her head back and drops her jaw, her face open and free and in the throes of pleasure. I slide my hand between us and massage her clit to help her come.

This is all I need. To watch Lucy Knox rock on top of me.

I wish I could convince myself that's all this is. That we're just sleeping together.

But that would be a lie, and I can't lie to myself.

There's a much bigger storm brewing inside me.

She gasps and moans my name again. That's the only name I want coming out of her mouth like that.

When we're both done, she opens her eyes and rolls off and next to me.

"Lucy, that was incredible," I whisper.

"Yeah." Lucy turns her head to me and smiles, post orgasm relaxation on her face. "You are so good at that."

"At what?"

"All of it."

I shift to my side and run my finger gently from the base of her neck down between her breasts and to her lower abdomen, then trace loops around her belly and back up.

Lucy moves toward me, and I admire the view of her full breasts, the valley of her waist, the rise of her hips.

I'm so fucking lucky to be here right now.

I can almost imagine that she's not trying to move to England. That her job with the Blizzard isn't temporary. That we started out real, not fake.

Lucy closes her eyes and snuggles toward me. I shift onto my back and pull her against me until her head lays on my chest, red curls tickling my biceps. I tug the sheet up over us, and she sighs, her breathing deep and steady.

Lucy Knox falling asleep in my arms in her mother's house on Thanksgiving? That was not on my bingo card for this year. But it feels pretty fucking good.

Almost too good.

Because I'm afraid of Lucy.

Afraid that I think she belongs here. With me. With me and Ava. Her and her stupid dog.

But Lucy seems totally okay with the fact that she's here for just one season. She's never wavered in her conversations about the job in England. Never doubted it's the right thing to do.

She might be okay with all that, but it's becoming increasingly clear that I am not.

CHAPTER 29

The Worst Skater

LUCY

Thursday, December 5

"Have you ever ice skated before?" Kellen chuckles as I cling to his arm like it's the last floating door and I've just fallen off the Titanic.

"Yes," I hiss. "A few times when I was younger."

It's late and quiet in the arena. Thanksgiving was a week ago, and our break up date isn't for another nine days.

I've had the most fun with Kellen over the past week. Sure, he's busy with practice and games and his daughter, but he'll stop by my office to say hi every day after practice. We sneak kisses and then he saunters out like it's nothing. On Tuesday, he was in the gym for an extra-long workout, and I worked late... And then we locked the door to my office and made out against the wall like a pair of horny teens.

The best part is that this relationship is HR vetted, so we don't even have to really hide. But we do because we've not told anyone this is real.

I haven't told him I love him. That would be stupid. I'm leaving. My life isn't here. And I don't even really believe that I'm in love with him. Except those words keep going through my head like a cable news headline whenever I'm with him and sometimes I have to bite my tongue so they don't slip out.

"Remember what we did out there?" Kellen nods to outside the rink where we had a mini lesson. Where it's safe and not slippery.

"Yeah, I remember."

"What are you supposed to be doing?"

"Small steps," I grumble.

"And what are you doing?"

"No steps. Just holding onto you so I don't die."

"I'm having a hard time understanding how your brother is a NHL player, but you can't even stand up on the ice."

"Shut up!" I attempt to let go and stomp off but immediately lose my balance. "It was so much easier when we weren't on a slippery surface."

Kellen grabs me by the waist and laughs.

"You should see Ava skate. She's pretty impressive."

"Good for Ava," I say, but I can't help but be impressed. That little girl is good at everything.

Last night the weather was unseasonably warm, so we got Ava's soccer team together for a fun reunion scrimmage on a lit field. The little kids screaming for me—*Coach Lucy, look at what I can do!*—warmed my heart. They begged me to play with them, so I did. I can at least keep up with the Snowballs. Ava is the biggest sweetheart of them all, which isn't surprising given how amazing her dad is.

Ugh. I'm such a goner.

"I was hoping we could pass a puck with each other, but I'm not sure we'll even get to the hockey stick part of the evening."

"This is hopeless."

"Try marching." Kellen lifts his skates up one at a time. "Might help you get a better feel for the ice."

"Like this?" I try marching and almost bite it. "I feel like you're trying to get me back for making you roar like a mountain lion on our hike." He cracks up, but marching helps, and I feel a bit steadier.

"How about some short, slow glides?" Kellen shows me what he means. The thing is, he looks like a graceful swan when he does it, and I'm sure I look more like an uncoordinated penguin.

I try though, and it sort of works. I make a few short glides without holding onto Kellen's arm, then I throw a giant smile backwards at him before falling.

I groan and prop myself up on my elbows. I think I broke my ass.

"How do you do this and play hockey at the same time? I don't understand."

Kellen laughs and holds his hand out. "It's second nature. Like walking. We've all been skating since we were little."

I reach for his hand, but instead of letting him lift me up, I tug him down onto me, and he lets himself fall. Kellen holds himself up on either side with a grin that makes my breath catch, then closes the remaining gap between us to kiss me.

"Come on. Let's get you up." His lips tickle mine as he speaks.

"But I'm much less likely to fall while I'm down here." I let him pull me up.

"Just stay standing and I'll pull you along," he says, facing me and planting his hands on my waist.

"Okay," I laugh. "Don't let me fall."

Kellen pulls me gently, and I'm impressed (but not surprised) by his ability to skate backwards.

We're laughing the whole time, and when we get done with a full lap, I tell him I need a break, then point to the side.

"Can we sit there?"

"Sure." Kellen grabs my hand and drags me to the penalty box —too quickly, and I see my life flash before my eyes—and pulls me onto his lap on the bench.

He kisses me deeply and lays a hand on the outside of my thigh.

"This is a lot more fun than when I'm normally in here," he says against my mouth, and I smile and keep kissing him.

Sometimes I wish we could be a normal couple. The secrecy is making us get creative about spending time together. Kellen teaching me how to skate is certainly more memorable than watching a movie.

I'm afraid it's making me fall even deeper in love with him.

And I get it. His family comes first. I'm a temporary person in his life. In Ava's life. As much as my heart twinges when I think about walking away from Kellen, Ava, MBM, my brother.

That secret—the one where I love him—will stay locked inside me forever. I won't tell Raleigh or January or my mom or Atticus or anyone.

And especially not Kellen.

CHAPTER 30

(Not Really) Sneaking Around

KELLEN

Saturday, December 14

"So you listened to me," Bri says.

We're standing at her kitchen counter. I'm chopping up a cucumber, and she's peeking in on the crockpot mac and cheese we made for a house full of Ava's friends, here for her sixth birthday party.

"What do you mean? I often block you out, so you'll have to be specific."

But I'm sure I know where this is going.

She puts her hands on her hips.

"Three weeks ago. We talked at the KFDPC meeting. About Lucy. Who was your fake girlfriend."

"Is? Is."

"See? That's what I'm talking about. Do you still not know what's going on?"

I don't make eye contact. *Slice, slice, slice.*

"Lucy's here, at our daughter's birthday party. Ava adores her. Ava's friends adore her. I even like her, which is unexpected."

I stop cutting and look up. "I don't see what the big deal is."

"Kellen." Bri rubs her forehead. "Lucy gave Ava her favorite birthday present."

"The stuffed dog that looks like Mister Barky McBarkface?"

"Yeah. That one."

I shrug. "Ava loves MBM. And yeah, she loves Lucy. That's all this is." I toss the cut cucumber into a bowl.

But my heart thumps in my chest as I know I'm full of shit. I know that's not all this is. And Bri does too.

Bri rolls her eyes and stirs the crock pot with a big spoon.

I grab a green pepper and chop.

"And remember, I also invited Atticus, Lachlan, and Harley."

I don't like how Bri can read the situation so perfectly.

Bri opens her mouth, but before she can say something back, Ava saves me by bursting into the kitchen with a trail of five- and six-year-old girls and boys behind her. They're making a conga line, one of them carrying an iPad with Taylor Swift blasting out of its tiny speakers. Lucy is right in the middle of it all.

Bri and I cheer as they march by, and Lucy throws the biggest grin at me, her cheeks flushed, her hair wild.

When they've descended the basement stairs, Bri spins my way.

"I'm not sure if you're in denial or you're lying to me. But... maybe figure your shit out." Then she stomps after the kids.

It's been a little over two weeks since Thanksgiving, but it feels like Lucy and I have lived an entire life together.

And my hockey game has definitely not suffered.

The Blizzard is on a winning streak, and during the last home game, I was on absolute fire. Not quite the hat trick from the first game Lucy went to, but knowing she was watching from the stands was everything. It allowed me to focus. To score. To assist Harley's goal. I easily ignored the other team's trash talk. I saved Lachlan from a fight. We won 4-0. Should've been an even higher scoring game, but I'll take it.

Lucy and I need to fit it all in because there's a timer on this relationship.

The KFDPC group chat had been blessedly quiet, up until yesterday when the conversation about our fake breakup kicked up.

Tomorrow. My insides twist thinking about it.

The main floor of Bri's house is much quieter with all the kids downstairs. Only the hockey boys' voices in the family room mix with the moms who stuck around for the party.

Lucy comes up from the basement without a trail of kids behind her. She moves next to me, looking around before ducking under my arm and wedging herself between me and the countertop.

"They're all downstairs," I say into mounds of curly red hair, breathing her in. She presses her cheek to mine.

Without thinking, I take her face in my hands and press my lips to hers.

Fuck, those lips.

I pull back and slide a finger under her chin, memorizing the scattering of freckles over her nose and cheekbones.

I thought we could get this out of our systems by hooking up all the time. That we'd get sick of each other.

But we haven't.

I want more.

The team has been traveling a lot over the past two weeks, but while home, I spent every moment I could with Lucy.

It even ate into my Ava time, which makes me uncomfortable.

But I cannot resist this woman.

I grab Lucy's hand and pull her around the corner into the mudroom area, strewn with shoes and jackets, but quiet and absent of children and interested adults. Lucy slides her hands up my chest, and I press into her, kissing her deeply, wishing we were truly alone.

The room falls away and there are only her lips, her curls tickling my neck, her waist under my hands, her warm breath in my mouth. We kiss as the world lazily spins, until a scream of delight from the basement startles us apart.

Lucy's cheeks are flushed, and her lips swollen with my kisses. Exactly as they should be.

"Wow," she says quietly, green eyes wide and locked with mine.

I nod. What else can I do?

"Lucy?" Bri calls.

Lucy detangles herself from me and glides out of the mudroom. Her and Bri talk and laugh, and then the door to the basement opens and shuts.

I press my palms on my eyes, willing my misbehaving heart to stand down. After a few deep breaths, I return to the counter and my half-chopped pepper.

"So your sister is working for the Blizzard?" one of the moms asks in the family room, around the corner and out of sight.

"Yup," Atticus says. "Just for one season though. Not even for the whole season, actually. She's trying to get a job with a pro soccer team in England."

"That's wild," another mom says. "So she's here temporarily?"

"If you want to know if Ava's dad is going to be single again soon, just ask," a third woman says. They think they're being quiet, but the voices carry to the kitchen. They must think I'm downstairs.

There are a few low laughs from the hockey boys, because they all know the real deal. Well, most of the real deal.

I've kept it purely platonic with all the single moms and women associated with Ava. No soccer coaches or ballet instructors or girl scout leaders. I've never wanted to get messy like that.

But I can't imagine anything messier than the situation with Lucy now.

"She worked for our father's soccer team back in D.C.," Atticus adds.

Lachlan appears in the kitchen doorway.

"Didn't know you were in here," he says and lowers his voice. "There's a mom in there that has a thing for you, I think."

I grunt and shrug.

"I can't date my daughter's friends' mom."

"But you'll date your teammate's sister?"

I look up, and Lachlan's eyebrows are raised.

The door to the basement bursts open, Ava leading the way with Mister Barky McBarkface in her arms.

"Piñata time! Come on, Daddy!" She leads a line of kids into the kitchen.

"Hold on!" Bri squeezes to the front of the group and points to the mudroom. "Everyone get your jackets and come outside to hear the rules. After, we'll have dinner."

"Come on, kids!" Lucy appears and leads the way into the mudroom. I wink at her as she passes, and she grins back. A curl hangs over her right eye, and I desperately want to touch it.

A herd of moms help with kids' hats and gloves and puffy jackets. Lachlan heads out back with Lucy, throwing his arm around her shoulders and whispering something in her ear that makes her laugh.

I sigh and hang my head. Lucy blends in perfectly with my family and my friends. With my life, really.

But tomorrow?

Tomorrow it's all over. My heart rate picks up, and I head out back to help manage the piñata.

I touch Lucy on the back as I pass by, letting my fingers linger on her jacket.

We'll have a public breakup. Then we can both move on with our lives. I can get back to focusing on only hockey and Ava. She can get back to trying to move across the Atlantic Ocean.

No matter how I feel about it, this thing with Lucy Knox will definitely be over.

CHAPTER 31

Fake Breakup

LUCY

Sunday, December 15

This morning, I felt like I was dressing for my own funeral. Last night after Ava's party was over, I stayed and hung out at Bri's house with Kellen and the boys. Everyone helped clean up, and Bri put on a movie. Kellen tucked the birthday girl into bed and then sat next to me on the couch, our thighs almost touching. The lights were dimmed low, and he put his arm around the couch behind me, not on my shoulders, but close.

I half hoped he would ask me to come to his house after the movie. But he didn't, and that's probably for the best, so I just shuffled out along with the others and left him standing on Bri's porch.

When I got home, there were text messages waiting for me. I had a surge of hope, like he'd beg me to come back.

But he didn't.

KELLEN

Thanks for everything tonight. I loved seeing
you with Ava. She loves you. She fell asleep
with MBM (the stuffed animal) tucked under
her arm

KELLEN

And thank you for helping with my situation.
You made everything better this fall. I'm so glad
you came to FoCo

KELLEN

Good night, Lucy

I pressed my phone to my chest and shut my eyes. What can I say to him? How can I sum up how I feel about him and Ava and this town?

I couldn't come up with anything that felt good enough.

ME

I'm glad I came too

ME

Good night

He didn't respond back.

I'm reading the texts again as I make my way up the stairs to the level of the arena with access to the corporate sponsorship box.

Those felt like goodbye texts.

They are.

But my phone buzzes in my hand and it's a new text in our chain.

I pause outside the second-floor stairwell to read.

KELLEN

Game's about to start. Good luck with our
breakup. I'm so sorry I can't be there to break
up with you in person 😂

ME

It was good while it lasted, puppy

KELLEN

Meh. Listen, sweet potato, I hate to say this, but I've had better fake girlfriends

ME

You absolutely have not

ME

And that's a repeat name

KELLEN

So is yours

I crack up, but there's an ache in my chest.

KELLEN

But I'm serious. Sorry you have to face them alone. Let me know how it goes

ME

Honestly? Savannah seems harmless

KELLEN

She does appear that way these days. But only because I've had you to protect me

ME

Thankfully. Because have you seen you? You definitely need protecting. You should try working out

He sends a laughing emoji and then a heart emoji, and my body warms.

Then I shake my head.

What am I doing in this hallway flirting with my soon-to-be ex-boyfriend? I take one last look at the text chain and enter the suite, my heart racing.

I've got my PR name tag on and if anyone asks, I'm looking for one of the local sponsors who I actually know is *not* attending. And if they show up? I chat with them. No big deal.

Savannah looks up when I walk in, and her eyes flit up and down my body, not unkindly. I'm wearing jeans, a Blizzard t-shirt, black flats, and a long black sweater. Much different from her belted gray dress and sexy black heels, high and expensive looking.

I'm not wearing Kellen's jersey.

A quick glance at the rink shows the players getting into position to start the game. I don't let my eyes scan the team for Kellen. I'm not here to watch hockey.

I spent all morning going over how I'll work into conversation that Kellen and I broke up. I assumed it'll be Savannah I talk to, and I'm right. She walks right over.

"Hello, Lucy. Come to watch Kellen?" Savannah's smiling at me and looks completely non-threatening. Sweet and lovely, actually. If anything, she seems lonely. She's looking for friends, just like the rest of us.

No wonder Kellen was nice to her. He's a good guy.

But here it is—the perfect opening.

I open my mouth to respond, but my throat tightens, and my eyes suddenly sting. These words are the last ones I want to be saying. I don't have to use my acting skills to appear like I'm getting over a breakup.

I'm really doing it.

"Actually, I wanted to see if one of the sponsors was going to watch the game, but it looks like they're not here." I make a show of looking around, and I hope she doesn't suggest I stay and wait for them to arrive. "And Kellen and I aren't together anymore."

Savannah's eyebrows shoot up. "Really? Oh no." She sounds genuinely sorry. "I thought you two were looking cozy at the coffee shop a few days ago?"

I shrug. One day last week we'd met up at Deep Roots Cafe for a coffee before work. It was kind of a bookend to the first public appearance we made back in early October.

"You okay? You just got really pale." Savannah reaches out and touches my arm gently, her face creased with concern.

"Yeah, of course. Things end. It's okay. I'm only doing a mat leave cover here anyway, so it wasn't going to last forever." My voice hitches on the word forever.

"What a shame." Savannah looks at me intensely, her gaze flitting from eye to eye. "Need anything? Girls night out? I'm meeting up with Lina for drinks right before Christmas."

I blink. "Um, I'm okay, really."

Actually, that sounds fantastic. I could use more women friends here in Fort Collins. I have Raleigh and January, but we're always scattered all over the place.

"Oh. Well, good." She drops her hand from my arm. "Glad you're okay."

"Savannah?" Paul calls from across the suite, then raises a hand to me.

"Enjoy the game." And with that, Savannah walks away from me, returning to Paul's side. The suited man he was talking to turns to her.

I stand for a few more minutes, pretending to wait for the fake corporate sponsor I mentioned to Savannah and watching the start of the game. My eyes find Kellen on the ice, and I watch him race around the rink with my brother and their teammates. I think about the disastrous but charming skating lesson Kellen gave me and regret we won't get to try again.

Why do I feel like my heart just got ripped out?

After the first period is halfway over, I slip out of the suite. I pause outside the door and lean against the wall, willing my heart to slow down, pushing away feelings of devastation mixed with relief.

That's it? That's the whole breakup?

Of course it is. What did I expect? A full-blown investigation? Savannah doesn't really care about me, or who Kellen dates. Neither does Paul.

I'll send one more text to Kellen. He won't get it until after the game.

ME

I guess now you're my fake ex-boyfriend

ME

It's been fun hanging out with you these last few months

ME

Hope you win today!

Hope you win today? Real smooth. I slip my phone into my back pocket.

That's it. No more texting. It'll only hurt. It already hurts. Hurts that I won't get to tell him all the random nothings of my day. No more stolen kisses. No more hanging out with Ava—oh, I'll miss that little girl. No more stupid food and animal pet names.

No more *us*.

I walk out of the arena, stopping by my office to grab my purse, and head to Atticus's apartment.

It's only when I'm almost home do I realize that Savannah might tell Paul how upset I looked, and Paul might tell my father, and my father might tell Ron—

And I don't care.

None of that matters.

CHAPTER 32

No Thank You

KELLEN

Sunday, December 29

It's been two weeks since Lucy and I broke up.

After her last texts to me confirming the breakup on that day, she hasn't responded to my messages. I guess I'd hoped that we'd continue our flirty banter and stolen kisses.

But now *I've* gotten the message.

Ava spent the night at my house on Christmas Eve, and Bri came over in the morning so we could both watch her open presents from us and Santa. I sent Lucy a Merry Christmas text. No response.

We're over.

Everything else in my life has been great since Thanksgiving.

The Blizzard is on a winning streak, and I've been at the top of my game. Paul gave me a *Good game, Bassey* on Monday.

Savannah acknowledges me, but it's not sketchy at all. There's been nothing about me and her on any gossip websites. I'll probably still keep my distance. I don't want to create any new problems.

But there's been no trade rumors posted about me or anyone

from the team. I'm feeling optimistic that I don't have to worry about that anymore. I've decided that I'm going to talk to Coach Jackson about my lingering concerns after the holidays, just to make sure.

"Hello? Kellie? Are you with us?" Lachlan snaps his fingers right in front of my face.

I shake my head and mentally return to the bar. "Yeah, yeah, sorry."

"Then take your shot, mate." Lachlan holds up a shot glass, and I clink mine to his and Atticus's, knocking it back. "We have no game tomorrow, and then it's New Year's Eve. So relax a little."

We got back late this afternoon from being on the road for the few days after Christmas. Lachlan and Atticus insisted we go out for drinks, and after I tucked Ava in bed at Bri's house, I met them downtown.

Atticus sighs and shakes his head at me. I hate that he's a daily reminder of my split from Lucy. His matching red hair and green eyes. I need to get over that—Atticus is my teammate and my friend, and he's not going anywhere.

"What?" I say.

"Are you still all messed up from what I told you about Lucy?"

"Huh? No. I don't even remember what you said."

Atticus rolls his eyes.

"I'll remind you, mate." Lachlan slaps his hand on my shoulder. "She's flying to England in the beginning of January to interview with her English soccer team."

"You know, her dream job." Atticus watches me, and I feel my right eye twitch under his assessing gaze. "The one she's been obsessing over all season."

"Good for her." I shrug, attempting nonchalance, but it feels like I'm cringing. I found out from Atticus while we were traveling that she'd been invited to interview in person.

"Another round?" Lachlan says, pushing aside a shot glass to pick up his mostly empty pint.

I shrug, but more alcohol is the last thing I need.

"Save the table, we'll get drinks," Atticus says to me, following Lachlan to the bar.

Lucy's really going.

Of course she'll get the job—she's freaking amazing. She's smart and confident and sweet and friendly, never mind beautiful and sexy. Maybe the slightest bit accident prone, but that only makes her more endearing.

I'm desperate to see her. I even bought her a Christmas gift, just in case the opportunity came to give it to her. It's stupid, really, a book called *A Guide to Hiking in Colorado*. There's a whole section on wildlife and what to do if you see a bear, a mountain lion, or a rattlesnake, among others. I put a few sticky notes throughout that chapter with some snarky comments I'd hoped would make her laugh.

I'm not sure I'll ever give it to her.

Because the thing is, even if we were really dating, even if none of it had been fake, it would still be ending. We'd be breaking up soon. Before she heads out of the country. So it's better to do this on my terms—*our* terms—and split before we got in too deep.

Unfortunately, I think I already am.

Lachlan and Atticus come back with drinks and girls. Three of them. One blonde, one brunette, and a redhead. All beautiful, smiling, and happy. Lachlan attaches himself to the brunette, Atticus the blonde, and the redhead slides next to me.

Are you kidding me? All I can see are Lucy's thick red curls, crazy around her head, and the way it felt to bury my hands in them.

"Hey, I'm Mel." Her red hair is long and wavy, and her eyes are blue, not green like Lucy's. She's got a scattering of freckles across her nose. They're different than Lucy's. Lighter, more subtle.

Is this my future? Where I compare every single woman to Lucy Knox?

Sounds fucking miserable.

"This is where you tell me your name." Mel smiles at me and cocks her head. She's wearing a low-cut dress that shows off her shoulders and long, creamy neck. Just enough cleavage is on display to be tempting but not overly showy. She's objectively hot.

"Kellen." I chug half of the fresh pint Lachlan pushes toward me. "I'm afraid I'm not much fun tonight."

She smiles at me, undeterred. "I'm sure we can make some fun together."

But I know we can't. I won't. She's pretty, but I'm zero percent interested.

I drain my beer as Mel tells me a story about her brother showing up to Christmas morning half drunk on Bloody Marys. I tune her out, nodding once in a while so she doesn't force me to engage.

My phone buzzes, and I pull it out so fast I lose my grip and drop it on the bar floor.

"Shit." I bend down to pick it up and flip it over as I stand.

It's a text from Bri with a picture of Ava cuddling the stuffed dog that Lucy gave our daughter for her birthday. She hasn't put that thing down since.

I can't believe Lucy hasn't changed that animal's name from Mister Barky McBarkface—sorry, MBM. Who keeps a name like that? After she swapped it once a week for months, and then she leaves it at the most ridiculous one of all?

"Why are you smiling? What's funny?" Mel has a tentative smile on her face when I clear my thoughts of Lucy and her dog and focus back on the woman in front of me.

"Oh, nothing, but it's my daughter. I need to get home."

"You're a single dad?" Mel looks even more interested. What is it with women and single dads? I think it's the inaccessibility. We're harder to pin down, so it makes them want us more.

"Yes. You have kids?"

"No, no." She shakes her head and widens her eyes. "I'm not really a kid person. I could be, I guess, but I'm just not around them very much these days. Ever, really." She goes on to tell me about her younger siblings who are fresh out of college and how none of them—her included—are anywhere near ready to become parents.

And this makes me think about the sweet relationship Lucy has—had?—with Ava. Bri tells me Lucy sends her pictures of MBM to share. She's still trying to stay in touch with my daughter.

Makes me love her even more.

I intake a breath sharply, and Mel stops talking.

I love her.

I'm in love with her.

As soon as I let myself think the words—embrace them—I know they're true. I've been pushing them away, hiding them, trying to make them disappear, but they've been waiting to pop up. Waiting for the moment I let my guard down.

And that moment is now.

"Shit." I squeeze my eyes shut.

I'm in love with Lucy Knox.

It's been dancing around my subconscious for weeks. Months. And now it's fully front and center.

"Everything okay?" Mel reaches a hand over and places it on my arm. I yank it away.

"Sorry. I have to go." I stand and look over at Lachlan and the brunette and Atticus and the blonde. They're very cozy, and I don't want to interrupt.

"Aw, are you sure?" Mel sticks out her bottom lip and tilts her head. I'm sure that pretty face works on most men. But not me. Not tonight.

"Yeah. Have a good night." I lift my hand to Mel and dart out of the bar.

Once outside, I flip up the hood on my sweatshirt. Fat snowflakes lazily drift from the sky. The cold air feels good. It slaps me awake. Maybe I should have worn a jacket to protect me from the biting winter, but I welcome the sharpness of the December air.

Why didn't I see the truth when it was all around me? When Lucy was with me?

Because I'm sure of it now.

I spent last fall not only fake dating Lucy Knox but also falling in love with her.

Maybe I loved her instantly.

Maybe it was the second I looked up from the ice during that practice back in September and saw her chasing her dog, her belongings flying everywhere, swearing and calling for Waffles.

Or maybe it took longer.

Maybe it was when I watched her as Coach Lucy with Ava, then evolve into Ava's friend.

Maybe it was during one of our fake dates.

Maybe it was at the retreat.

Maybe it was Thanksgiving, when I spent time with Lucy, Atticus, and their mom, and felt like they could be family.

Maybe it was during the skating lesson I gave her, or when I stole kisses from her at that one KFDPC meeting.

Maybe it was when I realized I'd trusted her from the moment I met her. With pictures of Ava, with my secrets, with my heart.

I'm now sure that none of it was fake.

But I've wasted all the time we had. It'll be January in a few days, and she'll fly to England and kick ass at her job interview for the English soccer club.

Then she'll leave.

"Fuck!" I scream into the deserted town center. The fountain is off for the winter, the stores shuttered for the night, and no one is around at this moment.

I love her. I'm in love with her.

I clench my fists as desperation twists into knots in my chest. I unlock my car, parallel parked a few storefronts down from the town square.

It's too late to make it work with Lucy. She's making her dream come true. A dream that doesn't involve me, or Ava, or MBM.

I rest my forehead on my steering wheel as a cold weight settles on my chest. Either I'm having a heart attack, or I've died inside.

I think it's the second one.

CHAPTER 33

(Almost) Midnight Kisses

LUCY

Tuesday, December 31

"Lucy, hurry your ass up and get out here!" January screeches at me from Atticus's family room. "We have pre-gaming to do."

"Coming, you psycho!" I glare down at my phone, anger boiling in my belly at the text from my father.

DAD/RICHARD/ASSHOLE

Happy New Year's, darling. I've been thinking about you a lot since Thanksgiving. I know things got awkward. I would love to talk about a new role I'm creating for you at DC FC. When are you free?

The man does not take no for an answer.

And he owes me an apology for inviting Ron to our dinner. But he would never apologize. Because he never thinks he's wrong.

Even after I brought Kellen to dinner, even after I assured him I am happy in Colorado and pursuing the England job, even after Kellen told off Ron in front of him, my father pretends none of

245

that is true or important. He pretends I didn't leave *because* of Ron. Because my own father didn't take my side.

But I'm really getting sick of thinking about all that.

I ignore the text and smooth my hair down in the mirror. January and Raleigh convinced me to get it straightened for tonight, and after hours at the salon, I look like an entirely different person. My hair is straight and much longer without the endless curls.

"I adore that dress, girly," Raleigh says when I stride out into the living room, MBM trailing behind me.

I'm wearing a short, black, sparkly evening dress with long sleeves off my shoulders and a plunging V neckline, showing a bit of cleavage.

"Thanks, you look great too."

"Not too much?" Raleigh looks down at herself and blushes. She's wearing a belted maroon, sequin wrap dress, sleeveless with a scooped neckline. Add in dramatic eye makeup and bright red lipstick, and she doesn't look like a boring pharmacist at all.

"If anything, too little, babes," January pipes in. She's in the kitchen preparing vodka tonics with an eye-watering ratio of vodka to tonic. "You're still giving pharmacist vibes."

Raleigh gasps. "Am I?"

"Definitely not, sis." I throw a dirty look at January, who shrugs and leans down to scratch my dog's head. He's behaving and not jumping up on us for the time being, which is good because I'll have to lock him in my room if he starts messing with our outfits.

"Hey, Janny? Can we not get trashed tonight?" I watch January add an extra splash of alcohol to the almost-full glasses.

January sashays over and passes me and Raleigh drinks.

"Why not?" She stares at me. "We're finally all together! It's been ages. We should celebrate."

January is wearing a lace jumpsuit probably designed for twenty-year-olds with zero body fat and perfect curves, but she pulls it off with ease. The wide-legged black pants lead seamlessly to a sleeveless black and silver lace corset. Paired with high strappy heels, she looks like a runway model.

I wish I could be that confident in myself. In my life. She travels the world, hopping from one city to another doing freelance consulting. January's managed to create a dream life for herself.

"Why not? Because this is my job. My boss will be there," I attempt.

"Your job for, like, a few more months, max. And you can't tell me this Lina person is going to be mad if you get a bit tipsy on New Year's Eve." January rolls her eyes. "Relax. You're gonna get the England job."

The morning after Kellen and I broke up, I got an email from Winchester FC inviting me to England for an in-person interview. Apparently, Lina had provided a glowing reference. And after hesitating for weeks, I asked the DC FC vice president of marketing and public relations for a reference. He had been my boss, technically, not my father. It still felt dirty to ask. I did it via email so I wouldn't have to have a long conversation with him. He agreed to be a reference and suggested we schedule a call to catch up, which I never did.

Everything is coming together just as I planned.

January turns her dark blue eyes to me and tosses her long, almost-black hair over her shoulder. She's basically a goddess.

"Where is Atticus, anyway?" Raleigh sets her glass down on the counter and spins it slowly.

I shrug. "With some of the guys. I'm sure the usual suspects: Kellen and Lachlan and Harley."

"You've been super interested in Atticus's whereabouts since we got here." January makes a face at Raleigh. "What's up with that?"

"Nothing's up with that. Just curious."

"Talked to your ex over the holidays?"

Raleigh scoffs. "No. I'm glad he didn't call. I'm especially glad I didn't have to spend Christmas with his family. What a relief."

"Why don't we try not getting married to the next man you date?" January downs her drink.

"I won't. I'm never getting married again."

"Weren't you on that new dating app earlier today?" January tilts her head.

"I'm just curious!" Raleigh throws her head back and sighs. "I'm not actually going to date anyone. Not anytime soon, anyway."

"I'll believe that when I see it."

"Hey!"

They banter back and forth, and I smile and quietly sip my drink, scratching MBM's head with one hand.

These are my people. January and Raleigh. My brother. My mom. I'm just here in Colorado for one season. If everything works out with Winchester FC, then I'll move to England. And if it doesn't, I need another plan.

Colorado will not be part of that plan.

* * *

The ballroom of the hotel in central Fort Collins is magically decorated for the holidays. Miles of white fairy lights line every door frame, table, and holiday decoration. Men in suits and tuxedos talk in groups, some older and some younger.

It's a holiday wonderland in here, but I'm having a hard time keeping my eyes off Kellen. Even the side view of him across the room is mouthwatering. He's wearing a black suit snugly fitted to his body, the jacket hugging his broad shoulders and perfectly tapering to his waist. No tie, but the top button of his white shirt is undone, adding a casual feel. He looks like he walked out of an advertisement.

Joy explodes inside me at the sight of him. This is the man I'm in love with. But then the joy fades as I remember we broke up, and I can't have him.

Uniformed servers walk around with hors d'oeuvres and glasses of champagne. One passes in front of us and January waves at him to stop, gesturing for each of us to grab a glass of bubbly. Then she leads us to the center of the room like she owns the place.

"Let's have a toast." She lifts her champagne flute. "To Raleigh, for officially getting rid of that dead weight of an ex-husband. Congrats on your second divorce, babes."

Raleigh moans but there's a smile behind the grimace.

"And to Lucy." January turns to me. "For getting railed by a hot hockey player."

"January! Hush!" I glance around the room. "You're practically shouting."

"Lulu, you were publicly dating him."

"Publicly fake dating."

"I'm betting more than one person in this room knows it went a bit beyond that. Certainly the entire Kellcy Fake Dating Planning Committee, which included like half the team by the end." January shakes her head. "Anyway! Not the point here."

"Hey." Raleigh grabs my hand. "You were so brave quitting DC FC, leaving everything behind to come here, and going for that job in England. You're an inspiration."

"Thanks, Raleigh." I squeeze her hand and swallow down the sudden lump in my throat.

We all clink and drink. Even though earlier I suggested we don't get trashed, what else do we have to do tomorrow besides sleep? I sneak a glance at the boys, who are now waiting in line for drinks, and Kellen's eyes lock with mine.

Even from twenty feet away, I feel his gaze rake over me. He nods and raises his empty glass before turning back to the line at the bar. Harley and a few others stay with him, but Atticus spots us and practically skips over, Lachlan trailing behind. Atticus has been desperate to hang out with us since my friends arrived and it invokes such delightful college memories.

"Hey, Luce. January. Raleigh." He nods to each of my friends. "You all look beautiful."

Lachlan clears his throat. "It's terrific to meet you stunning ladies in person, although I feel like I already know you from the Committee meetings."

"Man, shut up." Atticus glares at Lachlan, then turns back to us. "Just so you know, he's a total player, so don't be impressed by his stupid accent."

"Like you're not?" I make a face at my brother, who ignores me.

"You're not wearing a frat t-shirt tonight." Raleigh deadpans.

Atticus groans. "Because I'm twenty-nine years old and no longer identify as a fraternity brother. Will I ever live down those years of my life?" He keeps his eyes on Raleigh.

"No," we all say at once.

"What part of Australia are you from?" January asks Lachlan.

"Far North Queensland. The jungle, basically," he says and slides closer to her.

"I spent six months in Sydney a few years ago with a client," January says.

The two of them chat and Raleigh and Atticus tease each other, but their conversations fade into background noise as I watch Kellen, Harley, and a Blizzard player I haven't met walk across the ballroom.

Kellen's stopped halfway by Savannah, who is with another gorgeous woman. Both of them are in expensive-looking dresses, surprisingly conservative. Savannah doesn't put her hands on Kellen but instead touches her friend's arm and appears to introduce her.

The whole fake dating thing really did work. For Kellen, at least. For me? I'm not sure, but I don't really care about what my father thinks anymore.

The night goes on and we drink champagne, then red wine, then champagne again. My feet start to hurt in the heels, and I'm envious of Raleigh's more conservative shoe choice of flats. January seems not at all bothered by her towering heels.

Kellen and I don't talk. We orbit around each other like moons and never end up standing side-by-side when we're in the same group. At one point, January walks over to Lina with me, and we chat with her and Savannah. Before I know it, it's twenty minutes before the new year.

"Where's Raleigh?" I ask.

January hooks her arm in mine, and we scan the group for our friend.

"Where's your brother?" she asks.

"I don't see him."

"Interesting combination to disappear."

We look at each other and at the same time say, "Nah." Then burst out laughing.

"You're not going to find a hockey player to kiss? After all your speeches about what you and Raleigh would do when you got here?"

"Meh."

I crack up at her nonchalance, which I'm not sure I totally believe. She's way too chill about relationships and love. It's not natural.

"Harley's staring at you," I lean in to whisper in her ear.

"Harley has a girlfriend back in Maine." She shakes her head.

"You talked about it, huh."

January gives me a dirty look. "We were just making conversation."

For once in the evening, I'm not paying attention to where Kellen is. Not until he walks up to us with Harley and says my name.

CHAPTER 34

Just Once More

KELLEN

It's almost midnight, and Lucy Knox has me speechless. From the first moment I saw her across the room tonight, I lost my shit. Quietly, internally, but I'm a mess.

She's so beautiful tonight. Always, actually, but there's something about seeing her in that short black dress and heels.

I don't even know what to say to her. I feel like a teenage boy tongue tied around the hottest girl in school. I can't get her alone. I shouldn't, anyway. It's like she doesn't even notice me. She's the sun, with her fiery red hair, and I'm just some shitty planet too far away to feel her heat.

A waiter comes by with a tray, and I swipe two full glasses of champagne. I'm going to talk to her. What will I say? Fuck if I know. I'll ask her how she is. If she thinks about me.

If she realizes I love her.

Nope. Just the first one. I head in her direction with Harley, my heart pounding.

"Lucy," I say, and she looks up at me, her eyes filled with surprise and warmth, and maybe something like fear. Or is that heat?

I'm such a bad reader of people.

"Hi. Having a good night?" she asks, like we're two coworkers at a work event.

"Yes. Champagne?" I extend my hand toward her, and Lucy reaches out for the glass.

"Thank you—"

At that moment, Atticus walks up with Raleigh and Lachlan, and proceeds to throw his arm out mid-sentence. His arm hits mine, and the full glass of champagne I had for Lucy dumps completely down the front of her dress.

She gasps.

"Oh my god, shit, I'm so sorry." I spin to Atticus and shove the glasses at him. "Dick. Take this."

"Sorry, Luce!" Atticus grimaces.

"No worries. But that is really cold. And bubbly." Lucy cracks a grin but champagne drips down her chest into her dress.

"Come on." I link my hand around Lucy's arm, steering her away from the group. I lead her out of the ballroom and down the hall toward a distant women's restroom.

"Where are we going?" Lucy's breathless but follows my lead.

"There's a better bathroom over here."

She nods as if that's a perfectly reasonable excuse.

It is not.

But I saw a way to get her alone, and I'm going to take advantage. We walk down a long hallway in silence and thankfully a women's restroom appears. I push the door open and stick my head in.

"Hello? Anyone in here?" No one replies. "Come on." I pull Lucy in after me. There's an open area before the sinks and toilets with a chair, a clean counter, and a mirror. I grab a tissue from the box on the counter and turn to face her.

"There were napkins in the ballroom," she says. Her chest is heaving, and I don't think it's from the walk down the hallway.

"May I?" I don't respond to her comment but raise the tissue up so she knows what I'm asking.

She nods.

I dab the tissue around the hollow of her neck, not looking at her but staying focused on the spilled champagne, which is barely noticeable anymore. I can feel her swallow beneath my fingers, and I pause at the motion before moving further down, dragging the tissue. My heart pounds in my chest and I need this. I need this woman. I'm fucking desperate for her.

There's no more champagne to wipe up, but I let my hand move down between her breasts slowly, so she has plenty of time to stop me. My knuckles graze the side of her tit, and she breathes in sharply.

"I've missed you." I finally look up into her eyes and it's too much. I might not know anything about love, but I know there's fire there.

Lucy reaches her hands up and places them gently on either side of my jaw, sliding them back until they're behind my head, then in my hair. Leaving my hand between her breasts, I step forward, and her body lightly presses against mine.

"Come here," she demands, and I lower my face to hers. It's not sweet or gentle or soft, but hungry and needy. Wild. Our tongues wrap together, and I open my hand on her chest, moving over to massage her breast.

"Jesus, Lucy." I want to say more but she doesn't let me. Her body is reacting like mine. On fire as she tries to pull me even closer.

My knees wobble. My cock hardens. And my heart? I don't know what that fucker is doing.

Lucy makes a dirty, desperate squeak and grabs my hands, pushing them down onto her ass. Fuck, the feel of her under my hands. I squeeze her and press her against me, and she moans into my mouth.

This is too much and not enough. I kiss her like I'm never

going to see her again. I kiss her and try to tell her with my mouth what I'm feeling. That I love her. That I want her. I beg her to stay with my lips. But I can never say any of those things out loud. It's not fair to me. To Lucy. To Ava. To anyone.

Lucy moves my hand from her ass to between her legs, and she hikes up her short dress with her other hand. She's wet and willing and dammit, I want more than just sex, but I'll take whatever she'll give me.

Even though I know it'll hurt in the end. When she walks away. When she leaves.

I can't deny her.

"Lock the door." She nods her head to the closed door, breathing deeply as I rub my finger over the wet fabric of her underwear.

Who am I to say no? I step away for a beat and slide the deadbolt that's secured on top of the door to the bathroom. The look in her eyes when I come back to her, before we kiss, there's something there. Isn't there? Or am I just imagining it?

I back her up to the counter and push her dress all the way to her waist, then wiggle her underwear down before lifting her onto the counter and stepping between her legs.

I don't want to just fuck her; I want to make love to her. But that's not what she wants. She leans her hands on the counter and throws her head back, moaning as I slide a finger between her legs.

Lucy's never been more beautiful.

I stare at the way her breasts overflow from the dress, the fabric taut as she arches her back. I tug her dress down and they tumble out.

I pull a condom out of my wallet and then fumble with my belt and my zipper.

"Lucy." I lean forward and cup her jaw in my clean hand. Her skin is so soft under my fingers. I drink in her wayward freckles, those green eyes looking upward in pleasure, her lips so red.

"Yes?" She focuses on me.

"I want you. I've never wanted anything more. I *always* want you, Lucy. I'm not sure I've ever—" I stop speaking when she puts a finger on my lips.

She doesn't want to hear what I have to say. I'm glad she stopped me. Who knows where that was going.

"Just do it." Lucy doesn't want confessions of love or gentle caresses.

So I do what she wants and bury myself inside her. Being here feels like I've come home, and I never want to leave.

Lucy wraps her arms around my neck and pulls me closer to her. I rest my lips on her ear.

She gasps, and I push into her again and again until she moans my name and comes, fast and hard. I follow a second later.

We're panting, and she pushes me away, her expression already distant.

I zip my pants before leaning forward to kiss her neck and run my hand along her long, straight hair.

"I like your hair like this," I murmur into her ear. "But I love your curls."

She tugs her dress up and hops down from the counter onto her feet.

I don't want this to be it. I want to do this again, and again.

But Lucy's already pushed me away.

"We probably shouldn't have done that," she says, her face as serious as I've seen it.

"I'm glad we did."

But she doesn't respond, only reaches down to pull up her underwear, then watches me as I reach for her.

"We should get back," Lucy says, leaning away.

I lead her back to the ballroom. She doesn't let me hold her hand in the hallway.

The DJ is about to start the countdown to midnight. I hope she'll let me kiss her then, but she slips away to her friends, and I join Lachlan with the rest of the boys. Some of them have clearly had too much to drink and will regret it tomorrow when Coach Jackson kicks their asses.

But not me.

I'm not drunk. I'm in love.

CHAPTER 35

Dream Job

LUCY

Wednesday, January 8

"London is amazing." I moan and take in the view of the city from the twentieth-floor wine bar.

"Yes, ma'am, it sure is. Cheers." January holds out her glass and clinks mine. "To an amazing interview, and you moving to England."

"Don't jinx it, sis." I sip my dark red wine and enjoy the warmth it offers me. "But can you stay here too? I'll be so mad if I show up and you peace out a month later."

"I've thought about it. I do enjoy London." January rolls her shoulders back. "But I don't think I'll be here forever."

"Alright, ladies?" The bartender returns, showing off his gorgeous English accent. He refills our wine glasses from the bottle of Malbec on the bar.

"Thanks, Andrew," January coos.

"So how do we know the bartender's name?" I whisper when he walks to the other end of the bar to serve a group of men in suits.

January shrugs and flicks her hair out of her face.

"I have to keep busy somehow, don't I?"

We both giggle, and then a voice calls out from the entrance to the bar.

"Hello, ladies!"

"Stella!" January waves her friend over to us.

"You must be one of the best friends January is always talking about." Stella, a pretty, smiling woman with shoulder-length blonde hair, grins at me warmly and slides onto the bar stool next to January.

"I'm Lucy," I say. "Nice to meet you."

"You as well."

"Stella and I met through a work project," January says, nodding her head to her friend. "She's American but has lived in London for a decade. And is married to an ex-pro rugby player."

"Oh, no, not married. I don't do marriage." Stella laughs lightly. "But when you move here—"

"If I move here," I correct.

"*If* you move here, my partner's got plenty of hot rugby player friends I can introduce you to."

"Well, we'll see, I guess?"

I arrived in London last night after taking the train back from Winchester. The interview with Winchester FC went smoothly. I met with the head of HR, then the vice president of marketing and public relations—who would be my boss—and finally the club president. It's a big job, and that makes me both nervous and excited.

I know I can do it. Any of that job performance insecurity I had during my DC FC years is gone. My father had been intentionally holding me back, but that's over now.

But there's a stabbing in my gut when I think about walking away from the Blizzard. It's been so fun to work for Lina and with the team—and not just the Kellen part.

Too bad it's not even an option. And I can't imagine rejecting a job offer from Winchester FC. If I get one.

"She's definitely getting the job," January says to Stella, who nods in instant agreement.

Earlier today, we walked around north London, where January rents a flat. It's cold and wet and gets dark at four o'clock here, but she tells me that in the summer, it's light until well after ten at night.

And it's not like D.C. is nice this time of year either. Cold and wet and dark as well.

Fort Collins, though... there's something gorgeous about the snowcapped mountains and the feel of Colorado in the winter. Something magical. Maybe I can go back and visit Atticus next year. Soccer will always be my first love, but I've really fallen for hockey. The constant movement and excitement of the dozen players on the ice. The intensity of the crowd in the enclosed arena. The raw power of the sport.

But will I ever be able to separate my feelings about Fort Collins and hockey with the man who has dominated my time and thoughts since I arrived there?

"You'll love living in England. Oh, and I have a sister, Reese, who lives in Scotland with her Scottish husband, and another sister, Maddie, who lives in Ireland with her Irish husband. I'm trying to convince January to take a trip with me this summer to visit one or both of them." Stella sips her wine.

"I might join you, Stella." January shrugs. "But you know I have a hard time committing that far in advance. But Lucy—" January turns to me. "London is a short flight away from so many amazing places. It's incredible."

"Sounds like it," I say. I picture a whole new life here, one that January and Stella are doing an impressive job of painting for me.

"You'll be here by then. You can totally join us in Scotland and Ireland. If I go." January reaches over and touches my hand, but I'm in another world and hardly hear her.

"Oh, and both my sisters' husbands used to play for Winchester FC. I can't believe I didn't open with that."

"Wow, that's crazy. Wait—all three of you are with ex pro athletes?" My jaw drops slightly open.

"Um, yes." Stella sips her wine casually. "Why, is that weird?"

"I guess not." I shake my head. But I don't have interest in soccer players or rugby players.

Just a certain hockey player.

Kellen and I haven't talked since New Year's Eve. What was I thinking in that bathroom? I wasn't. When he wiped my chest with that tissue, I became desperate for him. It was animal instinct. Like if we hooked up again, maybe things would be different. He was looking at me with that intense stare of his. My neck heats just remembering.

As soon as it was over, I knew it had been a mistake. For my heart.

I'm so in love with that man.

My gut twists. I'm gonna beat that feeling down, stomp on it, ignore it, and fight it until it disappears for good.

But I can't get the words he said to me on New Year's Eve out of my head: *I've never wanted anything more. I always want you, Lucy. I'm not sure I've ever—*

Did I dream that moment? I had been tipsy, sure. But I heard those words. What was he about to say? I kissed him to stop him from finishing. It wouldn't do anyone any good to say things we can't take back.

"Stop thinking about your hot hockey player."

I scream in shock when January's voice cuts through my thoughts. She huffs a laugh and Stella giggles with delight.

"I've heard about this fake dating situation. You know, one of my sisters started out by fake dating her husband. It's not as uncommon a situation as you might think..." Stella's voice trails off, inviting questions, but I barely register her words.

"Why would you think I'm thinking of Kellen?" I attempt nonchalance and sip my wine.

"The state of denial you are in is extraordinary, babes." January rolls her eyes.

"I don't know what you mean." But my voice cracks, and I drain half my glass to soothe my throat.

"Lucy. You banged him in a hotel bathroom on New Year's Eve."

Stella gasps. "Amazing. Ethan and I have a thing for public places as well." Her face takes on a dreamy expression.

January grins at Stella. "And this is why I hang out with you." She turns back to me. "But that bathroom situation is so not you. It's never been you."

"That word is so harsh," I grumble.

"What word? Oh, banged? Could've been worse. I could've said fu—"

"Please stop."

"Okay. How about: made sweet love?" January raises her eyebrows. "On a public bathroom counter?"

I cringe. "Ew on multiple levels."

January and Stella laugh, and I join them.

"I was trying out being adventurous," I say.

"Bullshit."

"Please invite me to the wedding," Stella begs.

"Wedding??" I look at Stella and then January, who are both grinning.

"You and this hockey player. Because now I'm wondering how much of a chance we really have to convince you to move to London."

"Trust me, there's no wedding." I shake my head aggressively, then make a miserable sound and rub my forehead with two fingers.

"Yes. You're right, Lucy." January leans over and puts her hand on my forearm. "No wedding. But here's what *is* going to happen. You'll get this job and move to England. It will be amazing. You'll travel all the time to fantastic European cities. You'll make lots of new friends—like Stella. You'll meet a sexy English man who will make you forget all about Kellen Bassey. Could be a rugby player." She tilts her head. "Could be a Scottish man. Or Irish. French? They can be assholes but sexy as fuck."

"I repeat: rugby players." Stella nods knowingly.

"But what about my dog, Janny?" I stare at January with a hint of desperation.

"Not your dog, remember, Lulu?" January shakes her head.

"Yeah." I wonder how MBM is doing at the Delightful Doggy Palace. It's primarily a daycare, but they also have space to board a limited number of dogs. I've been checking the live video feed, but January's already swatted my hand away from my phone three times to stop me from obsessively peeking.

I might have found a permanent home for the stupid mutt.

Lina has a neighbor family who just lost their dog, and they're interested in adopting MBM. I already met up with one of the moms at a green area in the middle of Fort Collins, and she laughed and cooed at my dog, who traitorously licked her hand and her face. We made plans to meet again with the other mom before they make a final decision.

Fiona is returning to the Blizzard. She's scheduled to transition back at the end of February, so if I get this job, I'm free to go basically any time after that.

But what if I don't get the Winchester FC job?

And what if my dad comes through with a real job offer? Surely I can't take it, even if I don't get the England job. I can't do that to myself.

"Jesus, babes. Are you in there? Do you need to check your dog's social media feed or whatever?"

I laugh. "It's a live video feed of the kennel."

"Is this that dog palace place?"

"The Delightful Doggy Palace. It's where he goes to for doggy day care a few days a week."

January shakes her head at me, but she's got a smile peeking out.

"I bet you could get a ton of followers for him on social media if you shared some of his ridiculous stories."

I hate the dread in my stomach that manifests whenever I think about handing over that dog for good. It was never, ever supposed to be permanent. I simply accepted him when my ex dumped him on me. I'd give him one last adventure and find a good home for him in Colorado, a better dog environment than D.C.

In hindsight, I bet he would've been snapped up by a nice family at a shelter in D.C. Not be fed to a snake like I'd feared. Still, I couldn't bear it. I couldn't shove the little dog back into Ron's arms that day at my door.

The word *bear* makes me think of the name Kellen gave him when we went hiking. I groan and close my eyes.

"You'll start a new life here, Lulu."

I open my eyes, and January covers my hand with hers. "Don't let a dog or a hot hockey player lead you astray."

"But January, what if—"

"What if what? Did Kellen confess his love to you on that bathroom floor?"

"It wasn't the floor."

"The wall?"

I shake my head. "The counter."

"Lovely. Did he beg you to stay?"

"No."

"Did he even *ask* you to stay?"

I move my head slowly from side to side. He hadn't. What would I have done if he had? If Lina had offered me a job? I could continue with the life I'm building in Fort Collins. Working for the Blizzard. Hanging out with Atticus and the hockey boys. Maybe even be Coach Lucy to Ava on a more permanent basis.

But that's not what happened.

"He didn't ask me to stay." And I didn't ask him if he wanted me to.

January is quiet for a moment.

"Girl, he should've begged you." Stella sips her wine and watches me with clear blue eyes.

I sigh. "That was a weird night."

"Sure was. Did I tell you that I talked to Savannah for a while?" January twirls her wine glass. "You were chatting to Lina."

"No, you didn't." I furrow my brow.

"Hmm. Yeah. She was interesting. Did you know she has her law degree? And was studying for the Virginia bar before she moved to Colorado?"

"Kellen said something about her going to law school."

"Yeah. I don't even know how it came up. But then I told her I did one semester of law school and quit. She thought it was hilarious."

"Sounds like you had fun with her." I raise my eyebrows.

"She wants to take the bar in Colorado, but I don't think her husband approves." January shrugs. "I felt bad for her. But I guess that's what happens when you marry an asshole."

Stella scoffs. "Sounds like that woman needs saving."

"When I told her I broke up with Kellen, she offered to go out for a girls' night." I remember that day in the corporate sponsorship box when she'd showed such empathy.

"See? She doesn't seem so bad."

"I don't think she is."

"Right." January nods. "Kellen will do fine without you there. Savannah was never going to intentionally sabotage him, and I think she might now understand she should be careful with how her husband sees things."

"Maybe."

I need to get a hypothetical life in Fort Collins out of my head. I'm in too deep with the Winchester FC job. I've made a plan. I've committed to the plan, even if it's just to myself at this point. And the plan sounds amazing.

Why would I try to change that?

Because I think I'm in love?

How can I ever really know someone after what Ron did to me? I can't trust my own instincts or feelings.

Kellen's way out of my league, anyway.

In England, I'll forge my own way. Start fresh. I can be a new version of myself, without my painful past on display. No one will know who I am.

Everything will be better here in England. A fresh start.

So why do I feel like such garbage?

And why can't I get Kellen Bassey's gorgeous face out of my mind?

CHAPTER 36

Just Be Honest

KELLEN

Tuesday, January 14

"How was Lucy's interview?" As soon as the question's out, I pull my Blizzard hoodie over my head and hide for a few seconds inside the sweatshirt.

When I emerge, I see Atticus staring at me with narrowed eyes. I try not to fidget as he examines me. While I'm sure he doesn't know all the details of what happened between me and Lucy, he knows *something*.

"Good." He tosses dirty clothes into the laundry bin, then turns to his locker to pull out a clean sweatshirt.

"Really, Atter? That's all you're going to give me?" Frustration courses through my veins.

"If you care so much about what my sister is up to, why don't you ask her yourself? Or have you deleted her number from your phone?"

"Yeah, right." Lachlan snickers from next to him.

"Mind your business, Lach." I attempt to sound stern and throw a dirty look at our teammate, but he just chuckles and shakes his head.

"Leave Kellen alone," Harley says. "He's looking pretty pathetic right now. It's kind of sad."

"Shut up." I growl at Harley, then turn back to Atticus. "Seriously, man, it's just a question."

"And I'm being serious too. Between you asking about her, and her asking about you, I'm kind of over it."

"She's asking about me?" Hope surges, then fades. Why would that matter? It'll be better when she's gone from Fort Collins for good. Then I'll know for certain there's no chance for us. But while she's still here, I can't help but yearn for her.

"I don't remember." Atticus yanks the sweatshirt over his curls and grabs a baseball cap from his locker, settling it on his head backwards, red strands escaping from all sides. "Maybe she was asking about one of the other guys. You're not very memorable."

"Fuck off." I groan.

"As fun as this conversation is, I'm out of here." Lachlan follows Harley out of the locker room, and they leave me alone with my torturer.

I glance over through the glass window at Coach Jackson. I planned on talking to him about my trade fears, and now's the perfect time. But I can't let this go with Atticus. Not yet.

Atticus sighs, clutching his phone in one hand and a half-empty electrolyte drink in the other. But he doesn't walk away yet.

"Fine. But only because you are seriously pathetic right now. Lucy's interview went great. She saw January while she was over there, and I think she's all in."

"Oh." My heart drops, and my entire body sags.

"Sorry, man."

"She get an actual job offer yet?"

"Nah, not yet."

"Thanks." I sink to the bench and hang my head. "You go ahead. I'm staying to talk to Coach."

Atticus takes two steps away, then pauses and turns back.

"One piece of advice, if I may?" He's got a dead serious look on his face.

"Go ahead." I look up at him.

"If you've got something to say to my sister, say it. You have nothing to lose. She'll be gone soon. Far away. Don't have regrets about not shooting your shot while you still can."

I swallow the lump in my throat. There's a faraway look in Atticus's eyes, and I wonder if he's thinking about his own regrets. Then the look is gone, and he focuses back on me.

"But—" I run my hand through my hair. "What if it's pointless? It *is* pointless, I mean." So incredibly pointless. So pointless, I want to lay flat on this dirty locker room floor and close my eyes until the heavy feeling lifts off my chest.

"Just speak what's in your heart. No regrets, you know what I mean?" Atticus turns and strides out of the room.

"What the fuck was that about?" I say to no one.

But there's something niggling at me.

The light shuts off in Coach Jackson's office, and I sit up straight when he walks into the locker area.

"I was hoping to catch you, Coach."

"Great game out there. You're looking really sharp this season."

Coach Jackson is a good man. I know I can trust him. But still, asking about this feels awkward as hell.

"I'm worried about getting traded," I blurt. "And I wanted to get your thoughts on that."

"Why on earth would you worry about getting traded?" Coach looks genuinely shocked at my query.

I grimace. He doesn't know that I have good reason to worry about that.

"Paul hates me."

But... is that even true anymore? Sure, I got more than my fair share of dirty looks when the season started and that one humiliating talking to, but after things were happening with Lucy, it seemed to fade away. Then stop. Maybe Lucy and I were that good at fake dating.

Coach lets out a short chuckle and then looks around the room as if to confirm we're alone.

"Paul doesn't like anyone." Coach shrugs. "But he recognizes talent. He's a businessman first and foremost, and he wants to see goals scored and games won. If you're playing well and scoring like you are, I think it's safe to say *you* are safe."

I'm speechless.

"Safe as anyone is, really. You won't get traded. I heard the rumors about Markus last year. But he wasn't gelling with the team on the ice, and he was going to do better elsewhere. *That's* why he got traded."

Oh.

"Thanks, Coach." My shoulders slump, and I slowly blow the breath out of my lungs. I shut my eyes. All this worry. It's always been on my mind. Every game, every practice, every time I thought of hockey this season, it's always been in the context of getting traded and if I'd still be here in Fort Collins next season. If I'd be forced to live away from Ava.

I should feel incredible relief. And I do. But after the relief washes away, it's deep regret.

I got in my own damn way with Lucy, burned by a lifetime of broken trust leading to my extreme caution with letting people get close. Who deserves my trust? I guess that's the question.

I haven't even been able to trust myself.

Atticus, of all people, telling me to speak what's in my heart. That fucker is right, and that's what was niggling me.

Lucy.

I knew she was different right away, and then she showed me that I was right to let her in. I was right to trust her.

But I didn't trust myself.

I need to talk to her.

* * *

I head over to Bri's house to see Ava before bedtime.

"Hey," Bri says when I walk in the unlocked front door.

"Congratulations." I embrace Bri. "You're going to kick ass at your new job."

"Thanks, Kellen."

Bri's been beaming all week since she found out she got that better university job she'd applied to months ago, and she signed the contract today. I'm happy for her, especially now that I know I'm not going anywhere anytime soon.

Ava runs into the foyer and hugs me, clutching a soccer player Barbie in one hand.

"Do they really not make a hockey Barbie?"

"I'll put it on my Christmas list," Ava says solemnly.

"Christmas was like three weeks ago, Aves."

Ava shrugs, and I make a mental note to go online to search for a hockey player Barbie.

"Come have a snack with me, Daddy." Ava pulls me to the kitchen.

"Okay." I follow her to the table. Bri disappears upstairs, knowing from my texts that I want a minute with our daughter alone. "I have a question for you."

Ava slides into the pantry, pulling out a pack of fruit snacks and a chocolate chip M&M cookie. I give her a side eye when she deposits the sugar-filled processed food on the table, so she skips over and grabs a small apple to add to her pile.

"Are you sure that's enough snack?"

"Oh, can you get me chocolate milk too, Daddy?"

"No problem." I chuckle and grab the chocolate milk from the fridge and a pink plastic cup from Bri's cabinet.

"So what's your question, Daddy?"

"You know Lucy?"

"Coach Lucy! I love her! And Mister Barky McBarkface. He's my favorite dog ever."

"I know, sweetie." Ava only tells me every other day how much she loves Lucy's dog. Makes it hard to get that woman out of my mind.

"Can we dog-sit him again? I miss him sooo much."

"Maybe, I don't know. But listen." I open up the fruit snacks while Ava shoves the cookie into her mouth. "What would you think about me asking her if she'd go on a date with me?"

"A date?" Ava grabs the pack of fruit snacks and two fly onto the floor. "With Coach Lucy?"

"Yes."

"But I thought you already did that." She pops a strawberry shape into her mouth.

My breath catches in my throat. "Well, not really."

"Oh." Ava chews thoughtfully.

"Are you going to pick up what spilled?" I point under her chair.

"If we had a doggy, like Mister Barky McBarkface, he'd just eat them instead."

I can't help but laugh.

"My question, Ava?"

"Sure. But if you go out with Coach Lucy, can you get chicken nuggets and bring me home some?"

I nod solemnly.

"And can I pet her doggy?"

I nod again.

"Okay." Ava shoves the entire chocolate chip M&M cookie into her mouth, leaving the apple in front of her untouched.

There's only one more thing to do.

I pull out my phone and scroll to the Kellcy Fake Dating Planning Committee text chain.

CHAPTER 37

When It Rains

LUCY

Wednesday, January 15

I'm about to leave Atticus's apartment for work and stop in the kitchen to fill up my travel mug with hot coffee from my brother's carafe. It's going to be a busy day. We have a press briefing in the afternoon to announce a new sponsor, and I need to follow up with a list of publications we're working with to schedule features on Blizzard players.

And I got a request for a call with Winchester FC for nine thirty this morning.

All sorts of feelings swirl around inside me. I'm excited to hear what they thought of my interview. The job is perfect for me. The next step up in my marketing and PR career, in a foreign country, and no nepotism involved.

Most of the feelings are good.

When my phone rings as I'm sliding my laptop into my bag and reaching for the notebook containing my ongoing to-do list, I don't even think about it before answering.

When it's a split second too late, I see who's calling.

"Dad?" I freeze with my hand on the zipper to my bag.

"Lucy, darling. I'm in town." My dad's authoritative voice makes my skin crawl. "Can we meet for coffee?"

He's in town? I take my phone away from my ear and look at the time. Seven o'clock in the morning.

"When did you get here?" I put him on speaker.

"Yesterday afternoon. I had dinner with Paul Harrison. And I wanted to come see my daughter."

He was in town yesterday but didn't call me? Or Atticus?

"Ah. Okay. I have a busy day—"

"Paul said there's a lovely coffee shop called Deep Roots Cafe. He said he's seen you there before."

I swallow and shut my eyes tightly. I need to face him. I wish I knew what Winchester FC was going to say to me before I see my father again. I wish I had a job offer I could throw in his face.

"Have you talked to Atticus?" But I know he hasn't. My brother would have immediately told me if he had.

"No. But I might watch the game tonight. Paul's offered me tickets in the corporate suite."

I roll my eyes because Atticus could have easily gotten him tickets.

"Fine. I'll meet you at Deep Roots Cafe in fifteen minutes, okay?"

I click end. I didn't even think to ask where he's staying. I'm sure it's some bougie hotel that costs a thousand dollars a night.

As soon as I walk in to the cafe, I imagine myself there with Kellen. That first meeting with our first kiss, or one of the other times we'd gone to grab a coffee. I picture meeting Bri and Ava for hot chocolate so Ava could hang out with MBM.

But then I spot my father at a table in the corner, and all the happy feelings fade away.

"Lucy, darling," he says when I approach. Richard stands and pulls me into his arms. I let him, but keep my body stiff and only half-heartedly lean in.

"Hi, Dad."

"Shall we get coffee?" He gestures to the line of people, and I follow him over.

"What are you doing in town?"

"Both of my children live here, do I need another excuse?"

Yeah.

"No, I guess not." I shrug and try to smile. Maybe he is just here for a visit with no ulterior motive.

Dad orders us two large coffees with cream and sugar without asking me what I want. He doesn't care much for what other people want. He knows what he likes and assumes everyone will agree.

I prefer a vanilla latte with oat milk. Kellen had no problem remembering that.

We settle into a table in awkward silence.

"How are things with that hockey player?"

Shit. I shake my head. "Done."

"Right." He nods, like it all makes sense. "Like I told you at Thanksgiving—not forever."

My stomach twists, and I focus on not crushing the coffee cup in my hand.

"Nope. It was not forever," I say through clenched teeth.

"Maybe you should see Ron again? The time and distance might've been the perfect break. Now you can start over again together."

"No," I say firmly. "Remember how he cheated on me incessantly? There's no coming back from that." I have no feelings left for Ron. Maybe when I arrived in Colorado there was some lingering desire for him, but that's all gone now. I feel nothing for him. And it's a damn relief.

Richard raises his eyebrows. "Be honest, darling. That thing with the hockey player was a temporary interlude. Ron's the real deal. Same with your career at DC FC."

"Dad." I'm suddenly exhausted.

Richard shrugs, like he doesn't care to argue, like he doesn't care at all either way.

"Anyway, I might as well admit that I have an ulterior motive for being here." He flashes his pearly whites at me.

Of course he does.

"Go on." I wave a hand at him.

"I wanted to talk to you about a job opportunity. Like I texted you a few weeks back."

"Dad." I groan. "I'm not coming back to DC FC."

"Hear me out, okay?"

I want to say no. I want to stand and walk out. But he's my father, and he flew all the way here, and I almost always do what I'm told when it comes to him.

So instead, I nod and wait for him to continue.

"When you quit DC FC—" he pauses.

He says it as if I quit randomly and for no reason. Like I didn't do it because I couldn't face my ex-fiancé down the hall every day and think about how he cheated on me.

"—you were a director of marketing. I know you have ambition to do more. Be more."

"Yes. I do. But you've not actually really acknowledged that before." Annoyance in my gut turns to anger. "Whenever I've tried to talk to you about my career goals, you blow me off and tell me to be patient. But I'm done being patient. This is not only about Ron. This is about me wanting more. Me wanting the respect I deserve, both at home and at work." I clench my toes in my short boots and fury boils beneath the surface of my skin.

All these years, my father just wanted to control me. He only cares about my career now because I'm no longer under his thumb. I've managed to slip away.

"You know I had to be careful." He tilts his head. "It would look bad if people thought I was favoring you."

"Right. I get that. But at some point, you were doing the opposite of favoring me. You were ignoring me. Ignoring what I wanted. And when leadership does that to an employee, they leave. That's what happened with me."

Richard nods and leans forward. For a second, I wonder if he'll respond to my speech. Apologize for holding me back, controlling me, ignoring me.

"You know I deserved more at DC FC. But you just wanted to keep me under your control."

Richard nods like he's really thinking about what I just said. Okay. Progress. Is he really hearing me? Surely he'll apologize, tell me how he didn't treat me fairly.

"Lucy, I'd like to bring you back as the vice president of marketing and public relations. We'd have you hire two or three staff members, including your replacement, which we never found."

"What?" I freeze mid-sip. My mind struggles to catch up to what my father just said. It wasn't an apology or an acknowledgment.

It was an actual job offer.

"Mark is retiring early, and as soon as I found out, I knew I had to bring you back on for the job." Richard leans back in his chair, clearly pleased with himself.

Holy shit. I might have known about Mark retiring early if I'd agreed to catch up with him on a phone call instead of only asking for a reference via email. My brain tries to process it all. A VP role at DC FC? Except for the fact that I'd be working for my father directly, and my ex—

"And I've moved Ron to another role. Not with DC FC." His words startle me, but I make note that he doesn't apologize. Dad never apologizes because he thinks he's fundamentally always right. He won't apologize for holding me back at work. He won't apologize for not getting rid of Ron sooner. "You won't have to see him at work."

Ron's gone. Does that change anything? Everything? It almost feels like it does?

"You moved him?" A snake of suspicion wraps itself around my ankle and slithers up my leg. "Where?"

"He's doing a special project for me. Assessing a new venture." Richard lifts his chin, like he knows I'm going to pick on this detail.

"Not exactly a punishment." I narrow my eyes. "What's the new venture?"

Richard hesitates for a beat. "I'm looking at buying a NHL team."

"What?" I laugh bitterly and shake my head. "You didn't move him because of me." A sound rumbles in my throat.

"Sure, darling, of course I did."

"You basically promoted him." This all feels disgusting. Ron's not really gone. Just sent away for the time being. He could appear back at any moment.

And even if Ron was permanently gone, the perceived nepotism at DC FC—would it ever go away? No matter how many promotions or raises I earn, people at DC FC will always think it's because of who my father is. I'd have to deal with that every day. Again. Feeling like I'm not good enough for the job, even though I earned it.

"It all works out though. Now—" Richard grins and shows me his expensive smile. "—there's no reason for you to stay away. Not anymore."

He pauses and waits for my response, eyebrows raised. He expects me to accept on the spot. I know it.

"I'll think about it, okay?" But I don't want to think about it. I want to say no. And even though I finally managed to tell him how he's made me feel at work for the past eight years, I can't bring myself to reject his offer outright.

"Lucy. You need me. You always have." Richard leans forward and awkwardly touches my arm. "I'll take care of you. Better, this time."

I don't need someone to take care of me. Definitely not at

work. I'm capable. I'm competent. And here at the Blizzard, I learned I'm more than that. I'm valued and good at my job.

Still, something holds me back from saying no.

Richard and I make awkward conversation for another five minutes, and I call Atticus the second I walk away from my father and Deep Roots Cafe.

* * *

When it rains, it pours cats and dogs. Giant stinky dogs and feral sharp-clawed cats.

I have *two* job offers on the table.

"That's amazing news. Thank you so much for calling." To me, my voice sounds strained, even though I'm trying to infuse excitement into it.

I *should* sound excited.

"We're delighted to make you the offer. You are an outstanding candidate with a bright future, more than qualified to take on this role. I'll send through that written offer, and I look forward to hearing from you in the next week or so." Marcie Lancaster from Winchester FC reminds me of the deadline for responding and clicks off the call.

I drop my phone on the desk and lay my head on the cold, wooden surface. My stomach twists. With joy? Nerves?

Happiness, obviously.

I'm getting exactly what I wanted.

I should call someone.

My mom? She'd be so happy for me.

My father, to say no to his job offer? Now *that* will feel good.

My brother. He'll be supportive. Probably find something to make fun of me for.

January and Raleigh? Yes, definitely them.

My phone buzzes with a notification from the Delightful Doggy Palace that they've posted a new picture of MBM. I click through and smile at the image of my dog rolled onto his back with his tongue hanging out, practically smiling at the camera. There's another Boston terrier lying next to him.

The caption reads: *New friends Hulu and Mister Barky McBarkface having fun on Hulu's first day.*

Hulu. What a silly name for a dog.

MBM has no idea I'm scheming to give him to a family he's only met twice. No clue that I'll leave him here in Fort Collins and never see him again.

My betrayal stings.

A week ago, I met up with both of the moms from the family interested in adopting MBM. They loved him. And at the end of the visit, they told me their daughter wanted to rename him Max.

Max.

I thought they were fucking with me, but they were completely serious. And how would they have any idea what MBM's name history is? They explained that the little girl chose Max because of the movie *Secret Life of Pets*.

My dog hates that name. Despises it.

I didn't tell the new family that. They can name my dog—their dog—whatever they want.

Obviously, I will accept the Winchester FC job. It's my dream job, exactly what I wanted when I quit DC FC and headed to Colorado for just one season.

I can't be chickenshit and go crawling back to my father's soccer team, even if the title is good and the salary is more than I've dreamed of—he texted me a number an hour after we parted ways this morning.

Having choices is amazing. Two great job offers.

So why do I feel so bad?

But I know.

It's Kellen.

The hockey player I inconveniently fell in love with.

I want his blue eyes fixed on me. I want his smiles, his laughter, his steady presence. I want to be invited into his inner circle of people. For real. For good.

I want him.

I *love* him.

But if he wanted me to stay, he would have asked. I get why he doesn't. His top priority will always be his daughter and what's right for his family. And no matter how much I bonded with Ava, I don't fit in there.

Me leaving Fort Collins will make his life easier.

I'm so lost in my thoughts, I almost don't hear the knocking on my office door.

"Lucy?"

I look up to see Bri in the doorway.

"Oh, hey," I say, smiling. "How are you?"

"Good. I was just here dropping something off for Kellen. I thought I'd stop by to thank you for meeting me and Ava the other day for hot chocolate. She was absolutely desperate to see MBM."

"No worries. It was fun." I loved watching Ava wrestle with MBM and the gentle way he wiggled his body against her.

Bri stares at me.

"Actually," I say, because the silence is too much. "I just got the England job offer."

"Aww." Bri's eyebrows furrow for a split second. She crosses her arms and leans against the doorframe. "Congratulations. We'll miss you if you accept it."

"I'm going to accept it," I say firmly. But whether or not I'm trying to convince her or myself is unclear.

"Good for you." But Bri's not smiling, just watching me.

"And it's my dream job. Exactly what I want to do. Where I want to go. It's perfect for me." My voice hitches on the last word. With horror, I realize my eyes are filling with tears. I swallow hard and fight like hell to keep the tears in my eyes instead of dripping down my cheeks.

"Well. Before you go, maybe you should talk to him."

"Him?" As if I don't know exactly who she's talking about.

"Kellen." She says it slowly, stretching out his name, like she's explaining something to her kindergartener.

"About what?" I truly don't know. That chapter of my life is closed. Done and dusted. Completely over. "About the job?"

Bri shrugs.

"About me leaving?"

She shrugs again and cocks her head.

"About the fake dating?"

"Hmm. Was it?"

My throat tightens and warmth floods my cheeks. I bury a hand in my hair and push curls off my forehead.

"I don't know." I groan and shut my eyes.

"I do. And I think you do too." Bri fishes her phone out of her pocket and looks at the screen. "I gotta run." She lifts a hand and disappears from my doorway.

What was that about? As if I need another thing to think about.

Maybe she's right. Maybe I need to face Kellen before I leave. I don't know what I'll say to him. Certainly not that I love him. But maybe some closure will do me good.

I can't wait to get out of this town. That's the real closure I need. A plane ticket.

There's an empty cardboard box in the corner of my office. It's been there since I arrived in September. I grab it and start putting my few personal belongings in the box.

Obviously I don't need to pack right now. I haven't accepted the job and even when I do, I'll have time to tie up all my loose ends here.

But packing up my office is a symbol for moving on. Leaving. Filling boxes is when things get real.

And things just got really real.

I have two mugs on my desk, one is a DC FC mug with the team logo on it, the other a Blizzard mug with a fierce abominable snowman pictured on one side and the saying *Let's Go* on the other.

Both of them go in the box.

A picture of me and my mom and Atticus from Christmas a few years ago. Another framed picture of me, January and Raleigh, this one from this past New Year's Eve.

My chest aches as I move it all into the box.

CHAPTER 38

An Important Question

KELLEN

tticus texted me an hour ago.

ATTICUS

She got the England job

Those five words sent fear coursing through my veins. It makes my plan even more important, and more desperate, and potentially less likely to work.

ME

Thanks for letting me know

ATTICUS

Plus an offer from our father

Shit.

No matter how deranged it sounds, I'm going to try to win Lucy Knox's heart.

Last night, I had a long and ridiculous text conversation with the Kelly Fake Dating Planning Committee, minus Lucy. It culminated in a video call. Lachlan, Harley, Atticus, Raleigh, and Bri all joined. It was the middle of the night in London, so January was sleeping. And I refused to include Finn, Heath, and Romeo. Fuck those guys. They'd probably just pop some popcorn and laugh at me.

It was unanimous that I should do something big to try to win her back. Did I ever have her?

And yup, there was an actual vote.

My objective is simple: Tell Lucy how I feel and ask her out on a real date. Tell her I want her to stay and then leave it up to her. I need her to know that I want to be with her.

I push through the doors into the empty arena. I love this place when it's void of people, players, fans, and noise. There's a deep peace on the ice that means so much to me. It's carved my life into what it is today.

I can't give this up, and I'm torn about asking Lucy to walk away from the England job.

We could do long distance. Really long distance. I could spend the summers there and bring Ava along for some of it. Lucy could visit a few times during hockey season. Holidays together.

But that plan is unhinged. It would never work.

And it would involve me being away from Ava, which is what I've been trying to avoid all season. Ava's the reason why I've even been able to get to know Lucy.

Right now, Lucy is at a press briefing. Atticus told me that as well. She asked him to pick up MBM from the Delightful Doggy Palace at four o'clock.

Apparently, she thinks her dog has been spending too much time in daycare. I don't understand how Lucy thinks she's giving that dog away. She's clearly obsessed with him.

I pause at her office on my way to the stairwell, wondering if I can catch her before she heads to the briefing room. Her door is cracked, and I knock and slowly push it open.

She's not there.

But there's a cardboard box on her desk, filled with her belongings. For a second, my feet are frozen to the floor. She's really leaving.

Fuck. I have to hurry.

I jog to the stairwell and take the steps two at a time up to the second floor. Down the hallway past the corporate suite.

The thing is, Lucy's spent years thinking she's not good enough. I get that now. Her asshole ex cheated on her. Her own father wouldn't promote her at work and certainly wouldn't defend her against her ex.

They don't respect her. They don't think she's good enough.

They are also idiots.

I need her to know she's more than good enough. She's better than I deserve.

The door is open to the last conference room—the big space is used for formal team meetings and press briefings.

It's quiet as I approach, but then I see that there are a few rows of journalists already seated, notebooks in their hands, press badges clipped to their shirts. I step into the room and remain in the back.

Lina is talking at the podium. Next to her is Paul, a few corporate leaders like Claire Morgansten, the HR woman who interviewed Lucy and I back in October about our relationship, and a handful of people I don't know.

And Lucy.

She's wearing a long, dark blue cotton dress with short sleeves and a scooped neckline. Her curls are off her neck in a messy bun, and two tendrils lay along the side of her face.

I watch her. She doesn't see me yet. I can't believe I did so wrong by this woman. That I used her to protect myself from Paul and Savannah and then went along with the breakup like she didn't mean everything to me. I hid behind all the excuses in the world: my trust issues, Ava, hockey, anything to avoid my feelings.

Especially after I fell in love with her.

I'd like to spend forever making it up to Lucy.

"We have an exciting new sponsorship to announce today," Lina says. "We've been hammering out the details for a few months now." She glances at the people I didn't recognize and smiles. "I'll let Paul say a few words."

Paul steps to the podium, and I completely tune him out. The sponsorship representative joins him up front. *Christ, the press must be bored to tears.*

I'm about to make it a lot more interesting for them.

My gaze is drawn back to Lucy, and I find her staring at me, eyes wide. Her gaze is like a beam of sweet summer sunshine.

I smile at her, but she looks even more confused.

"Anyone have questions?" Paul asks.

One reporter asks about the previous headline sponsor. Paul answers that one. Another reporter asks if the players have any new individual sponsors. Lina steps forward and speaks.

Then the room falls quiet. It's time for me to prove to Lucy that she's good enough.

Starting with one date.

Heart pounding, I shoot my hand in the air. Lucy mouths *what are you doing* and shakes her head.

"Oh, hi Kellen," Lina says, an easy smile on her face. "Did you have a question?" Her expression says *of course you don't*, and *did you get lost?* and *what are you doing?*

"Yes, I do." I push away from the back wall and take three steps up the center aisle. The reporters turn and look at me expectantly, most of them smiling.

"Go on."

"I wanted to ask Lucy Knox if she'd go to dinner with me."

There are smiles and chuckles from the audience, who's

looking between me and Lucy. Lina looks over at Lucy with wide eyes.

"Don't worry, everyone," I say. "I cleared it with HR." The HR woman raises her eyebrows and looks less than amused, but the journalists chuckle.

Lucy is staring at me, her mouth dropped open, and her pink cheeks are the cutest thing I've ever seen.

"A little off the agenda—" Lina sneaks a look at Paul, who shrugs and half rolls his eyes. He's the most chilled out I've ever seen him.

"—but I guess I'll allow it." Lina throws her hands in the air and waits for me to speak.

"Lucy?" I take a deep, filling breath. What I'm about to do might be career-limiting, and this time it's mine, not Lucy's. Despite his nonchalant look at the moment, Paul might be disgusted with my display. The press might destroy me. Lina might cease recommending me for sponsorships. I'll certainly get called into HR.

"I am so sorry that I let things end between us. It was a huge mistake, and I'll never forgive myself for losing the past month with you."

I don't talk about fake dating. Not sure we need the reporters to put that in their articles. And god knows it was only fake for the shortest moment.

I take another few steps, my thighs feeling like jelly, my heart racing.

Lucy doesn't say anything but bites her bottom lip in a move that makes me want to kiss her until she can't breathe.

"I want to start over. With dinner. Will you go out with me? I mean, can I take you out? Because I'm not sure if you know this, but I really like you." I glance at the row of Blizzard staff, who are staring at me wide-eyed, then at the journalists, who are looking way more lively than before. "I really like her."

Lucy stands but stays cemented in place. Her face turns darker pink beneath those adorable freckles.

"Actually, I more than like you. I'm in love with you."

There are literal gasps from the press, plus a few chuckles. Phones are raised, and I'm sure about a billion photos and videos are being taken. They'll definitely end up all over the internet.

"Kellen," Lucy whispers and steps forward.

"Please know that every moment we've spent together since you got here last September has been incredible. And I know you might leave—that you're most likely going to leave—but I don't want to waste another minute without you."

Lucy's chest heaves up and down and she presses her lips together.

"I love you," I say. "I want you to stay here in Fort Collins, but even if you can't, I still want to be with you. Whatever pieces of you you'll let me have, I want them all. I want you. And MBM, if you end up keeping him. I want you to be a part of my life, and Ava's life. Because she loves you too."

Lucy lets out a huff of a laugh when I mention her dog and crinkles her forehead when I mention Ava.

I wish she'd run down the aisle and leap into my arms. Wouldn't she do that if she felt the same way? But I'm asking too much of her. I know it.

I can't control how she reacts. I can only control what I say and how *I* react. I take three more steps forward, and now we're a few feet apart.

"I know it's complicated. We can figure out all the details later. I'd also like to note that the—" I lower my voice. "—the KFDPC completely approves of this. They even voted on it."

Lucy laughs, and the sound is the sweetest to my ears.

There's some murmuring in the crowd.

Meh, they won't figure that out.

Lucy's laugh tapers off, and she's staring at me intensely,

tugging at the waist of her dress. She's thinking. Considering. She swallows, and I watch the ripple of her smooth throat.

Paul scoffs loudly, but when I glance over, he's not glaring at me, but instead looking mildly amused.

I turn back to Lucy.

CHAPTER 39

One, Two, Three

LUCY

Kellen's in love with me?

Shock has frozen every muscle in my body, including my vocal cords. I'm filled with all the feelings. Love. Joy. Happiness.

But also much worse ones.

Sadness. Desperation. Because what good can possibly come of this?

Kellen Bassey just made a literal formal announcement of his love for me. With an audience of so many people. Journalists! And now he's stopped right in front of me. Cautious, his hands are out like he's approaching a skittish puppy.

"I know you've had a lifetime of hurt from your father." He says this in a low voice, just for me. "And your ex-fiancé is an absolute piece of garbage. He was the stupidest man on the face of this planet to lose you."

Warmth cascades through my body, encasing the sadness and desperation until those feelings are unrecognizable. I make a soft sound but can't get my vocal cords to work quite yet.

Kellen squeezes his eyes shut. "I'm not much smarter. I lost you too."

"It was sort of a scheduled loss. Remember? The KFDPC voted on it."

His eyes fly open, and one side of his mouth turns up. "You always make me smile, Lucy Knox."

The conversations in the room grow to a low murmur as people talk to each other, check their phones, and watch us. I look around, briefly meeting Lina's eyes. She raises her eyebrows, and I can only imagine what she's thinking. *What the hell,* probably.

I press my lips together and glance down at Kellen's hands. He clenches his fists, then releases. It's like he's holding himself back from reaching for me.

"And it's not true, what you said." My voice cracks.

"What part of it?" Kellen asks.

"Do you know what? I think that's all for today," Lina announces to the group, who quiets down. "If you have any follow-up questions—" The journalists all raise their hands. "—about the sponsorship—" All the hands go down. "—then shoot me an email or call me. Have a great week."

Relief washes over me. There was no way I could continue this conversation with such an audience.

The people of the press slowly gather their things and stand, looking not in a rush at all to leave the room.

"Come on, come on, get out now." Lina shoos the journalists toward the exit.

Paul walks our way, pausing for a beat to clap Kellen on the shoulder.

"Sucker," Paul says, but he has a good-natured scowl on his face. I didn't know the man was capable of anything good-natured. He strides out of the room, not stopping to talk to anyone.

"Lucy? What part of it isn't true?"

"The part where you said you aren't much smarter." I stare at Kellen, this man who I love, as he looks back at me so intensely.

He lets out a murmur and takes a deep breath.

"And the part where you said you lost me." I said I'd never confess my feelings for him. I'd never tell him I love him. And with good reason. I'm leaving. I need to move forward in my life, accomplish all the things I know I can.

But here I am, about to spew those feelings all over him.

"Really? Lucy?" The hope in Kellen's eyes envelops me.

Because maybe I am good enough for Kellen Bassey.

All along, I've thought I wasn't. Like I wasn't good enough to impress my father or keep Ron interested, I knew I wasn't enough for Kellen, his daughter, his teammates, his life.

But he just showed me he doesn't want to hide me away any longer. He could've waited till after the press briefing, when we could talk privately.

He wants everyone to know how he feels.

I shift on my feet. My bare feet because I had a shoe malfunction right before this briefing. Who has a shoe malfunction while wearing flat shoes? I do. Of course I do.

There's something like hope on Kellen's face. His eyes flit to my arms and then down to my feet.

"Where are your shoes?" he leans closer and whispers.

"The side of my shoe got caught on my office chair and completely ripped right before this meeting. I hoped no one would notice me barefoot since my dress is long." I'm a hot mess. As always. But this man is looking at me like he doesn't care. Like maybe he likes me *because* I'm a hot mess.

"Don't you keep spare flip flops in your office?"

"Oh my gosh." I gasp. "I totally forgot about the ones I tucked in my drawer. How did you know that?"

"You told me once." Kellen's grin fades. "Lucy, I really need to know what you meant by I was wrong about losing you. Please, tell me what you're thinking."

What am I thinking? I'm going to England. What's the point of entertaining this fantasy?

But he asked me to stay. He wants me to stay. Relief and joy cascade through me and blend together into brief happiness.

Brief because I can't imagine saying no to the Winchester FC job. I couldn't live with myself if I sacrificed my dream for a man. I want to be selfish in this next stage of my life. Confident and focused and strong enough to go after what I want.

What do I really want?

I've grown to love Fort Collins.

And MBM. I can't let his name become Max.

Kellen wants me to stay.

But there are so many reasons to go.

Kellen runs his hand down his face, where there's a five o'clock shadow.

All the love I've been suppressing for this man escapes from the cage I've tried to contain it in.

Because now everything feels different.

But is it?

I want to reach my hand out. I want to throw my arms around his neck and kiss him. I could do it right now.

"Lucy?" Lina says from behind Kellen. She'd left the room with the others and now stands inside the entrance. "I know you're busy, but can I steal you for just one minute? It's very important. And relevant." Lina points to Kellen. "Kellen Bassey, you stand right there and wait. This will only take a second."

Lina waves me to right outside the now-empty room. I let out a huge breath.

"Did you know he was going to do that?" I ask, my voice shaky.

"No, of course not." Lina puts her hands on my shoulders. "Are you okay? Do you need rescuing?"

"Absolutely not," I say without hesitation. I'm itching to go back in there before I wake up and realize it's all a dream.

"I didn't tell you this before, especially after you told me about the Winchester FC job offer, but I feel like now it might be useful information." She slides her hands off my shoulders and glances back through the doorway to Kellen. He's standing with his hands in his joggers, facing the podium.

He turns and our eyes meet.

Devastation makes my stomach twist. I can't give up everything for this man, even if I'm in love with him. Look what happened with Ron. With my mom and dad. With Raleigh's two marriages. With basically every marriage and long-term relationship I've seen up close.

"Fiona isn't coming back to the Blizzard."

"What?" I swing my head back to Lina sharply.

"She called me earlier this week to confirm it, but she's been considering for a while. Said she can't bear to leave her baby. He's had a few health issues, although he's fine now."

Lina tells me the short story of Fiona asking for an extension of her mat leave, then another extension, then finally telling Lina she doesn't want to come back at all.

"I didn't want you to feel pressured but now might be the right time to tell you that if you want it, there's a job here for you with the Blizzard in Fort Collins. We've all loved having you on the team. You've been a great asset, and a wonderful person to work with." Lina reaches out and squeezes my hand. "Everyone loves you, Lucy."

"You're offering me Fiona's job?" My mind races to catch up.

Holy shit.

This could change everything.

"It'd be senior director of marketing and public relations, which you've proved you're completely qualified for. The same level as your Winchester FC job offer. We can talk salary and benefits, if you want."

Lina tells me the estimated salary, and I nod. It's good. Not as good as the job Richard is dangling in front of me, but similar to Winchester FC.

"Thank you." I look back inside. "I think I better get back in there."

"Okay." She releases my hand. "Hey, call or text if you want to talk."

And with a quick hug, Lina's gone. I stand in the hallway alone.

I have *three* job offers?

I picture Atticus dropping me off at the Denver airport, about an hour drive from Fort Collins. Getting on a plane to England. Flying thousands of miles away from this place. Away from Atticus. Kellen. MBM.

The thought fills me with dread.

What if I stayed here?

I allow myself to consider the idea. I'm filled with the opposite of dread. Elation. Hope.

Love.

I head back in to see Kellen.

"Do you mean it?" I walk quickly up to him, the scratchy corporate carpet rough on my bare feet.

He turns to me and nods his head. "Every word. Lucy, I—"

"I love you too." I say it so quickly, he blinks and his forehead crinkles. I close my eyes and intake a steadying breath.

That's not enough. I have to explain why I love him.

I open my eyes.

"I think I fell in love with you in Wyoming when we kissed under the carpet of stars behind the resort. Or maybe it was as far back as the first hike we went on when you saved me from the rattlesnake."

Kellen chuckles and reaches his hands out to mine. I let him entwine our fingers together.

"You would've been okay."

"Well, you definitely saved MBM."

"I think it was Bear at the time. But yeah, he might not have been okay."

I huff a laugh.

"Kellen, you made me feel something again. Not just something. Everything. You had no judgement. You laughed with me when my dog was ridiculous. So basically all the time." I shrug. "When I was ridiculous. Also all the time."

Kellen huffs a laugh, but I keep talking, this time with a smile behind my words.

"You laugh when I do stupid shit like spitting water all over you or breaking my shoe before a big press conference."

"I love you because you're ridiculous, not in spite of it, Lucy."

I close my eyes for a beat and breathe in. I want to hear those words over and over out of Kellen's mouth.

"You're brave and strong and care so much about your daughter. You treat your teammates like your family and are generous and kind. And the way you look at me?" My voice hitches. "The way I feel when you touch me?" I glance down at his lips and let the warmth from his fingers spread up my arms and into my chest.

"You make me crazy for you, hot sauce," Kellen says, dead serious.

"Now I'm a condiment?" I burst out laughing and Kellen shrugs sheepishly. I step closer. "I love you too, Kellen. I love your daughter. I love everything about your life."

"Thank god." Kellen lifts a hand and pushes back a curl from my forehead. It immediately springs forward. "I can't lose you, Lucy. That's why things went so far on New Year's Eve. I was heartbroken at the idea that you'd be gone forever soon."

I love this man.

I don't want to leave.

I can't leave.

"Kellen." I pull my hands out of his and reach up to his face. His eyes burn, and he slides his hands on my waist, pulling me against him. I can feel his heart thumping against mine. "You're not going to lose me."

"I'm not?" His face is open and vulnerable. He looks less like a tough hockey player and more like a man who is naked and baring his soul without knowing what will happen.

"Kitty, I can't believe you said all those things at a press briefing," I quirk a smile. "Wow, that name really doesn't work. Sounds like an eighty-year-old woman rocking a water aerobics class."

Kellen laughs. "I had to convince you that I was serious. I meant every word." He squeezes my waist. "Can I kiss you now?"

I nod, unable to squeak out an answer aloud. Kellen leans down and presses his lips against mine, and it's everything I've missed since our fake breakup. Since New Year's Eve.

Everything I can't live without.

I relish the feel of his soft, warm lips. His kisses are a seal to our love. A promise. A confession.

"I missed you," he says when he finally pulls away.

"Me too." I press my forehead against his and try to catch my breath.

"So will you? Go out with me?"

I laugh.

"Of course, I'll go out with you."

"And... when are you leaving for England?" His voice is tortured.

"I'm not." I shake my head. I've made my decision.

I can't leave Fort Collins.

This town is giving me all the opportunities in the world to build a life here: family, a job, friends, my dog, Kellen.

"What?" Kellen's brow furrows deeply.

"Lina just offered me a job. Fiona's not coming back."

Emotions swirl in his widened eyes.

"You can kiss me again," I say.

He smashes his mouth on mine. I press my body up against him and move to my tiptoes. Kellen's phone buzzes in his pocket, pressed firmly against my thigh.

"Want to check that?" I say, my lips moving against his mouth.

"That's probably the Kellcy Fake Dating Planning Committee text chain. We should fill our friends in."

I release him from our embrace so he can pull out his phone, loving the sound of *our friends*.

Kellen flips the screen around to show me, keeping one hand on my hip. There's a stream of texts coming in a group titled Kellcy Fake Dating Planning Committee (No Lucy).

I'm not sure if I'm offended or touched.

A little of both, I think.

LACHLAN

It must be over by now. What happened, mate?

JANUARY

Kellen, you have five minutes before I call Lucy to find out

ATTICUS

Give it a minute in case my sister just wiped the floor with him

RALEIGH

That's not funny, Atticus 😦

ATTICUS

Who said I was trying to be funny? You know it's a distinct possibility

RALEIGH

You wouldn't know funny if it knocked you into the boards

ATTICUS

Aw, she used a hockey reference

HARLEY

Give it a rest, you two

BRI

He'll update us as soon as he can. Have patience

"Holy crap, they are persistent," I say with a laugh.

"Sure are. Here, let's do this." Kellen presses the camera button and holds the phone back, capturing both of us on the screen. "Photo evidence?"

"Perfect," I say, and Kellen takes the picture.

CHAPTER 40

A Dog Named Waffles

KELLEN

Friday, January 17

It's the first night Lucy is staying over at my house. The fact that we get to do this thing between us in the open now is an incredible feeling. Never in a million years did I imagine that fake dating Lucy would end up like this. I didn't think it was in the cards for me to feel this way about someone.

There's a knock at the front door and Ava comes bursting in a second later.

"Daddy!" She throws herself into my arms. I'm ready for her, squatting down and lifting her up for a quick twirl, love and affection bursting from my chest.

"Hi, sweetheart."

"You took forever at dinner. Did you bring me chicken nuggets?"

"Obviously." I nod toward Lucy who's holding a paper bag with chicken nuggets and french fries inside. Lucy's dog runs circles around us, desperate to get to Ava.

"Yes! I already had dinner, but I can have this for snack time, right, Mom?"

"Sure, Aves." Bri steps inside. "Lucy, are you sure we can borrow MBM overnight? Ava's been desperate for a doggy sleepover."

"He will love it. He loves Ava. And you, too, Bri." Lucy smiles warmly at Bri, then down at my daughter.

Bri laughs and shakes her head. "I don't need him to love me. But he's pretty cute."

Lucy is the only woman I've dated that Bri has enthusiastically approved of. The only one she's smiled at, supported, welcomed into our lives. That's gotta mean something.

"No, Mommy, that's not right." Ava wiggles out of my arms and looks at Lucy.

"What's not right?" Bri asks.

"Lucy? I had an idea." Ava clasps her hands together.

"What's your idea, sweet girl?" Lucy cocks her head and waits for my daughter to continue.

MBM jumps up on Ava, and she wraps her arms around his body, kissing his head and giggling.

"I was thinking about all the names you gave Mister Barky McBarkface."

"Well, you gave him his latest name, although I shortened it to MBM."

"What were all the names again?"

Lucy scrunches her face as if she's thinking really hard. "He started out as Max, but he is definitely not a Max. Then he was Oscar, and by the time I got here he was Waffles. Then Zeus, Taco, Harry, Prince Harry, Bear, and now Mister Barky McBarkface. MBM."

Bri and I both chuckle. Lucy gives us a stern look as Ava is tapping her chin dramatically, clearly thinking hard.

"Yeah, but I think it's too long. It's hard to say. And I don't really like MBM as a nickname." She shakes her head.

"Ava." Bri crosses her arms.

"It's okay. She's right." Lucy nods, her face completely serious. "Do you have a recommendation?"

I groan and laugh. "Careful what you ask for, Lucy."

"I think it should be Waffles," Ava says.

"Really?" Lucy bursts out laughing just as her dog barks wildly.

"See, he likes it!" Ava gets on her knees and lets Mister Bark—Waffles—lick her face in a way that grosses me out just a little.

"Hmmm. Maybe he likes it." Lucy appears to consider the idea of renaming her dog, but I already know she's going to do it.

"You really don't have to." Bri shakes her head.

"It's perfect. I think it was always my favorite name," Lucy says. Ava cheers. "But this has to be it. His name is permanently Waffles."

"Yes!" Ava squeals.

"I can finally get an engraved nametag. I knew I was waiting for a reason."

"Do it!" Ava jumps up and lets Waffles lick her hand. Lucy clicks the leash on Waffles's collar and hands it to Bri.

Once they're gone, Lucy settles on the couch in my family room while I grab a bottle of Merlot and two wine glasses from the kitchen. I can hear her sigh happily from the other room.

"That restaurant was amazing," she says when I return and hand her a glass. "I didn't even know I loved French food, but apparently, I do."

"I'm guessing you meant our dinner, not our chicken nugget stop." I settle next to her and rest my arm on the back of the couch to let her snuggle right next to me.

"I'm pretty sure that fast food place isn't French."

I laugh. I must be the luckiest man on earth.

"There are a lot of good restaurants in Fort Collins. I can't believe your brother hasn't recommended any of them to you."

"Since when does Atticus eat at nice restaurants? He's more of the pints and hitting on women at a sports bar kind of guy."

"True. And he and Lachlan are always the most likely to take those women back to the hotel when we're traveling. Found at sports bars, usually."

"Ew. I didn't need to know that." Lucy makes a face.

"Sorry."

We clink glasses and take a sip, then she puts her drink down. I want to see if she comments on the wine, and I don't have to wait long.

"This is so good, what kind is it?"

"A Merlot. From your mom's vineyard."

"What??" Lucy's mouth drops open.

"I really enjoyed the wine while we were there for Thanksgiving, so I ordered a case and shipped it here."

"Oh my god, you didn't."

"I did."

"I didn't even know she shipped wine. Or sold cases." Lucy smiles. "This is amazing." Lucy leans in and presses her lips against mine. "Thank you."

"For what? I get to drink it too."

"For everything." She settles back against my arm and shoves a loose curl out of her eye.

I swear, this woman doesn't know how incredibly hot she is.

Lucy's effortlessly gorgeous tonight. Her red curls cascade down her shoulders, and she's done up her green eyes so they pop. She's wearing a mid-length gray dress, and I haven't been able to keep my hands off her all night.

"Thanks for letting me take you out."

"I needed it after the calls I had to make today, so thank *you*."

Lucy had a conversation earlier today with Winchester FC to tell them she was turning down their job offer, and I know it's been weighing on her.

"Are you sad?"

She looks at me and shakes her head. "Not sad. I know I made the right decision. The job with the Blizzard is just as good as the

England one. I love working here. And I no longer feel the need to run so far away from my life."

"This is far enough?"

"This is the perfect distance." Lucy sips her wine and runs her hand down my thigh.

"You've had more than your share of rough conversations today."

She shrugs. After she called to tell Winchester FC she was staying here, she called her father. He didn't take the rejection well. He's not used to any kind of rejection.

"My favorite part was when I told my father to let Ron know I'm doing fine." Lucy chuckles. "And he admitted he will probably come back to DC FC if the NHL team purchase falls through. There were just so very many things wrong with that whole conversation." She growls and shakes her head.

"Asshole." I shake my head.

"Yup. I told him I need space from him. A break. At first Dad thought I was talking about Ron. My father does not live in the same reality that I do." She shakes her head.

"I think space from Richard is a good idea."

"I'm gonna go full no contact for six months. Then I'll reevaluate what role he gets to play in my life."

"Our life."

"Our life." Lucy nods.

"Well." I lean forward and kiss her, breathing in her scent, tasting the deep red wine on her lips. "I'm thrilled you chose here. Me. Us."

She smiles against my mouth.

"Hey, I have something for you. Don't go anywhere." I stand and leave my wine glass on the coffee table.

"Where would I go?" she calls after me.

I smile and dart into the study to grab Lucy's wrapped Christmas gift from where I left it on the desk.

"Here." I hand her the present and sink back beside her.

"What's this?"

"A Christmas gift I never got to give you. It's not a big deal, I promise."

Lucy rips the abominable snowman wrapping paper off and chuckles when she reads the title of the book.

"*A Guide to Hiking in Colorado?*"

"Yeah. I put a few notes in there, like around what to do when you encounter wildlife. There's a whole chapter on rattlesnakes, mountain lions, and bears."

"I am never going hiking without you." She flips through the pages, fingering the sticky notes with my scribbles.

"Deal."

"Thank you." She lays the book on her lap and kisses me. "I don't have anything for you."

"I don't need presents. I much prefer to give them than get them."

"That's sweet." Lucy sighs and rests her head on my shoulder.

"I had another idea, but didn't want to do it until I talked to you first."

"What is it?" Lucy tilts her head up.

"This summer, do you want to go on vacation with me? I'm thinking England. We can visit January in London, then tour around the countryside. Maybe go up to Scotland and see Edinburgh and the Highlands."

Lucy doesn't respond, so I rush through the next part of my speech.

"Maybe we can check some boxes off so you don't have any regrets about not moving to England."

Lucy stands and launches herself onto my lap and into my arms, one knee on either side of my hips, her dress gathered around her thighs. The weight of her on me feels like a heavy blanket keeping me warm on a cold Colorado night. Lucy's the first sip of an ice-cold beer on a hot day, the best dessert after a perfect meal, the sweetest sight for sore eyes after being away with the team.

I can't wait to come home to her again and again.

"That's perfect." There are tears in her eyes. Lucy slides her hands on either side of my jaw and presses her lips to mine.

"So you'll go with me?"

"I'd go anywhere with you, but definitely to England and Scotland." She kisses me again.

"I know you were looking forward to living there." I say when she leans back to take a breath.

"Being here is my choice." Lucy presses her forehead to mine. "It's partially about you, but it's also about me. Atticus. Waffles. The career opportunity."

"I totally get it. The world does not revolve around me." I let Lucy kiss me again, and again.

"Don't expect me to marry you or give everything up," she says when she takes a break from kissing me. "And if we break up, I'm not going anywhere. My life is here now."

"We're never going to break up, Lucy." I could kiss her on this couch forever. "Remember how much I love you? I'll take whatever you'll give me."

I lean back and breathe in, not moving my eyes from her, soaking in every bit of Lucy Knox.

I would truly do anything for her.

"I love you, Lucy."

"And I love you."

It's only been a few days since I confessed my love to her at the press conference. A few days of bliss and happiness and pure joy.

I know it won't be easy with my job and Ava, and Lucy building her own life here as well. But we will make this work. Because I'm in love with her. And she's in love with me.

I deserve to be able to trust someone like her with my heart.

And she deserves to know she's more than good enough for me.

"What do you want to do now?" she asks as I lean forward to

kiss her neck, breathing in her scent, wishing for this night to never end.

"I'll do whatever you want, my red-hot chili pepper."

She laughs, her head tilting back.

"It's not fair, you have better options for names. I keep getting stuck on farm animals."

"You can call me sloth or hedgehog or duck, for all I care. I'll answer to anything that comes out of your mouth."

Her eyes light up. "Okay, my blue-footed booby."

I burst out laughing, lifting my face from Lucy's collarbone, which is at my eye level since she's still nestled on my lap.

"What? It's a funny blue bird that lives in Mexico. I saw it in a video."

"Whatever you want."

I intend on making the rest of our lives whatever Lucy wants. I'm all in. This woman who saved my job and my family by fake dating me has also now stolen my whole heart.

And I wouldn't have it any other way.

A Dog Person

LUCY

EPILOGUE

Springtime

"Yes, a dog parade. Well, it's a Boston terrier parade. And then a bunch of food trucks and tents with crafts and other dog stuff." I attempt to smooth my hair back into a messy bun—all my buns are messy with curls like mine—and tug my makeup bag across the counter toward me.

I'm in my own bathroom, in my own small one-bedroom apartment.

It was kind of great living with my brother and getting to know him again, but I was so ready to have my own place.

I love Kellen, but I think it'll be a long time before I give up this kind of independence again.

If ever.

"What has happened to you, babes?" January says with a deep frown through the video call. "I can't believe you're fully a dog person now." She raises her eyebrows and hums. "Actually? This was totally predictable given how you swooped in to save Waffles from your ex like a red-headed knight in shining armor."

"I think it's adorable," Raleigh says. "Just you and Kellen and Ava?"

"Yes, I think." I swipe mascara on my right eye. "Atticus isn't coming." I do my left eye and then glance down at the screen.

She blushes furiously. "Why would I care what Atticus is doing today or who he is dating?"

"Who was talking about Atticus's dating life, sis?" I swipe both eyelashes once more and steal another look at my friends.

"Not me!" Raleigh squeaks.

"If it makes you feel any better, or worse, I dunno, Kellen says he's not taken home a girl while they've been on the road for months."

"Really?"

"Your magical kiss on New Year's Eve did not cure that boy of his sluttiness, Raleigh Durham." January shakes her head.

"I still can't believe you snuck off and kissed my brother and didn't tell us until weeks later." I pull out a concealer stick and dab under my eyes.

"It wasn't a big deal. And I don't care if he takes home girls when he travels. Or that he hasn't done that recently." Raleigh scrunches her face.

January groans.

"You are almost six months out of your second divorce being final and that deserves celebration." January points at the camera. "So go sow some wild oats, or something like that."

"I am. I've gone on a bunch of online dates. And I've been chatting with this one guy who lives in Utah."

"Okay, great, but slow your roll, Raleigh. Nothing wrong with taking your time getting back out there." I brush light blush on my cheeks and grab lip gloss.

"I know." Raleigh rakes her fingers down her face. "I'm thirty-three years old, and I've been divorced twice. And now I'm online dating. What a fucking disaster."

"Aw, sis. Do you need another trip out to Colorado? It's supposedly amazing here in the summer."

"Maybe," Raleigh says.

"Really? Come this summer!" I look down at the screen and zip up my makeup bag. "Please? We'll only be in England for a few weeks."

"Well. Maybe. I might have a lot of free time coming up." Raleigh bites her lip. "Let's get back to this dog parade."

"Wait—" January asks. "What do you mean by *I might have a lot of free time*?"

"I just might, okay?" Raleigh's cheeks turn red. She combs her fingers through her thin, shoulder-length blonde hair.

"Raleigh!" I pick up the phone and switch off the bathroom light.

"I don't know." Raleigh's voice is miserable. "I've been thinking of taking a break from work."

"Like a long vacation?" I furrow my brow.

Raleigh's always had the most stable career of the three of us. She went to pharmacy school after we graduated college and has had a good paying, stable job since then.

Her love life? Not quite as stable.

"I'm burning out. From this town. From this job. From everything."

"Okay. We should talk about this more, but I really need to run." I grab my water bottle and fill it at the refrigerator, balancing the phone in my other hand.

"Me too, actually." Raleigh looks relieved. "Love you guys, talk soon."

"Wait," January says. "You're avoiding the conversation."

"I have to think about things. And I need to get ready for my shift. Bye!" Raleigh disconnects.

January and I stare at each other. Something's definitely going on there.

"That was weird."

"Yup." January laughs.

"You know you are always welcome here too. Savannah asked about you last time I talked to her."

I followed my instincts and actually started being friendly to Savannah. Turns out, she's sweet and supportive and funny as hell. And she needs a few more good friends in Fort Collins.

So do I.

"She's registered to take the Colorado bar."

"Good for her," Jan says. "I follow her on the socials, but she hasn't posted anything about that."

"Not sure if that's social media material."

"Maybe not." January shrugs. "I'll think about visiting sometime. Maybe I'll come for New Year's again."

We agree to tie Raleigh down for the next video call as soon as possible and then say goodbye.

Waffles sits at my feet, staring up at me, tongue hanging out of his mouth.

"Ready for the parade, Waffles?"

He barks and smiles. Fine, maybe that's just his face, but still, it looks like a smile. His name is perfect for him. I don't know why I didn't see it at the beginning.

Fifteen minutes later, I spot Kellen and Ava as I approach A Good Book. I take a moment to appreciate the sight before me.

Kellen's crouched down in front of his daughter, saying something in her ear, making her laugh. He stands and takes her small hand in his large one. My hot hockey player boyfriend is in a snug long-sleeved gray t-shirt and jeans that probably cost more than all my pants put together.

He turns to look at me and when his eyes meet mine, his smile is brighter than the sun that shines on Fort Collins. And the sun shines 300 days a year here.

Ava spots us and squeals, running full speed and skidding to a stop to let Waffles jump up on her chest and give her a billion kisses.

"He's wearing his new name tag!" Ava touches the soft leather tag clipped onto his collar. I got one back in January, but Ava wanted me to get another one with a bit more bling. So he's got a glittery silver name tag that says *Waffles*, surrounded by pink and purple gems.

"Hey," I say when Kellen steps around Ava to kiss me softly. My cheeks warm, and I'm filled with all the feelings.

"Hi. Ready for this?"

"I suppose?"

"Hey! It's Kellcy!" Atticus's voice rings out, and I jerk my head in his direction.

"What are you all doing here?" I groan but can't keep the smile from my face. Atticus, Lachlan, and Harley are all lined up waiting behind Kellen.

"Quick, get your cameras out!" Lachlan's Aussie accent causes a few heads to turn around us. "We can sell pictures of them to NHL Tea!"

"Sorry." Kellen shrugs and ignores Lachlan. "I couldn't keep them away."

"Mind if we come along?" Harley asks, always the polite, reasonable one. "None of us have ever been to a dog parade."

"Sure, might as well."

"Oh, and Bri's joining us as well." Lachlan whips out his phone. "She's here." He looks up and waves at Bri, crossing the street to meet us.

"It's an official Kellcy Fake Dating Planning Committee reunion." Bri hugs Lucy and then Ava.

"What about Heath, Romeo, and Finn?" I ask.

"Don't you dare," Kellen says with a laugh. But then his eyes widen as he sees those very boys heading our way on the sidewalk. "Are you kidding me?"

"Romeo, Romeo," Atticus calls to the approaching group. "Glad you could join us."

"This is ridiculous." Kellen shakes his head, but I can't help but laugh.

"I adore dogs," Romeo says with a wide, toothy grin. He squats down to pat Waffles's head.

"Hello, Miss Ava." Finn nods his head to Kellen's daughter, who smiles up at her father's teammates. Heath stands next to Finn, quiet as usual.

"Just one more," Atticus says. "There she is." He points to Savannah, approaching us with a wide grin.

"Hey, Savannah." I smile at the woman, and she stops and greets me.

"We are our own parade." Kellen grumbles under his breath, but I know he loves it.

"Should we video call your friends?" Atticus asks me.

"Video call? At a dog parade? Nah. I just got off the phone with them anyway." My brother looks disappointed.

"Let's go, you guys. The start of the parade is a block over." Kellen smiles at me.

"Can I hold Waffles's leash, Lucy?" Ava asks and reaches her little hand out.

"Of course." I pass the leash to Ava. Six months ago, I wouldn't have trusted Waffles to behave with a six-year-old at the end of his leash, but months of dog training have significantly helped.

Kellen reaches out and grabs one of my hands, weaving his fingers with mine.

"Can I hold your hand too, Lucy?" Ava looks up at me with big, beautiful blue eyes.

When I got to Fort Collins last September, I didn't know what I really needed. I thought I knew. But I had no clue what was coming.

I didn't know that the mountains of Colorado, this small

town, and a job with the Blizzard were what I wanted. Being around my brother and the hockey team. Stopping at Deep Roots Cafe and A Good Book and making new friends. Celebrating the New Year with January and Raleigh and getting them to promise to come visit me again. Not knowing what I'd do without Waffles.

I didn't know that the devastatingly handsome hockey player next to me and his adorable six-year-old daughter are exactly what I want in my life.

But now that I know all that, I'm gonna hold onto it with everything I have.

I reach out and grasp Ava's tiny hand in mine.

Kellen leans over and kisses me, his lips expressing the things we talk about all the time.

"Let's go, Daddy! Let's go, Lucy!" Ava says. But then Waffles darts over to a fire hydrant. Ava pulls us forward to follow him, and Waffles immediately picks his leg up and pees.

Ava cracks up, and Kellen looks at me and smiles.

"Waffles," I groan.

THE END

If you enjoyed *Just One Season*, leave a review, it helps so much!

Check out Kellen & Lucy's spicy and sweet bonus chapter by signing up for Chrissy's newsletter on her website! Also get free hockey novella *Zamboni Kiss* and bonus chapters for each book.

In the meantime, check out the completed Hart Sisters Trilogy:

If We Pretend is Reese & Oliver's love story. It's a fake dating, divorced mom, ex pro soccer player light sports romance set in Scotland.

Unless It's You is Stella & Ethan's love story. Set in London, this romance is a second chance, enemies-to-lovers, bucket list novel.

Since We're Here is Maddie & Patrick's love story. It's a grumpy sunshine Irish romance.

One Hundred Lights is a prequel novella to The Hart Sisters Trilogy and is a holiday romance featuring Britt & Adrian, both morally grey characters who can't stay away from each other.

Stay in touch:
Instagram: @ChrissyHopewell
Facebook: ChrissyHopewellAuthor
TikTok: @ChrissyHopewellBooks
Email: Chrissy@ChrissyHopewell.com
BookBub: ChrissyHopewell

Acknowledgments

The best part about writing books are the readers and other writers I've met along the way. Thank you so much to all of you readers who have read this book or one of my other ones. I can't believe there are people out there who get excited when I publish another book... I am forever grateful for all of you! Thanks for sticking with me!

Thank you to my trusted betas: Sarah, Lillian, Ericka, Cate, and Paris, and my hockey betas: Jillian, Lou, Melissa, Andrea, Shania, and Emily. Thanks to editor Dani Galliaro and proofreader Jenny with Owl Eyes Proofs & Edits. Thanks also to my closest writing friends who are there for every complaint and rant, and my high school besties who are always around to brainstorm ridiculous things for me and argue amongst themselves about plot points and things like if a pro hockey player would really have two nannies for his daughter (the answer is yes).

Thanks to my family, including my husband and four delightful children who really don't understand what I'm doing with my life (same same).

Until next time!

Love, Chrissy

About the Author

Chrissy Hopewell started her love for romance novels by sneaking her mom's steamy books in middle school. She has spent varying amounts of time overseas, including working at a pub in Dublin, waitressing at a hotel in the Scottish Borders, and studying and living in London. Because of these experiences, international flair and accents often show up in her writing. Chrissy now lives in the suburbs of Cincinnati, Ohio with her family, and she no longer has to sneak what she reads.

instagram.com/chrissyhopewell
tiktok.com/@chrissyhopewellbooks
facebook.com/chrissyhopewellauthor